P9-CQU-473

FORT WORTH PUBLIC LIBRARY

3 1668 03544 8908

Praise for Natl

"Mackey's poetry is a smoking mirror: what appears briefly dissolves into mist, alternate forms invite us into its slow-burning, world-tribe dance. His poetry leaps from reason, rhythmically utters in fevered lyrics, images and references that pitch the reader into tribal ceremony. It follows the course of storms that navigate the reader into a realm of language that burns the reeds and melts the saxophone buttons and returns the fire to weaver of words, braiding threads of language to splice them again in new designs, where we renew our souls by seeing a waterfall not as a waterfall but as a jaguar tongue."   —citation for the 2006 National Book Award

"Mackey's vast epistolary novel might just as easily be perceived as an extravagantly inventive essay on music, African American history, and the relation bet...... ...."   ......*-forum

"Macke   ng
African   ."

                                                                               er

"Mack   al
listene   .-
ters ar   -
provis   s,
and to   x

"Mack   g
theme   .-
turnin   a
piece t

EMS   FICTION MACKEY 2008
Mackey, Nathaniel
Bass cathedral

Shamblee   06/16/2008

SHAMBLEE BRANCH   n

"Mackey is a lyric poet whose probing of wounds and the whir of words reaches into epic dimensions." —*The Nation*

"Mackey's prose is witty, satiric, at times hothouse in the endeavor to translate regions and terrains of music into language; it is philosophically and erotically intimidated, which is to say sincere." —*The Sun*

"Mackey, with his nuanced knowledge of jazz, convinces the reader that music operates like a language, with all the power to convey, say, a specific feminist critique of male-centered jazz culture, or to acquire levels of symbolism that would make Dante wonder if he should have taken up sax." —*Publishers Weekly*

"Mackey's writing (much like the best of Ornette Coleman or country blues) rewards close reading with resonances of real experience." —*Village Voice*

"Mackey is a sure and skilled and *author*itative composer/compositor. . . . The workings of his words indicate an uncontestable care and loving respect for . . . the most subtle and resonant nuances of language." —*African American Review*

"Mackey's rampant alliteration and his reconfiguration of words on the phonemic and morphemic level create a sonic atmosphere that enacts a state of jazz." —*Boston Review*

"We hear the echoes of African shores painted by drum brushes and the stutter of jazz lead rhythms. This cross-cultural mélange is what Mackey is best known for." —*Rain Taxi*

"Mackey's multi-cultural cross-references combine in a rich fabric of fantasy, psychology, and symbolism." —*Pulse!*

BASS CATHEDRAL

ALSO BY NATHANIEL MACKEY

POETRY BOOKS AND CHAPBOOKS

Four for Trane

Septet for the End of Time

Outlantish

Song of the Andoumboulou: 18-20

Four for Glenn

Eroding Witness

School of Udhra

Whatsaid Serif

Splay Anthem

FICTION

Bedouin Hornbook

Djbot Baghostus's Run

Atet A.D.

CRITICISM

Discrepant Engagement: Dissonance, Cross-Culturality, and
    Experimental Writing

Paracritical Hinge: Essays, Talks, Notes, Interviews

ANTHOLOGIES

Moment's Notice: Jazz in Poetry and Prose, *with Art Lange*

RECORDINGS

Strick: Song of the Andoumboulou 16-25

BASS CATHEDRAL
NATHANIEL MACKEY

WITH A PREFACE BY WILSON HARRIS

A NEW DIRECTIONS PAPERBOOK ORIGINAL

COPYRIGHT © 2008 BY NATHANIEL MACKEY
PREFACE COPYRIGHT © 2008 BY WILSON HARRIS

All rights reserved. Except for brief passages quoted in a newspaper,
magazine, radio, or television review, no part of this book may be reproduced
in any form or by any means, electronic or mechanical, including photocopying
and recording, or by any information storage and retrieval system,
without permission in writing from the Publisher.

Bass Cathedral is volume four of *From a Broken Bottle Traces of Perfume Still Emanate*,
an ongoing work. Volumes one, two and three are *Bedouin Hornbook, Djbot Baghostus's Run*
and *Atet A.D.*

Sections of this book have appeared in *Cahiers Charles V, Callaloo,
Detroit Metrotimes, Jubilat, mark(s), New American Writing, Nocturnes, /nor, Tripwire* and
ZYZZYVA.

Manufactured in the United States of America
New Directions Books are printed on acid-free paper
First published as a New Directions Paperbook 1097 (NDP1097) in 2007
Published simultaneously in Canada by Penguin Books Canada Limited

Library of Congress Cataloging-in-Publication Data

Mackey, Nathaniel, 1947–

   Bass Cathedral / Nathaniel Mackey.

      p. cm.—(From a broken bottle traces of perfume still emanate; v.4)

   "A New Directions paperbook original"—T.p. verso.

   ISBN 978-0-8112-1720-0 (pbk.: acid-free paper)

   1. Jazz musicians—Fiction. 2. Bands (Music)—Fiction.

   3. Musical—Fiction. I. Title.

PS3563.A3166B37 2008

813'.54—dc22   2007034666

NEW DIRECTIONS BOOKS ARE PUBLISHED FOR JAMES LAUGHLIN
BY NEW DIRECTIONS PUBLISHING CORPORATION
80 EIGHTH AVENUE, NEW YORK, NY 10011

for Joe, Naima, Daemon, Ella and Ian

PREFACE

Bass Cathedral by Nathaniel Mackey is an open-ended epistolary novel, the fourth in an ongoing series commencing with *Bedouin Hornbook* in 1978. Such elements—in a context of irony, subtlety, capacity and power—make for a rare, literary achievement.

In *Bass Cathedral,* N., who is a composer and multi-instrumentalist in a band known as Molimo m'Atet, writes letters, once again, to Angel of Dust.

The first letter (29.x.82) is inclined to be "rushed" in depicting "more pieces than we originally planned" and the necessity to make a "three-record" rather than the "two-record" set that had been anticipated. This heightens the tension between past and future musical events through "the mere bit of melody which has held me up."

Yet—despite having been held up—N. has made an advance in the pieces of music he brings to Angel of Dust. A creative, open-ended weight to speculations within and beyond the precise narrative in the letters N. writes thus develops. Figurations of the genesis of music—how it may move within and beyond the absolutes of place to trace the joys and ailments of Mankind—are left "open" to imaginations intensely aware of straitened and narrow forms of expression.

We see this in the next letter (8.xi.82) in which one learns of a "demiurgic rumble" experienced at Lambert's where members of the band meet to ponder on the mystery of music. Lambert is a prominent member of Molimo m'Atet.

What is a *demiurgic rumble*? Here perhaps may lie an important clue to the important nature of the letters N. writes. Gnostic intimations—which have been banished from civilization by the Catholic Church and are entertained now by open-minded persons—encompass a demiurge. References to this crop up again and again throughout the novel. The demiurge in gnostic philosophy may be interpreted as an inferior height which civilization fixes to itself without quite sensing—sensing fully, so to speak—that it does so. Thus we become prone to realistic measurements—a storm, rising seas, melting ice at the poles, have nothing to say except within themselves—whereas there are *immeasurable* realities through which we may become aware of heights, depths, widths, in gaining some notion of the stresses in ourselves and in unpredictable natures.

Perhaps the "mere bit of melody" that held N. up in his compositions, which were advanced nonetheless, as though by a twin, quantum psyche, may be converted into a fleeting but indestructible electron with a spin which produces immediately a twin effect in another electron across vast distances *without a material connection*. This is known *technically* but it has no bearing on the creative, re-creative origins of art or music. Yet we may glimpse a sensation of qualities beyond conventional assumptions. We may perceive a "lack" in fixed traditions, we may perceive a "leverage and levity" which share roots to leave a mediation in ourselves about absolute structures. Much in *Bass Cathedral* revolves around a "lack." Can this "lack" be filled by dream and performance pointing through itself into purposes we may begin to glimpse?

Do the balloons that appear and disappear as they arise from Aunt Nancy's instrument—Aunt Nancy is another member of the band—represent a "levity" even as they bring about a "lack" of leverage or purpose within mysterious heights and depths? Does the "straw" on her guitar carry a hint, an "itch," of a dream of the stars?

N.'s letter (15.xii.82) lifts Lambert and himself—as if by hidden strokes of music—to a shop not far from the Hollywood Boulevard Exit. They come upon plastic busts of Beethoven, Bach and Mozart.

"It was hard, stepping inside, not to step on or stumble over a saxophone rest, a music stand, a bass drum or some other object on the floor."

These are presented on the "arc" of music as subsiding into waste properties close to "straw." One is inclined to ask oneself: What do they "lack" in the deepest sense? Merely a hint is established or given as to the revolutionary essences that are cast out in making them stereotypes of sound in which flesh is to be honored in one corner of the market or exploited brazenly in another.

In this "lack" of a real connection between honor and exploitation Lambert tells Fred, who is in charge of the shop, that he is searching for a "mouthpiece," but "it wasn't sound he was after . . . *sound commodified or fetishized* . . . the charm of sound . . . to let listeners bask in the fullness and beauty of tone . . . and to be intermittently startled or made ecstatic." Basking in sound—without a deeper reflection of the chasms between peoples—is prevalent everywhere but it wasn't what Lambert was after. Does this not bring us back indirectly to the context of music in which Bach and Mozart are involved?

Bach's music has affected the Church across centuries but has not invoked a reflection of the slave trade or the agonies of the Middle Passage. Perhaps we feel we hear differently in the singing, crying, mocking voice of Billie Holiday or in the laughing/serious trumpet or horn of Louis Armstrong. The genius of Mozart—regarded as the greatest composer in Western music—has not portrayed, in any real, psychical or creative sense, the gravity of the wounded, human body which becomes a property set apart as inferior in a hierarchy of history.

I know that Western music gives deep pleasure. But is this pleasure a basking in sound? This is what Lambert objects to. He is intent on a sound to which we listen differently in the core of ourselves. Such a core is not stereotypical. It is the highest task of creativity.

The "Dream Thief"—which the band plays—brings the core of humanity into play. The Thief steals from within humanity, steals his/her dreams, and gives back a portion of what is stolen, but steals again. Thus word, image, sound, tone, and every expression in art, are—in some degree—bereft of the wholeness of meaning. They are left incomplete. Yet, in this incompletion, we may no longer bask in sound but seek to hear what is stolen, we may go beyond stereotypes in search of a kinship with originality. Such originality may prove a new beginning in Man, a new creative, re-creative quest that may never be realized but gives us a vital sense of "leverage and levity."

"Straw" and "balloon" take on deeper and higher aspects, beyond themselves within themselves. One is taken forwards and backwards in an open-ended, ceaselessly unfinished process.

The "Dream Thief" suggests that there is no material connection uniting art in itself, art and art, music and language, yet art belongs to all humanity in ways that require new listenings, new active, problematic links.

One may be led backwards and forwards, forwards and backwards, in trailing the mind of music, the mind of art. *Bass Cathedral*—in its open-ended sensibility—takes us back from Hollywood Boulevard to an earlier occasion. We view Aunt Nancy's bass solo in which she makes "a cave of herself, an esoteric recess, whose bodily husk housed rhythmic disbursements of thump and strum." She becomes an "antiphonal church" in which, through which, the others join in, Drennette, Penguin, Djamilaa— antiphonal yet a "flirtation with voicelessness." Djamilaa—"availing herself of Aunt Nancy's crabwise aisle"—while Lambert dances "endlessly" a dance "that borders on imbalance." Are they less encased in a single culture and more open to the core of humanity?

The core is an endless pursuit of possibilities; it may begin by invoking incompletion, an incompletion we do not normally see in ourselves. It demands therefore a crucial visionary adjustment that looks through the grooves of creativity we have planted within us.

After an immense dream-dance with "petticoated facticity" N. "lay immobilized by romance and revolution's failure . . . I lay bodiless and divided, dateless, my head in one place, my heart another . . . This, though, had to be a dream I knew. . . . I did so kicking the covers off the bed."

Kicking the covers off the bed is an allusion to "wizened kin, fled brethren," age and those who have vanished or are dying, on "a divine-divinatory bed of aroused bramble." Humanity may sleep but is called upon to awaken. The arousal of bramble may be a trick but a sign that it will.

N. puts it well. "Rub and refusal have their say . . . exacting a toll having to do with wizened kin, fled brethren, a brer patch as much as a briar patch . . . Brotherhood of Breath . . . quantum-qualitative sputter, a divine-divinatory bed of aroused bramble, burr, thistle, a divine demiurgic spread of prestidigitator spiral and stir."

Qualities of height are hinted at, tricked into subjective spirals by the slender leaves and branches of plants and trees.

There are many ways of achieving the compass of such a rich and complex novel as *Bass Cathedral* in which there are tricks a conjurer might play as well as sober and far-reaching realities, all in a blend of dream and performance. I trust the approach I have attempted is a pungent and illuminating one.

In essence *Bass Cathedral* gives us a vision to retrieve essentials in music and art that have been so suppressed in their variety—by an undeviating order or value—they are virtually lost or sent into exile.

In retrieving, or bringing them back, we face a complicated focus on the nature of originality which is open to vulnerabilities across the spectrum of humanity, to *incompletion* where least seen, and to a potential wholeness to be derived from the creativity of all cultures—unlike classic fixtures—in breaking themselves from the one-sided triumphs of a hierarchy of history looming large still.

WILSON HARRIS

BASS CATHEDRAL

Dear Angel of Dust,

I've been meaning to write for a while now, a while that seems like years though it's only been weeks. A bit of melody held me up, the beginnings of a piece I've been wanting to write but can't. It would be a piece, were I able to write it, the sleek skein of whose retreat would limn an interpolative truth. Retreat, I mean, would imbue the receipt the piece would bestow—imbue and ambiguate such receipt (grudging receipt). Which is where the wrench or the rub I've been up against comes in: how to ambiguate receipt without foreclosing on receipt. Foreclosure is the risk I've run and evidently succumbed to, unable, as I've been, to get on with or get beyond the mere bit of melody which has held me up. Grachan Moncur III's "Frankenstein," however, encourages me to believe I can. That he wrote it as a waltz, more exactly, keeps me from giving up. It seems he speaks to retreat and receipt's cautionary rhyme and revision by pushing waltz's restrained embrace a bit further, furthering such restraint via titular monster-held-at-bay (extenuation confounding stark, Frankensteinian stitch with *Ur*-rhapsodic stitch). I've let myself be taken up with this more than I probably should have, tending more toward shutting down on other fronts than makes any sense. Still, sense or no sense, that's how it's been. Sorry to've been silent so long.

We've made some decisions regarding *Orphic Bend* you should know about. Here are the pieces we've decided will be on it, in the order in which they'll appear:

"Prometheus" (Take 1)

"The Slave's Day Off" (Take 1)

"Tosaut Strut" (Take 3)

"Our Lady of the Lifted Skirts" (Take 1)

"In Walked Pen" (Take 2)

"Udhrite Amendment" (Take 1)

"Drennethology" (Take 1)

"Like A Blessed Baby Lamb" (Take 1)

"Half-Staff Appetition" (Take 2)

"Dream Thief" (Take 1)

"Bottomed Out" (Take 1)

"Tosaut L'Ouverture" (Take 2)

"Feet, Don't Fail Me Now" (Take 1)

"Altered Cross" (Take 3)

"Opposable Thumb at the Water's Edge" (Take 1)

"Sun Ship" (Take 1)

"Aggravated Assent" (Take 2)

These, then, are the pieces you should base your liner notes on. Having taken so long to get this info to you, I hate to rush you, but the sooner you can get the notes written the better, as we're about to send the album into production. The jacket will be the last phase of the process but, even so, it's not all that far away. You should also know that since we're including more pieces than we originally planned we'll have to make it not a two-record set as we thought at first but a three-record set. And instead of the Limelight design, with booklike leaves and three-dimensional pop-outs, we'll use the three-panel folding design Atlantic used for their *Passions of a Man* Mingus release three years ago.

Let me know if there's any more info you need for your notes.

Yours,

N.

_____

Dear Angel of Dust,

We got the test pressing of *Orphic Bend* this morning and got together at Lambert's to give it a listen this afternoon. It was during Aunt Nancy's bass solo on "Dream Thief" that what I'm writing to tell you about happened: the balloons appeared again. With the very first note she plucked a balloon emerged from the point where the needle and the vinyl met. Enclosed in it were these words: *I dreamt you were gone. A preemptive dream I knew it to be even as I dreamt it, as if to dream it was to preclude its coming true. But to know that or think that, I thought as I dreamt, was to weaken its power to preempt itself.* A rest of half a beat cleared away this balloon, its place taken by another as Aunt Nancy plucked again, enclosed in which were these words: *To know that or think that flew in the face of post-expectant aplomb, unprepossessing (non-prepossessive) aplomb. To know that or think that rolled web, record and wreckage into one, though at the time I had no way of knowing this, notwithstanding what I otherwise knew or thought I knew.* Another half-beat rest cleared away this balloon, another emerging as soon as Aunt Nancy plucked again. Enclosed in the third balloon were these words: *It was all only a dead expanse. My unravelling sweater picked me wishbone clean. The ground a demiurgic rumble, cloth was the country I came from. The backwater rag around my head worn see-thru thin, I was dressed to kill. I strummed a gut wanting the world to relate.* Another rest followed, clearing the third balloon away. Following this rest, Aunt Nancy left off plucking and proceeded, à la Jimmy Garrison, to strum the bass, another balloon emerging, enclosed in which one read:

The ground shook, tore my threadbare voice—chthonic rent. I bent my wrist as I strummed, addressing flat guitar strings made of straw at an acute angle. It was as though if I could only get the right sort of leverage all would be well again. Here followed another rest, ever so slight, the balloon disappearing, its place taken by another when Aunt Nancy resumed her strumming. Enclosed in this fifth balloon were these words: *No, no "as though" about it: if I could only have gotten the right sort of leverage all would have been well again. Cloth was now the country I came to as well as from, the backwater rag around my head pulled tourniquet tight by chthonic rent—so tight, albeit see-thru thin, I saw stars. My head spun in outer space.* After another ever so slight rest Aunt Nancy went back to plucking, the fifth balloon's place taken by a sixth, the solo ending with a run which brought it oddly full circle, these words enclosed in the balloon: *I came to in a country of cloth, torn cloth, dreaming you gone to be free of you going but no less bound even so. The leverage I sought escaped me. Cigar box, broomstick, straw—the crude components of my flat guitar—bore the lament I laid your leaving to rest with.*

Needless to say, this came as a surprise. It had never occurred to us that the balloons might put in an appearance at something other than a live performance, so much the issue they seemed to be of breath, bodily bearing, notwithstanding our not, until now, having thought it thru in exactly this way. Their now having arisen from a vinyl surface returned us to the question of what exactly they are. Urgency vied with agnostic resignation as we pondered what manner of emanation they advanced. Inference? Interference? How to tell which? Such questions were given a sharper point by Aunt Nancy's reply to Drennette asking her who the "you" was the balloons went on about so, went on about, she (Drennette) assumed, at her (Aunt Nancy's) behest. "Hard to say," Aunt Nancy said. "I'm not sure those are the words I'd have used. Of course, it's been a while since the recording date. I'm not sure I can reconstruct what was on my mind as I took that solo." This piqued our sense of intrigue all the more. It went beyond whether the balloons put words in Aunt Nancy's mouth. It was more a question of where exactly the point of enunciation was, exactly whose mouth, so to say, the words came out of. The bass's? The record's? The needle's? None other than the balloon's itself? What Aunt Nancy had said was perhaps all anyone could. Each of us, at any rate, the more we talked, ended up echoing her at some point: "Hard to say."

The balloons' comings and goings appear to be something we'll just have to live with. We've had no luck trying to make heads or tails of why they show up when. The only point on the test pressing where they appear is Aunt Nancy's "Dream Thief" solo, yet even there they don't show up every time it's played. We played *Orphic Bend* twice all the way thru but found no other point at which the balloons emerged. We played "Dream Thief" nine times. The first four times the balloons emerged but on the fifth and sixth they didn't, only to reappear the last three times. Whatever principle of whim or caprice governs their appearances, however, doesn't seem to extend to the wording they bear. Each time they appeared the words inside the balloons were the same: *I dreamt you were gone*, etc.

Whether they'll show up on the final pressing and whether, if they do, it'll be on every copy or only on some remains to be seen. The consequences of that, should it turn out to be the case, we don't dare even think about yet.

Yours,
N.

_____

Dear Angel of Dust,

Aunt Nancy says she's given the balloons a bit more thought and that the more she thinks about it the more they seem to be time-lapse translations of thoughts and feelings extending much farther back than the moment of the "Dream Thief" solo. They partake of an order of telescopic retrieval, telescopic *récit*, lens and crystallization rolled into one. The balloons know something, she says. They see deep into the past and present and magnify what they see, a rhapsodic swell akin to the Penny dream's oracular "eye made of opera glass." She says that she didn't see it at the time, didn't make the connection as the balloons emerged from the test pressing of *Orphic Bend*, but that there actually was a cigar-box guitar in her life.

Djamilaa told me this. Aunt Nancy told her and she told me. She seemed agitated, put upon, Djamilaa says, pestered by a gremlin or a ghost. When she (Djamilaa) remarked as much, told her so, Aunt Nancy said, "Yes. The ghost of my father." She went on to say that although she'd forgotten or failed to see it ("as though it were light-years away" was how she put it, Djamilaa says), the fact the balloons led her to recall was that her father, who died when she was five years old, had made her such a guitar when she was four. It wasn't exactly the same, she admitted, but close enough to make it clear, even so, that this was what the balloons were getting at. The guitar her father made her he made with a cigar box, a sawed-off broomstick and rubber bands, not straw. Straw was the balloons' time-lapse revision, their bent, oblique way of speaking, an oblique, refractive indictment equating string with tenuous grip, slipped grip, string with problematic address. She now, she said, saw that he was the "you" of "I dreamt you were gone," that the balloons implied or suggested that she reached out for him as if grasping at straws.

Aunt Nancy, Djamilaa says, went into the particulars of her father's death and the senses of loss it left her with—complex, largely inchoate feelings she said she felt she'd spent her life building walls against. Chief among such walls was something she termed her "appetite for absence," the attempt at a preemptive strike whereby she repeatedly sought, in her words, "to beat loss at its own game." She gradually, Djamilaa says, moved away from the strictly personal and adopted a generalizing tack, asserting that straw attested to an itch for leverage, an infectious itch to be effica-ciously angled, athwart, possessed of a levered purchase or approach. She grew almost giddy, Djamilaa says, with the sense of this as a universal itch, repeatedly coming back to the word "leverage" in concert with "levity," "lift," "making light," stirring "light-years" into the mix as well. It was as if the remedy she sought proposed a pedigree among the stars. "Straw," Djamilaa recalls her summing up, "scratches a rendezvous with absence light-years away. We have no choice but to make light of it, take liftedness as high as it'll go. Leverage and levity share roots in the sky."

As the balloons would say: no "as if" about it. Aunt Nancy resorted to interstellar space as an Archimedean fulcrum with which to pry her-self loose, disengage herself from an incumbency of loss endemic to Earth, move, if not the world, herself at least. I couldn't help thinking of Sun Ra as Djamilaa spoke, couldn't help recalling the time I went back-stage to see him after a show several years ago. I remembered him bend-ing over at one point to pick up a small trunk filled with equipment. He paused to look up at me while still stooped over, announcing, "Now, this is what you call a space lift," then proceeded to complete the otherwise ordinary act of lifting the trunk up onto a table. Otherwise ordinary, I say, meaning nominally otherwise. Ra's bend and divergence from nom-inal routine sought, like straw, an angled flight from flat abidance, an ad-mission of flatness meant to decry flatness, jimmy its way past it. As with his unexpected announcement, so with straw, the balloons' antithetical springboard starward. Sprung resonance deepens otherwise nominal space.

Some will call this compensation. I'll agree but not go along with the putdown implied. Compensation apportions lack and possession. The latter we tend to forget. What I get from Aunt Nancy's revelations is this: Straw, the balloons' antithetical spur, is as much an affliction as the Ndembu's *ihamba* tooth, as much a boon as it is an affliction. Compensation is a claim cutting both ways. The balloons, one can say, are a compensatory, outward-moving edge we're bitten by, a grief- or grievance-driven seizure of and by premises presumed out of reach.

As ever,

N.

Dear Angel of Dust,

Thank you for your letter. You raise questions I can't give the space I wish I could. Why Aunt Nancy's guitar spoke to me so I can't say. Straw had to do with antithetic detour, resonances coaxed from unprepossessing "string." Foothills burnt brown in the summer came to mind, dry grass, dry weed and dry scrub's inauspicious remit. It seemed I wandered those hills and heard voices, beset by antithetic audition, endowed with a recondite ear. Straw sought an accord with laryngitic declivity, an eviscerated call or cry, swallowed cry. Straw may well have been—I sensed it had to be— scratch to laryngitic itch, retrospect epiphany (suspect epiphany) rendered moot. Still, an advancing choir filled the dead summer air with faint, unlikely sound, tangential voices or intangible voices, all diaphragm and throat, no lips, no tongue. What I wanted was to endorse, not further encumber, Aunt Nancy's guitar.

That I'm not alone in having been so spoken to became evident the other night during our gig at Onaje's. Between sets Drennette suggested we begin with "Dream Thief" when we went back out, a suggestion no one had any problems with. So, back onstage for set two, that's what we did. It was during Aunt Nancy's bass solo that what I'm referring to took place. She'd been at it a short while, eyes closed as they usually are when she solos, head tilted back a bit. She now brought her head down and leaned over the bass and began to strum, punctuating her fingers' address of the strings by thumping, every now and then, the wood of the bass. She thumped with her thumb and with the heel of her hand, sometimes one, sometimes the other, a now halting, now hortative colloquy of thump and strum. Leaning over the bass, hunched over the bass, she increasingly made a cave of herself, an esoteric recess whose bodily husk housed rhythmic disbursements of thump and strum. Colloquy and cave rolled into one, she and the bass effected a unified or unitarian house of sound, a first antiphonal church of thump-inflected strum. It was into this church that Drennette stepped in making a move that took us all by surprise.

As Aunt Nancy delved more deeply into the strum-and-thump line she pursued, eyes closed, her back to the wall, it seemed, of the cave she made of herself, Drennette picked up the duffel bag she keeps on the floor near the foot of the high hat, the bag she keeps cowbells, maracas and such in. She picked it up and reached into it, taking out not a cowbell, maracas or such but a small guitar, a rough-and-ready affair she later told us she herself had made by attaching a sawed-off broomstick to a cigar box and using fishing cord for strings, so moved she'd been, she said, by the test pressing balloons. No balloons came out of Aunt Nancy's bass on this occasion, but Drennette, in an allusion to the test pressing emergence which, surprising though it was, was obvious even at the time, took out the guitar and began to play. Aunt Nancy, hunched over the bass, eyes closed, hardly expected the answering strum she heard coming from where Drennette sat. She opened her eyes and saw what the rest of us, no less unexpectedly, already saw: Drennette strumming and plucking the cigar-box guitar, out of which a damped, sotto voce, seeming shell of a sound emerged. Damped, sotto voce, seeming shell notwithstanding, it advanced a hip, infectious, ditty-bop rasp and reach of irredentist huff. Drennette's guitar sought annexation of pluck-inflected strum by thump-inflected union— unification, it said—with Aunt Nancy's bass.

Drennette, when she plucked, pulled the string out as far as she could and let go, letting it snap against the box to make a rattlish, raspy sound. She hummed, grunted and moaned as she played, a sotto voce run of extenuated voice which brought Delta blues to mind. Even more it brought Bazoumana Sissoko to mind, the "Old Lion" of Mali, the guitar sound more that of an ngoni than that of a guitar. Together, she and the guitar put forth a rolling, multiply-pitched rumble, gruff and apparently offhand but so exact it could not not've come of considered application. They put forth an entwined, sotto voce commotion that both spoke to and took a step farther Aunt Nancy and the bass's antiphonal church.

Aunt Nancy, nonplussed albeit a bit taken aback, didn't miss a beat. She now not only strummed and thumped but also plucked, snapping the strings and letting them buzz against the low end of the fingerboard. Her low-end buzz took up with the guitar's ngoni-like rasp, consorting with it for a long enough stretch to become its escort, a fuzzed, otherwise ictic escort limning a wider aisle in a now much larger church. She somehow managed to work into the strumming, thumping and snapping a steady four-beat walk Leroy Vinnegar would've been proud of, a walk she implied instead of stated outright as often as not, its implicit feet felt in the strum, thump or snap she interrupted it for. She and Drennette were the true heroines of ictic tenancy, spooked apostles of a first-tabernacular iterance/itineracy, antiphonal kin whose blue devotions mourned a felled or, if not yet felled, failing body, the church's first and most reliable house.

This was the annexation Drennette sought. She and Aunt Nancy now walked as one, an ictic promenade which acquired a crablike meander and drift. Her cigar-box guitar seemed a diminished, cautionary doppelganger to Aunt Nancy's bass, a ghost or, better, poltergeist of a claim to connection. She too, that is, now widened her repertoire, now not only strummed and plucked but also thumped, rapping the box with her thumb and the knuckles of her third and fourth fingers. The sotto voce falsetto she now and again got into so lent itself to such thumps it seemed she tapped at a séance table. It was a rough-cut, mystical side of Drennette we don't often see.

Aunt Nancy's bass solo was now clearly something else, a lank, double-jointed duet which, loose and on speaking terms with lateral drift, made its availability or amenability to other voices abundantly clear. Penguin was the first to so avail himself. He quickly slipped backstage and returned with a broom he'd evidently noticed earlier, an old-fashioned cornstalk broom he came back onstage holding like a guitar, strumming like a guitar. He seemed intent on reminding us that the guitar the balloons told of was strung with straw, not fishing cord. He ran his fingertips across the cornstalk straws and extracted what sound he could, an even more diminished, meager ghost of a sound than what came out of Drennette's guitar, a sotto voce flirtation with voicelessness which, like the guitar but even more so, put one in mind of an ngoni. He made his way back to the mike and held the strummed, straw part of the broom close to it, signaling to the fellow working the mix at the back of the room for more volume. That helped some, but it was still a forced, meager sound, pointedly hoarse and laryngitic, mostly gesture if not all gesture, ictic tease. Whenever he left off strumming he plucked, taking a straw between the nails of his thumb and his forefinger (part mime, part makeshift mudra), pulling it out and letting it go and exacting a clipped, anticlimactic pinch of sound. There was next to no snap, absolutely no buzz.

Penguin advanced a philosophic rapport with deficit sound if not with outright lack of sound, so measly and pinched, so miserly or deprived were the dry pricks of sound his plucking produced. It seemed he scratched at the straw for sound, strained at eking what sound out of it he could. A thirsty man on a desert scratching water from sand, he stood elated at the daunting odds he faced. He strummed and plucked, strummed and plucked, elated, oddly geared up. Strumming's dry ripple of sound in concert with plucking's dry pricks of sound introduced a thread of dry humor as well, a philosophic, self-deprecating thread seeking leverage on Drennette and Aunt Nancy's churchical exchange, urging them to lighten up but not without designs on churchicality itself, no sooner urging them to lighten up than advancing its own blue-ictic amen. Several people in the audience laughed. Fierce, funny, desperate in its odd, elated way, Penguin's broom contributed an element one felt was absolutely apt, notwithstanding one would not've known it belonged had it not been there.

Djamilaa was the second to avail herself of Drennette and Aunt Nancy's crabwise aisle, the widening promenade or prospect that all the more showed itself able to accommodate any and all who'd come, having found room for Penguin's wry, blue-ictic sashay. At the piano, she took a Monkish tack, issuing plinks, anxious plunks, hesitant fills, gradually building up to longer runs. She added to Aunt Nancy and Drennette's percussive thumps by stomping her foot every now and again, sometimes her left, sometimes her right, lifting her leg and letting it hang for the time it took to conclude a phrase, bringing her foot down hard on the floor to announce and reinforce having come to the end of the phrase. She had a way of delaying the final note of the phrase, leg suspended, not hitting it until a micro-beat after her foot came down on the floor. A shade late in coming, the note had been held up, it seemed, by some impediment stomping her foot on the floor dislodged. She'd angle her body when she lifted her leg, leaning to the right and away from the piano when she lifted her left, to the left and away from the piano when she lifted her right. She too, it took no genius to see, sought leverage, an oblique, dislocating fulcrum furthering her own blue-ictic stroll, pianistic strut.

Stride and strut were decidedly what she built up to. The others picked up on this, each greeting every impeded note she stomped her foot to free with a micro-beat hitch and a shade late reinforcement of his or her own: an explosive thump from Aunt Nancy's bass, an impulsive pluck from Drennette's guitar, straw's abstract snap or extrapolative snap from Penguin's broom. These became more staggered, dispersed, strewn about as things proceeded, micro-beats and more intervening among stomp, thump, pluck and snap. The blue-ictic aisle became an eruptive expanse in which, hiccup-like, these detonations took one another by surprise.

This was the expanded, eruptive aisle Lambert now stepped into, not with his horn, it turned out, but to dance. He drew abreast of the aisle's blue-ictic tread, its resident walk, starting off with a pointedly long stride to the center of the stage. Once there, he extended his arms in front of his body, hands hanging limp, the classic or stereotypic sleepwalker's pose though his eyes remained open. His arms were extended for balance one soon saw, as he now leaned back on his heels, letting the front of each foot come up off the floor. His heels alone touching the floor, his legs locked at the knee and at a 75° angle with the floor, he proceeded to step in time with the music, walking backwards in a counterclockwise circle.

Lambert's dance endlessly bordered on imbalance, warded off imbalance. He ran a constant risk of leaning too far back, a risk he fought or compensated for by constantly adjusting and readjusting the position of his upper body, fought or compensated for with the quickness of his feet.

His backwards walk was a levered appeal to curved earth, a conserving abandon he sought to enlist or to align himself with. It made a virtue and a game of being caught out, found an awkward beauty in finding itself on the verge of coming apart, a sustained and concrete play on being taken aback.

Lambert bit his lower lip as he danced, a look of resolve, chagrin and cool assurance all in one. The lids of his eyes lowered the longer he danced, never completely closing but according with the sense of a sleep-walk even so. The floor was flat rather than curved one saw, but Lambert's walk reminded one this was mere appearance, so fraught was each step he took with the risk not of falling to the floor so much as falling from it. He staked a claim for ultimate stakes, intimating that to lose balance would be to vanish, disappear.

Aunt Nancy and Drennette's felled or failing body came to mind of course, supported and propped up by the note of ultimacy Lambert struck. Drennette let this note take the humming, grunting and moaning she disbursed a step further, finally having recourse to words as though Lambert's walk advanced an answering talk. She resorted to words in what she now sang, albeit words as often as not not entirely clear. If you've heard cante jondo or Nelson Cavaquinho or that Billie Holiday album *Songs & Conversations* Paramount put out a few years back, you'll have an idea of the way she made a music of slurred speech. She took up with and played with the title of the piece in a now no longer sotto voce run, a run which reminded us we don't yet know what singing is, haven't yet exhausted what it can be. She sang as though she talked out loud in her sleep, a ripped, insistent talk that was garbled and articulate by turns, thick-tongued, inebriate talk in which "dream" and "thief" kept coming up. She held forth with a tone of categorical insistence, what sounded like categorical insistence, vehemently declaiming, expostulating, exhorting. But for all her vehemence one couldn't make out whether dream was what was stolen or itself the thief, her point evidently being that no clear line separated the two, a cloudy line separated the two.

The coupling of categorical tone with cloudy assertion was a tour de force, a slurred swerve into phatic, non-predicate iteration. Lambert meanwhile continued his backwardswalking dance, Djamilaa her stomp-inducted strut, Penguin his dry ripple and pinch, Aunt Nancy her pluck-accompanied, strum-accompanied, thump-accompanied walk. It now fell to me to make a move. I stood put upon by a phrase I heard inside my head. "Given all one has to mourn or lament" were the words which said themselves, it seemed, again and again, words which began a sentence I couldn't complete. Possessed of a non-predicate truth or the tease of a truth which put completion on the tip of one's tongue only to withhold it, I had no choice but to put a horn in my mouth. All I wanted was to feel the reed vibrate against my lip, the sense of extension, completion even, the horn, a straight one, would give my tongue. I took up my soprano and put it in my mouth, content with merely percussive bleeps and blurps to begin but surprising myself by falling in with Lambert. It was an impulse I followed without giving any thought, joining the dance he continued to make of courting imbalance, the backwardswalking circle he went round and round in.

I fell in behind Lambert (that is, facing his back) but in another sense in front, dancing backwards myself as though I led the way Pied Piper-like. The soprano was the pipe I enticed him with, charmed him with, his already sleepwalk-seeming tread all the more so now. Percussive bleeps and blurps gave way to a more sinuous vein, a snake charmer's vein. He followed my lead, mesmerized, it seemed, although it was I who had followed his—a reversal or a confounding of back and front which augmented or extended Drennette's confounding of "dream" and "thief." I walked flatfooted at first, backing round and round as I played, but the more I played the more I continued to in fact follow Lambert's lead. The more I played the more I leaned back, finally letting my toes and the balls of my feet leave the floor, dancing on my heels as did Lambert, my arms out in front holding the horn, elbows raised for balance. I too leaned at a 75° angle. My raised elbows felt like wings. It seemed I'd fly backwards, lift off at exactly that angle at any moment. Though that moment never came, I felt for a sustained, seemingly endless instant how right Aunt Nancy had been. We were each the arm of a universal itch, a shared, angling arm eternally bent on leverage, though—Archimedean crowbar, crack in the cosmic egg (call it what you will)—whether it was an in or an out we sought we could not have said.

We did find our way to the bridge in due course, did get back to the head and wind up the piece. It was evidently one of our best that night. Later, as we left the club, we saw several people who'd been in the audience milling around on the sidewalk outside. One of them spotted us and yelled out, "Yeah! 'Dream Thief'!" He then leaned back at a 75° angle and proceeded to walk backwards on his heels, arms out in front.

Yours,

N.

_____

Dear Angel of Dust,

I dreamt last night I was back in a place I'd once been in. It's a dream I keep having, a dream I can't keep from having. I knew it was the same dream even though the setting wasn't the same. Without having the same look it had the same feel. Nor did the people look at all like the people I'd dreamt of before, let alone like the people who'd been in this place when I was actually there. Still, I knew it was a place I'd once been in I was dreaming about, knew the dream I was dreaming was again the dream I'd often had before. I knew this even though so little about it seemed the same. Mostly what I felt, how I felt, made it the same. I felt a sense of arrival, almost of never having left. Though the woman who drew me there mixed intimacy with distance, intimate yet immune, never again to be caught out, I had a sense of belonging, of being back where I belonged. I'd gotten there soon after she'd woken up. We sat in her living room, talking. "I was afraid I'd never see you again," she said. And then, abruptly, "We're not the same." Just as abruptly the room filled with people, none of whom was anyone I knew or had ever seen. A party had been planned and this was it, though not, I found, a party for me. Even so, the sense of being back where I belonged persisted. Everyone milled around, standing or sitting, talking in groups of two, three, four and five. Talk of the woman who'd drawn me there was on everyone's lips—so much so it was as though she wasn't there. No two groups referred to her by the same name and none of the names any of them used was the one I knew her by, but I nonetheless knew it was about her they were all talking. This was finally confirmed when a man came thru the door referring to her by the name I knew her by, at which point I left the room in search of a bathroom down the hall. The hallway, however, led not to a bathroom but to a small pinball arcade and, from there, to what appeared to be the entrance to a theater. Walking thru that entrance, I ended up, as the dream inconsequentially ended, out on the sidewalk of a busy street.

I woke up upset, unable to get back to sleep, bothered to be put upon again by something I'd long since been done with, long since put away. Presumably put away I suppose I should say, for the dream seems intent on calling closure premature, presumptuous even. A fiction so wishful and so entrenched it could afford to dispense with its usual trappings, it all but gloated, leaving it to me to see thru its disguise. That I so easily did so helped it make its point. I lay awake thinking about this afterwards, unable to get back to sleep, convinced the dream had come to confirm Drennette's ambiguous equation, her cloudy confounding of "dream" and "thief." Yes, a dream can at once debunk and prolong its own wish, I had to agree, steal from itself as it replenishes itself. Yes, I had no choice but to continue, it disrupts ostensible contentment by insisting on lack, a dream in two senses (what's wanted, what can't be had), looter and loot, a thin line, if any, between. Yes, I continued, unable to stop, it invites and discourages in a single sweep, offers and refuses at the same time. This went on, me unable to stop, for quite a while.

It turned out to be a long night, but it got me closer to getting the piece written I wrote you about a few letters back. The sense of grudging receipt I've been after, I came to see, not only has something to learn from the dream's concatenation of theft and recognition but would be better served by brass than by saxophone. Call it brass epiphany. I listened a couple of times to Henry Threadgill's new album *When Was That?*, the one with his new group, the seven-member sextet. Craig Harris and Olu Dara did it, the latter's cornet work in particular, that cracked or cut-into whimsy or wisp of a sound he so often gets. A bird with cracked wings, it reconnoiters and reconceives the music's bugle-corps roots, a militarist call it shades with misgiving, mystic affliction, oddly beguiled and soliloquistic but leading the charge. A feel for confronting long odds (one of the tunes is called "10 to 1") sustains a sense that its apparent play on cavalry and calvary might amount to more than play. It's as though a bitter medicine puckered his mouth, a stiff potion of rescue and duress meted out as one. That, I decided, is what I want for the piece I've been thinking about. It sent me back to my trumpet, which, it made me realize, I tend to neglect.

The intimate-immune reception the dream subjected me to also bears on the piece. Grudging receipt, the dream seems keen on announcing, borders on gnostic receipt, a resolute wish to wake up, gnostic resolve not to be caught out. "Reverie's Reveille" is the title I'm toying with.

As ever,

N.

_____

Dear Angel of Dust,

Thank you for the liner notes. Who but you could've written so movingly about *Orphic Bend*? It seems you've removed at least one wall (perhaps two or three) between reflex and assignation. We ourselves now hear the music in another light. I say so using that expression after a great deal of thought. Isn't it the otherwise nonevident pulsation of light, an achievement of tension between tendency and torque you apprize throughout, the bent, burnished body of tone or intimation torn toward the other meaning of turn (to go sour)? Isn't such an aggrieved or aggressive turn, severing wisdom and resignation, glare's rough acoustic approximation? You lend such light an ear it wouldn't have were it not for you and we follow suit. Your words become the ax we each unwittingly played, an interpolative wrinkle apportioning lapse and oblique sustentation. It's as though your notes were the music's destiny all along, unbeknown to us, axial immensity's come-up largesse. We read our music in what you've written and the ear you lend it amplifies ours. Who but you could do that?

Speaking of liner notes, I just picked up Frank Lowe's *Skizoke*, which carries a reprint of an interview he did with *Cadence* on the back. I'm struck, especially in the wake of the brass epiphany I wrote about in my last letter, by him talking about stealing licks from trumpeters to get away from Trane's influence. I'm even more struck by how he puts what this led him to, the "experiment in time and colors" he calls "just having the horn sound like it's having a big laugh." He mentions Lester Bowie in connection with this, shedding new light, without referring to it outright, on Lester's trademark lab coat, allowing one to see such attire in relation not only to Miles's "We were like scientists of sound" and his divergence from Satchmo, but also to Satchmo's Elizabethan clownish license (as Ellison puts it). One would want to stop short of calling mad scientist or mad professor Lester the synthesis of Miles's antithesis and Louis's thesis, but the near rhyme of Lester's coat with jester's cap bespeaks a need to keep alive, if not sublate, the two contraries. Such attire, in concert, so to speak, with Lester's decidedly tongue-in-cheek instrumental tack, re-dresses both (Miles, for example, on "Dreaming of the Master" on the Art Ensemble's *Nice Guys*, Satchmo on "Hello Dolly" on his own *Fast Last!*). Ripped and retributive, Lester's coat and jester's cap's near rhyme reveals a need or an appetite for (or the need or the appetite of) mad science, knowing's need to laugh at itself or lose its head, know it doesn't know. Coat and cap augur a no longer mystic (no longer only mystic), suddenly scientific (mad-scientific), post-Hiroshima mushroom need to clown, cloud one's knowing, a need steeped in parody, pastiche, mad profession.

So maybe "Reverie's Reveille" isn't a matter of switching over to trumpet but of playing trumpet-in-cheek tenor, lending tenor trumpet's bluster and blare. Frank also mentions Roscoe Mitchell, who, I realize now, does exactly that. Listen to his tenor solo with the Art Ensemble on "Unanka" on *Bap-tizum*. A vaguely brass timbre at the solo's outset eventuates in a profusion of quasi-brass cackle (mad profusion), a "trumpeted" sense of urgency, seizure, stampede. Bluster, yes, and blare, but, even so, it works an aroused, otherwise quietist impulse, annoyed, it seems, at the very need to make sound. As if to announce, à la Rufus Harley, "I didn't ask for this," it begs off its calling, besets vocation with qualms. One hears brass implied in some of Roscoe's alto work even—as in "Sing/Song," on the *Snurdy McGurdy* album, when his descending figure on alto emerges to call the "noise" passage to a halt, only to at once give way to Hugh Ragin's bread-and-butter new-bop trumpet, as though trumpet, if not, granted, in his cheek, had been up his sleeve.

To be rubbed off on by an alternate ax is to question one's calling, pose an alternate calling. Gnostic resonance or residue accrues to such rubbing, an exquisite receipt rendered moot by ensuing detour. And if not rendered moot made to answer to a need to buy time, bartered rapport translating quizzical grip to "inquisite" grasp. I want that to be what "Reverie's Reveille" does.

Yours,

N.

Dear Angel of Dust,

Thanks to brass epiphany I've been thinking about Dizzy's ballooning cheeks. As my wording may have already made evident, they strike me as of a piece with the balloons we've been visited by, in some oblique, subterranean way related. Dizzy's trademark cheeks comply with a principle of exertion and exaggeration, factoring inflation and elasticity in as well. Still, them being a visual trademark may well be their signal feature, trademark visuality itself the signal fact worth attending to. Trademark visuality, it seems to me, wants to domesticate or mask an acoustic risk the music otherwise runs, the risk of acousticality itself. I've touched on something like this before, I realize, but bear with me long enough to consider Dizzy's recourse to scat and his affection for "oo" ("Oop-Pop-A-Da," "Ool-Ya-Koo," "In the Land of Oo-Bla-Dee," etc), his love affair, more generally speaking, with the vocable, as an explicit, so to speak, vocalization if not verbalization of the occult clamor whose risk he runs on the horn. Please also consider an apparent need to eclipse or in some other way recuperate such clamor by way of the purchase visuality provides or appears to provide. Does trademark visuality sugarcoat, for the public at least, the bitter pill of occult clamor? Does the public seize upon consumable, commodified visuality, trademark purchase, as a hedge against acousticality's furtherance of itself, risk of itself, a furtherance and risk the public wants but only on its (the public's) own terms? I'm thinking of Sonny Rollins showing up for a concert in Japan without his Mohawk haircut and the audience not believing it was him. Bird's "Another Hairdo" takes on new meaning, prophetic meaning, and I'm wondering if Dizzy foresaw this problem as well. Are his ballooning cheeks a bone he throws the public or a bone he picks with the public? Or are they, in some way we've yet to understand, both (bone-in-cheek)? I've suggested before that the balloons we're visited by are the shadow visibility casts on the music. Are they also a bone in our collective cheek, a bloated bone we let rip or let go?

This is only a quick note, a kind of addendum to yesterday's letter. Were it to eventuate in music entailing balloons they would beg off being balloons, enclosing words to, say, the following effect: *"A psychopompic foray into occult acousticality . . ."* *So began the balloon, the aborted balloon I glimpsed in the interstice between thought and articulation, waking and sleep. "Spied 'er" was the thought occurred next, balloonless but at large it seemed, in the air if not itself the air. It hung there, a whisper ubiquitous lips momentarily shaped, the lips as well, albeit invisible, in the air if not themselves the air.* (Pause, new balloon.) *"Spied 'er's" apostrophized "h" intimated excision, absence, yes, but also a withheld expulsion of breath, an exclamatory burst born of eight-limbed embrace held under test-tube arrest. It had to do with goings-on in Hotel Didjeridoo, keyhole inquiry, door-peep surmise. Someone assumed himself to have stolen a peek at the proverbial "her," the proverbial muse animating industry and art, the anansic muse on whom "Spied 'er" shamelessly punned.* (Pause, new balloon.) *A random scrap of song, a strung bauble of sound rode a gust of air, a strangled address as of cotton caught in a singer's throat. Sheer insistence held it aloft, sheer anxious energy, adrenal straw, ambient strain drawn of combinatory qualm, coaxed emolument, cracked air's ambient whoosh . . .*

In other words, a bone within a balloon picked by shaman and showman alike.

Yours,

N.

_____

Dear Angel of Dust,

Yes, the balloon I saw the night I sat in with the Crossroads Choir, the balloon the audience batted about while I played, no doubt can be said to have anticipated the comic-strip balloons we've been visited by. I haven't wanted to go down that road, really, but you bring it up and it's all I can do to keep the rush of recollection and reflection in check. The sense or sensation I had that my breath had been taken away, literally sucked away by and bound up in the balloon I saw rising toward the ceiling, is one I'll never forget. It was an impossibly sustained or extended sense of breath as inescapably bated, subject as such to sudden increase, quantum increase, quantum hyper-anticipatory inflation. As a child I thought it was "baited" people were saying when they spoke of bated breath and such was the sense I had as I watched the balloon rise toward the ceiling, a sense of the breath it bound as anticipant no matter how much one struggled to the contrary, hooked. The balloon, empty of all but air but endlessly inviting even so, was bait and bound breath rolled into one.

The other side of it was that, depleted, breath spirited away, I availed myself, it seemed, of someone else's lungs, someone else's breathing. Someone stepped in, stood where I stood, notwithstanding I stood there still. Breath Ex Machina I'd call that someone, except the mechanicality putting it so implies fails to do what I sensed or seemed inhabited by justice. Someone momentarily spelled me, stood in my place as the balloon bore my breath away. Breath Absconditus I'd call the balloon, except it didn't entirely bear my breath away. Understudy, stand-in, second wind (call it what you will), the someone who stepped in drew breath from it, a cardiognostic lung, it seemed, upwardly displaced. I was afraid I'd pass out but it quickly came back down, alighted like a bird inside my ribcage, ensconced, I couldn't help feeling, for all time. I was both cheered and chastened to know that something or someone I couldn't claim to be me had come forth to curtail crisis, something more syncopal than sheer continuance, cardiognostic wind and wing rolled into one more than mere persistence.

The balloon's rise rode my sunken heart. Held in reserve, breath held on high buoyed me up, made my recourse to problematic romance pan out. A subterranean bubble the balloon struck me as having once been. It had risen like gas, a chthonic belch given off by realignments taking place underground. Such realignments gave lost love a seismic stage, a geologic if not cosmic theater and thrust monitoring would-be redemptive history from afar—inward, intimate and one's own yet oddly remote. Rift and realignment amended bedrock truth. Balloon binding bespoke loose (albeit bedrock) truth, elastic truth, a seismic stretch or substratum my sunken heart sought to rise up from. Loose truth's advocate or avatar it was. "Only One" was its cardiognostic disguise.

I could say more but, as they say, don't get me started . . .

As ever,

N.

Dear Angel of Dust,

My mind wandered while I was reading this afternoon and I heard exactly the trumpet sound I want. It was in an in-between place that I heard it, half here, half gone. It began as a flinched expulsion of air, ambient excitation albeit low-key, a flutter of sound with a pendency not unlike that of a feather, the proverbial feather one could've been knocked over by. It emerged abetted by a low-lying, slowly advancing musk, a low-lying perfume, a low, universal blow seeping under a door at Hotel Didjeridoo. It was "air" to the low blow's "earth" but at the same time "earth" in its own way—a cave (albeit an aerial one), an acoustic recess cut in the air by the feather's edge. A rough, sculpted cut the feather rode as well as inflicted, it welled outward and emptied inward, an abrupt, incommensurate cyst. I saw, with my ear's eye, the ground transformed into grotto, cave into alcove, an eluant transfer not available otherwise. What spoke to me most was the impression of breathlessness behind it, a mereness of effort or an insufficiency of effort (a miscalculation of effort as with, in basketball, an air ball perhaps), the exact airiness of a merely imagined caress. Such mereness or insufficiency or miscalculation (an aroused or merely asthmatic shortness of breath) bespoke or seemed intent on singing the obstructedness of all endeavor, as though singing were somehow other than endeavor, so saying short of would-be speech, meaningfully so. Meaningfully less than speech, it spoke nonetheless, a sound or a cyst of sound on the verge of exhaustion. All those stories about trumpeters blowing themselves breathless on a high note and keeling over backwards came back to me, bound up in that cyst and the knockdown feather it'd been carved out by. Mereness (meaningful lack) floated free but also fraught with recollected duress, a sweet tooth for duress one nursed and had a need for and knew in the simplest intake of breath.

Could I have caught it in a bottle I'd have been the happiest man on Earth. Still, I knew that to bottle it would have been to betray it. This made it all the more an emotional shorthand I could only hope to someday manage on the horn. It hung in the air, not exactly of the air. It exempted itself of the ambient complication it caused or occasioned or (so it seemed to insist) merely rose coincident with. It hedged, haloed itself. It augured against exactly such perturbation as it brought about, an emotional feint or a philosophic forfeiture I found myself intimately ambushed by. Intimate ambush was augured intimation and it bestowed an innerness on the halo it wore, a cutting innerness and a perimetric edge it swelled against, grew to be constricted by.

I sat entranced by what I heard for no telling how long, half here, half gone. What brought me out of it and broke up the sound was another sound—the sound of knocking. Someone was at the door. It was Lambert, it turned out, showing up as we'd arranged earlier on the phone. We were to go to a little music shop up in Hollywood, a tiny place tucked away on a backstreet above Hollywood Boulevard just below Franklin. The fellow who runs it is beginning to get a reputation among saxophone players for customizing mouthpieces. Lambert's been suggesting for a while that we go by there sometime. He's done so a bit more often, a bit more insistently of late, due, it seems, to my recent turn toward brass. He's let a remark or two or three slip since I first mentioned it to him and the rest of the band, remarks about me, as he puts it, "forsaking the reeds, not keeping the faith." He's done it jokingly but I suspected from the first it wasn't just a joke. His insistence of late that we check the music shop out, see what the fellow there might be able to do for us mouthpiecewise, seems to be an attempt to, as he sees it, save me. That notwithstanding, I agreed to go.

We got going right away and on our way out to Lambert's car he said he'd been knocking for quite a while before I came to the door. I proceeded to tell him why as we got into the car, began talking about the trumpet sound I'd heard while half here, half gone. We pulled away from the curb as I went into it, struggling to find the right words, Lambert's eyes on the road in front of us, only on the road in front of us. He seemed unusually intent on the road and on his driving and I went on talking, wrestling with trying to translate what I'd heard into words. Lambert's eyes remained on the road, him not so much as nodding in response to me talking, not turning to make eye contact until I was finished. Even then he waited a moment before turning to me and speaking.

"What next? Violin?" This caught me offguard.

"Well, I happen to like 'Snowflakes and Sunshine,' " I said, calling him on his allusion to Ornette, "but that's not the point." His comment had caught me offguard but before I knew it I knew what to say.

"Okay," he said. "Touché. But this trumpet thing worries me." We were on the freeway now, his eyes no longer glued to the road as they'd been before. It was just the opposite. He looked me in the eye for a long stretch, neglecting the road, looked me in the eye as if to make me break down, confess. I wasn't clear what I was expected to admit and had no intention of doing so in any case but I began to talk. My beginning to talk made him ease up on the eye contact, return his attention to the road, much to my relief. We barely missed rear-ending a car that had pulled into our lane while he was looking me in the eye.

What I had to say about "this trumpet thing" was a repeat of what I'd already told him and the rest of the band, a repeat as well of what I've written you. I not only repeated but elaborated on what I'd said and written before (the longer I talked the longer his eyes remained on the road). I eventually got into an aspect of this I hadn't yet gone into either with the band or with you.

"And who's to say this has nothing to do with my early church upbringing, all that business about Gabriel's trumpet announcing the end of the world and waking the dead, Joshua's trumpet toppling the walls of Jericho?" I rhetorically asked. "Who's to say it's not the horn's apocalyptic pedigree at the root of all this?"

Lambert's eyes were no longer on the road. He glared at me as if I'd insulted his mother. "Apocalyptic?" he all but spat. "Who cares? The sax-ophone is the more epochal horn, the more Promethean. You do remem-ber that piece I wrote, don't you? And what's this 'church upbringing' bit? Trane's father was a preacher. You can't get any more church-brought-up than that."

I answered yes but that for me the horns don't preclude or compete with one another, that it's just that of late I've wanted to get back in touch with what brass can do. It was an argument he wasn't ready to hear, had no patience for, and I found that the more he spoke on the saxophone's be-half the less both/and the tack I took became, the more I responded in kind, pro-trumpet. It soon got to where we went back and forth without either of us really hearing the other, to where it seemed we spoke two dif-ferent languages. Gabriel vied with Prometheus, epoch with apocalypse, Hebrew with Greek as Lambert's eyes, now on the road, now on me, were off the road much longer than on.

The impasse we'd arrived at was easy enough to see, so easy it com-bined anticlimax with saving grace. It left little else to do but laugh, which we did. We laughed at ourselves and at the argumentative whim we'd been ridden by. We laughed at its possession of us and, especially, at Lambert's incommensurate pique. Even he had to admit he'd gone off.

We took the Hollywood Boulevard exit and we soon found the shop. Its looks were inauspicious. It was a long, narrow tunnel of a place, walls lined with instruments, books, merchandise of the usual sort, a bit on the dark side, light coming in only thru a display window to the right of the door. Also to the right of the door, as one entered, was a long counter atop a display case, immediately catching one's eye on which, right beside the cash register, sat plastic reproductions of the human skull interspersed among plastic busts of Beethoven, Mozart and Bach. There was a great deal of clutter in the place, which, small, truly a hole in the wall, was packed past the bursting point. It was hard, stepping inside, not to step on or stumble over a saxophone rest, a music stand, a bass drum or some other object on the floor.

The owner of the shop sat on a stool behind the counter reading a book, a short, stocky fellow with a ruddy face and medium-length brown hair. He looked up from his book and said hello as we walked in. We said hello and Lambert asked if he was Fred who does work on mouthpieces. He answered yes and went on at once to exhibit the trait we'd heard a lot about, been warned about: once he started talking it seemed he'd never stop. Yes, he was the Fred who works on mouthpieces, he began, then, asking who we'd heard of him from but not stopping for an answer, he launched a long spiel in praise of his work. No, he wasn't surprised we'd heard of him, since, after all, no one knows mouthpieces better than him and some of the best players in the world visit the shop, like Pharoah Sanders who'd been in just the week before last, etc, etc. He boasted, he bragged, he opined, he told anecdotes—on and on and on, etc, etc, no end in sight.

It was Lambert who finally broke in, his voice raised a bit above normal to get Fred's attention. "Yes," he said, "we wouldn't be here if we didn't already know all that." It was on the brusque side, somewhat abrupt, but we'd been told that's what one has to do, cut in, that there's no way to get a word in otherwise. It did the job, for a while at least.

Fred stopped talking and Lambert and I introduced ourselves. At the mention of the band Fred was off and going again. Oh yes, he'd heard of us and may even have caught one of our gigs, let him think. No, he couldn't pin when and where down at the moment but he was sure he'd heard us, etc, etc. Lambert and I looked at each other and I cut in to say we were sure he had and to ask if we could look at some mouthpieces. "Absolutely," he answered, beginning to walk toward the back of the store while motioning for us to follow. "What kind of sound do you want?"

He didn't give us time to answer before asking had we brought our horns along and then, noticing the cases we carried, said never mind, he could see we had. He then asked again about the sound we were after, "The bottom-heavy, dark, Dexter Gordon end of the spectrum or the light, floaty end à la Stan Getz?" Again he didn't give us time to answer before, barely taking a breath or waiting a beat, pointing out that, speaking of bottom-heavy, Joe Henderson comes into the store from time to time. "Do you want to hear a funny story about Joe?" he asked, already laughing.

"We're sort of in a hurry," Lambert shot out quickly.

Fred stopped and Lambert immediately added that it wasn't sound in some inert sense he was after, that manueverability among certain subtle alterations of attack was what he hoped a new mouthpiece might help him with. This wasn't to say, he went on, that a meatier sound in the middle register wasn't something he'd welcome, only that it wasn't about sound per se, sound commodified or fetishized, sound as magic wand. He said he hates it when a player relies too much on the charm of sound, loads up on its aura, that, frankly, that's a problem he has with Pharoah's playing of late, that Pharoah seems content to let listeners bask in the fullness and the beauty of the tone he gets and be intermittently startled or made ecstatic by his trademark sandpaper screech. He used a phrase for this that stayed with me, "paralytic aura," saying that Pharoah's transit between beauty and terror, between what he (Lambert) took to be intended as beauty and terror, had become too pat, pure hypostasis, that Pharoah's mind seems too made up as to what these two things are. Compare, he went on, his playing while he was with Trane, his actual choice of notes and dynamics and the proportions plied by quandary and duress, with his playing of late and we'd see what he meant.

It was a mouthful, more than a mouthful. Lambert went on for some time, caught up in the distinction between sound per se and alteration of attack, unintentionally beating Fred at his own game, for a time at least. It was a distinction I'd heard him expound on before, but never with quite such adamance or insistence. He was upping the ante on Fred's mention of Pharoah but it was also not lost on me that what he said might also have been aimed at my having gone on about the trumpet sound I heard.

It was classic Lambert—fussy, painstakingly discerning, cavalier. Fred, who seemed at first only to be biding his time, only half-listening while awaiting his chance to begin talking again, gradually appeared to be drawn in, to take genuine interest in what Lambert had to say. The look on his face changed. It was as if he'd been relieved of his compulsion to talk, as if such relief were what, without knowing it, he truly wanted, as if compulsive talk disguised a latent wish to be so genuinely engaged as to gratefully fall silent. So it seemed for a time at least.

Lambert began to repeat himself and Fred's attention began to fall off. He no longer seemed relieved of the compulsion to talk. At the third or fourth repeat of the distinction between sound and alteration of attack he cut in, admonishing, "There's no getting away from sound." With that he was off again, going on to add that in music sound is what alteration of attack is made of, that by virtue of attending to one you attend to the other. He qualified this latter assertion by explaining that it was neither as automatic as putting it so made it sound nor as reciprocal, that what he really meant was that you can't attend to alteration of attack without attending to sound, though, yes, Lambert was right, you can, as too many players, he agreed, nowadays do, load up on sound without regard for alteration of attack. He went on to talk about Joe Henderson as a case in point (he seemed intent on talking about Joe Henderson one way or another, funny story or not), citing his use of alternate fingerings as not simply a question of dynamics, the facilitation of certain transitions alternate fingerings afford, but as a matter of sound as well, of aural distinctions arising from the fact that the same note differently fingered sounds different—subtly so, granted, but appreciably so nonetheless.

Lambert cut in to agree but also disagree, off and going again, not repeating himself now but putting forth a number of new ideas, angles, wrinkles, Fred eventually cutting in to in turn agree but also disagree. This exchange went on longer than I thought it needed to, so I opened my saxophone case, took the horn out, put it together and strapped it on. Lambert and Fred noticed me do so, watched me do so, but went on talking. It wasn't until I put the horn to my mouth and loudly played a run that they stopped, at which point I took the horn from my mouth and suggested, "Maybe it's time we got down to specifics." They agreed.

It was then that we really dealt with the matter at hand. Fred had me and Lambert play our horns from bottom to top, every note, alternate fingerings included. We talked about each note, how it sounded, was it the sound we wanted, what about it, if not, wasn't right, what it was it needed. He had each of us play whatever runs or transitions or turns of phrase had been giving us trouble or that we wished to go elsewhere with, asking what it was about it we found a problem, what it was we wanted we hadn't been able to get to yet. It was striking how different he now was—not overly talkative, not at all talkative really, just asking questions and looking at us closely as we played. He had a notebook out on which, not unlike a shrink, he jotted everything down. He had us take the mouthpieces off and looked each of them over closely, jotting down more notes and making sketches as well. He then selected a mouthpiece for each of us from among those in the store and had us play again from bottom to top, every note, him asking questions and jotting things down. It was a long process, made all the more so by being interrupted a couple of times by other customers coming into the store.

Fred finally said he had all the information he needed, that some of what we were after a change of mouthpieces could address—some, he emphasized, not all, specifying which—and that he'd get to work, as he put it, "doctoring the mouthpieces up." He was busy, backed up, he said, but he could have it done in a couple of weeks and would contact us then. We let him know how we could be reached and after another jab or two between him and Lambert regarding sound versus alteration of attack we said so long and were on our way.

Once outside, we saw that we'd been in the shop quite a while. The sun had just set. The sky bore streaks of orange, pink, yellow and gray. Lambert suggested we get something to eat and I said good idea. We headed for a place he likes a lot in Chinatown called Yang Chow.

We'd been there long enough to be halfway thru a bowl of wontons when a woman suddenly sat down in our booth right next to Lambert, sliding in so close the side of her body pressed up against his—flirtatious, forward, yet so emphatically so, outright so, the gesture seemed less intended to woo than to make a point. Lambert and I, surprised of course, taken aback, looked up from our wontons. As soon as Lambert saw who it was, as soon as his eyes met hers, a beaming, toothy smile lit up her face. "Hello, stranger," she said with a mock-melodious lilt, her voice low-pitched and a bit breathy, insinuating pillows, perfume, rumpled sheets. Lambert returned her smile, almost laughing really, said hello while taking hold of her left hand with his right, leaned forward to bestow a dry, ceremonial kiss. A simple peck whose gallantry and restraint made it almost lewd, it too suggested bedspreads and blankets tossed aside. The two of them seemed unaware, for a moment, that I was also there in the booth or that there was anyone in the whole restaurant but them.

It was only a moment. Lambert turned to me and introduced us. Her name was Melanie, he and she were old friends, they'd met while in college back east. She was glad to meet me, I was glad to meet her. She explained that she was there with a couple of friends, that they had just walked in and that as they did she'd spotted Lambert, whom she hadn't seen in months. She looked at Lambert as she said this last part, emphasizing "months." He laughed and said yes, he'd been scarce lately but that weeks was more like it, emphasizing "weeks," insisting it had been two, maybe three at the most.

Melanie brought Mingus's title "Vasserlean" to mind. It may have been the mention of college back east that did it but if it was it wasn't only that. A fetching mix of pretty and unprepossessing, she was well-scrubbed and well-spoken, thin of limb and thin of torso as well, a hint of lubricity borne to the bone, it seemed, in the way she carried herself. A certain salience of tooth and bone, the hard parts of the body, bestowed a hard-won, rough-and-ready allure, a close-to-the-bone bodily sway and sashay never all that far from barebones come-on, skeletal courtship, boned embrace. Her close-cropped hair highlighted the bones of her face, the closeness of skull below the surface of skin. Countering the obduracy and closeness of bone was the fleshiness and fullness of her mouth—generous, pliant, large, barely short of overly so. When she smiled, which she tended to do a lot, it was, as I've already said, toothy—toothy and tending to show, when she laughed, a lot of gum. Her dress's exposure of jutting clavicle and shoulder further brought bone to the fore, as its drape of jutting albeit close-to-the-bone breast and curvaceous hip equally did for countering flesh.

Melanie stayed at our table a while, pressed as close to Lambert as when she first sat down, sampling his bowl of wontons at one point, talking to me as well as to him. When she left to rejoin her friends Lambert's eyes and mine followed her across the room. Turning back to him, I asked, "Girlfriend?"

"Sort of," he said, shrugging his shoulders. "We kick it around from time to time."

"She seems ready to kick it around some more," I said. He said nothing, a bit abstracted, lost in thought, showing no sign of wanting to go into it further. I let it go.

We talked about a good number of other things as we ate. After we'd left the restaurant and were in his car on the freeway, however, he brought Melanie up. It was then that he went into their involvement in more detail, calling it on-again, off-again and again referring to it as kicking it around. He spoke almost as if thinking out loud, especially so as he tried to characterize what it was about her that he was drawn to, "the certain something," as he put it, "I love but grow weary of but can't help, even having grown weary, going back to again and again." He spoke of ambivalence, mainly his, but also of her not being wholly free of it. He spoke of beauty, her beauty, a certain lack of abashment, a certain forthrightness, "a sexiness, a readiness," as he put it, "that borders on overly bold, borders on brazen." He paused before asking, "You know what I mean?"

I knew what he meant. It was the outright or forthright appetence I've been calling close-to-the-bone. "Yes," I answered, "bordering on brass."

He threatened to stop the car and put me out.

Yours,

N.

Dear Angel of Dust,

There are stretches of time that seem outside of time. This is one of them. It has to do with seasonality, countered expectations of seasonality, the not only normal departure of L.A. weather from the wintry scenes associated with Christmas but the more than normal departure we've been experiencing the past two days. It's been unseasonably sunny and unseasonably hot even by local standards: temperatures in the nineties, the sky all but without smog, there having been enough wind, if that's what it takes (or enough, if not, of whatever it takes), to blow most of what there was of it away. Now, though, there's no longer wind or even an inkling of wind, the air eerily, ominously unmoving. It's what, especially farther north, they call earthquake weather. The air and the sky have a burning, bright but oddly muted intensity to them, as though their apparent forthrightness were no more than apparent, deceptively clear. This makes for an even greater sense of displacement or dislocation, of things being out of joint, multiply out of joint. It's as though we were not only out of step with the season, our own as well as the holiday season, but had migrated north if not stepped outside of time, seasonality, altogether. In the latter respect, it's as though we'd migrated south or been visited by a region farther south, unexpectedly hosted a mesoamerican visitation. It's as though, that is, the five leftover days at the end of the Mayan year, the five dangling or dateless or stray, orphaned or unlucky, rogue days at the end of the year that are not really, in a sense, a part of the year, a part of time, had arrived early, ahead of themselves, ahead of time, landing us outside of time.

Everything's odd, a bit off, curiously shadowed by syncopations not of time so much as of brightness, light, as though brightness or light turned its head or turned around to inspect itself, turned to catch a glimpse of itself, catch itself offguard. Brightness or light, possessed of a darkling wish, wants not only to enable sight but to see itself so enabled, more than simply conditioning sight. In so doing or, short of doing, wishing, it induces a waver, a wrinkle, a fold in the accoutrements of sight which, even so induced, shears or shades over into undoing.

Spinning my wheels? Maybe. But that's what what I'm talking about makes one do. It makes what appear to be waves mount like rungs of a ladder, a ribbed, etheric lake at what appears to be asphalt's end. At rehearsal today it crept into our music. We trudged up a hill beyond which to walk was to accept that light fell unequally on the world. Chiming rungs which were synthesizer strings bore us over. Our acceptance of light's inequality implied prismatic recompense, insisted on it, made it our own. The earth was unequal light's jagged consort, a course cut in haggard pursuit. From somewhere beyond or in back, that is, a synthesized aura sought instrumental extension, sought more to be played than to preside it seemed, eight or eight hundred years into the future, eight or eight hundred years after the fact. We were trying to make it home or to heaven, hoping to make them one and the same. We were trying at the very least to make something happen. A synthesizer keyboard lay before and in back of us, each key a chromatic step we took.

Then, too, there was the extent to which the "we" was in question albeit as close as our very breath. Lambert's audible exhalation etched an aspirate sigh. In so doing it exacted of each of us an answering sussurration it was all we could do not to be whisked away by, borne thru the wall he thereby embroidered. "We" was the churchical wall he not so much wailed at as blew the dust from, a particulate cloud and a kind of clemency, the grit of what we knew would pass. His aspirate sigh, which we made ours as well, was meant not to conceive an alternative, however much it did so or may seem to have done so, but to extenuate the cause that gave it rise. A wall of glass it was of sorts or in certain parts, a window occluded or colored by aspirate wind's unwieldy arrest, maculate print one may have taken for stain but, even so, could not but be moved by the light it let thru. All this was abetted by Aunt Nancy's totemic bass, its intimation of an arachno-erotic web, eight-limbed embrace, a "we" pressed well beyond erotic-elegiac snag, as though capture, perhaps, arose only to be obscured if not outrun. No one could not be moved by her uptempo "walk."

So, as well, there was the fact that it was, in many ways, a chthonic window, notwithstanding the light and the color it let in. It sat within a wall only recently evolved out of mud, across from an alcove whose cave ancestry was abundantly clear. Bass Cathedral Djamilaa's synthesizer keyboard called it, a handle she proffered cautiously given the fall of Hotel Didjeridoo. Even so, color and light were now undeniably synthetic aura, sympathetic trap, a magico-mimetic snare cave stain or cave painting introduced us to. A piece or a pocket of time had torn loose we now knew, a before-the-fact catch or a prepossessed capture Bass Cathedral built on as well as wanted to enshrine. Yes, we readily agreed, Bass Cathedral, no sooner ratifying than naming it anew, Bass Calendar, temple and temporality rolled into one, we saw, insisted, possessed of southerly color's reckoning spin.

As ever,

N.

PS: "We," it almost went without saying, was an eroding wall Penguin's oboe assailed, wanting to ascend. To one side of Aunt Nancy's "walk" and from an angle of address Lambert's churchical stain imposed on the eye, one watched him serenading Drennette. Drennette ostensibly stood on the balcony under which he played but she was visibly on the ground right in back of him, seated at her drumset, playing along. Penguin pointed his oboe up toward the balcony, eyes closed, head back, blowing as though each breath were his last, playing his heart out. What came out of the horn were not balloons but a bouquet of milkweed, sourgrass, dandelions and such. One was led to hear not only *would* in the horn's "high wood" root but *weed* as well, leaf given rise to by root. It wanted one to recall the vacant lot among whose weeds Drennette turned a cartwheel, the vacant lot the balloons apprised us of in Seattle. It invited one to hear not only *would* and *weed* but *would* and *we, we'd,* as well, albeit *we'd* was as much *we had* as *we would* one immediately saw. Either way, past or past perfect or conditional, it bespoke a deprived present, a "we" that was yet to act as one or that once had but was now done with doing so. Launch or lament, *we'd* was high wood's wager, *wed* apostrophized. A leaf Penguin put in his pipe, it addressed a union otherwise not there, lost or never had but hoped for, would-be union gone up in smoke or induced by smoke.

An abraded wall born of would-be union, blown smoke, it unveiled an eclipse one could otherwise not have witnessed, an opera staining the glass one, protected, held up to one's eye, salting one's ecclessial surmise. One saw Drennette lean back as far as she could on the drum stool, her back at a sharp angle to the floor, looking as though she'd fall over backwards. Arms extended, locked at the elbow, she let the sticks mark time on the snare's head as though biding her time, equating *we'd* with infiltration, having none of it. She kept her distance, eyebrows raised, increased her distance, insisting on the equation of *we'd* with rank profusion, insisting on its homophony with *weed,* unwanted growth, insisting *wed* wasn't even to be considered. What one saw one called "Entropic Duet (Penguin and Drennette Virgin)," a cracked or a creaking aria one could elicit only an excerpt from.

_____

Dear Angel of Dust,

I'm enclosing a new after-the-fact lecture/libretto. I feel a need, ever since the piece or the pocket or the capsule of time tore loose the other day at rehearsal, to move in a somewhat new direction. I feel a need to literalize operatic inflation via the presence onstage of what I call puppets, moot puppets, large polyethylene bags filled with air, clear but colored bags or balloons, each intimating elastic bottle, beached whale, lung, slug and more rolled into one. By moot I mean beside the point, by puppet pointedly so, what exactly they are not really mattering, that being the point. There would be two of them, each about twenty-five feet long, seven or eight feet tall, seven or eight feet wide, wine-bottle green in color. They would lie each to one side of the stage, attached to the floor by wires and open at the attached end, a blower blowing air in thru the opening, small slits along the sides letting the air out. The rate at which the air is blown in would vary, now speeding up, now slowing down, causing the bag to expand and contract and to otherwise move, an unpredictable wiggle and writhe. So they'd lie moot but not inanimate, lie, I'm inclined to insist, in wait, an evolutionist ambush erratically spawned on this or that abstract premise (churchical wave within cathedral arrest, breached arrival washed eventually ashore).

The Hollywood Bowl, given its trademark shell, would be the ideal venue, letting _marine_ infiltrate _bass_, albeit short of changing names outright. An acoustic beachhead or, even so, Marine Cathedral is what the setting should be, beach a kind of balcony, sand anabatic serenade, staged antipathetic spin climbing skyward (glass away from grain, grain away from timbre), staged interstice, turn. The production style should run the gamut, alternately juicy and dry, a *dropped* opera. I want it to combine elements of overblown opera with blasé gig. I don't expect it'll ever make it to the Hollywood Bowl, so puppet show, shadow play, sitcom and closet drama should meet and mingle within it as well.

Yours,
N.

ORPHIC SHORE

or, The Creaking of the Word: After-the-Fact Lecture/Libretto
('Nansic Breach)

B'Loon and Djbouche lay marooned on an abstract beach neither
knew what to make of. They lay on the sand changing shape with every
shift in the wind, no matter how slight, not unlike bubbles at the breeze's
mercy, metamorphosing, blown glass in its molten state. What to make of
themselves was an ancillary question.

They were there to testify to see-thru containment's aliquant advance, an advance into datelessness. Their sponsoring scribe, long known
only as N., had only of late been able to move beyond initial constraint,
donning the name Natty Dredge. Signing his letters that way, he now
dated them "Dateless." He had acquired the name, filled out his name,
taken it beyond a mere first initial, the night that he, Lambert and Penguin
stood serenading Djeannine beneath her bedroom window.

B'Loon and Djbouche remembered it well. "Too much has been made
of music's role in this," they again heard N. insisting. "I myself, I have to
admit, have been as guilty as anyone."

Irritated, annoyed, Penguin, just as he had before, had interrupted by
asking, "Why do you keep bringing that up?"

N., just as he had before, had ignored the interruption, continuing,
"Music is only a deficit we expend in pursuit of an equation beyond its
reach. It neither explains nor characterizes anything. However much it
may appear to speak to the task, it's only to say, ultimately, 'Hush, now,
don't.' "

It was this repeated caveat, repeatedly met by Penguin's interruption, that had earned him the name Natty Dredge. All this now came back to B'Loon and Djbouche. Unable to take it any longer, Penguin, they recalled, had finally poked fun at N.'s apocalyptic tone by teasing, "Dredge, Natty, dredge." Remembering what he then went on to say, neither B'Loon nor Djbouche would have been able to keep a straight face had they had faces. "You wear highwater pants," Penguin had spat out. "The Flood dried up ages ago."

Penguin's quip had drawn a round of laughter. B'Loon and Djbouche could all but hear it even now. Lambert had laughed and Djeannine had laughed. Natty Dredge himself had soon given in and laughed, whereupon Penguin let himself laugh at his own joke.

When the laughter subsided they'd gotten back to the serenade, taking it up exactly where Natty Dredge's caveat had cut if off—not exactly not missing a beat albeit closer to that than one would've thought possible. Penguin's, as it had been before, was the lead voice, but the jovial mood his quip had reinstated had come crashing down when Djeannine, moved by the music, seductively cooed, "Yes, sing it to me, Rick."

Penguin, crestfallen, had stopped singing. Lambert and Natty Dredge, seeing that Penguin had stopped singing, had done the same. It was in this way that the serenade had crested and fallen, fallen short of cresting, crested short of cresting and fallen with a resounding crash, a crash the wave washing B'Loon and Djbouche ashore echoed when it broke.

The plan had been that at serenade's end Lambert and N. would discreetly slip away, leaving Penguin and Djeannine alone, at which point Penguin would ask Djeannine out on a date. The whole thing was Penguin's idea. Lambert and N. had come along at his request. They both had had reservations but had come along nonetheless (in N.'s case waveringly so, as the caveat he repeated had made clear).

Lambert and N. had been there as backup, moral as much as musical support, there to reinforce Penguin's resolve. Such resolve had entirely disappeared with the cooing encouragement Djeannine offered "Rick." That dreamgirl Djeannine and realgirl Drennette's ex might be an item had entirely blown Penguin away. As embarrassed as he was crestfallen, he'd beaten a hasty retreat. Lambert and Natty Dredge had given Djean-nine a puzzled look before they too beat a hasty retreat.

Thus it was, B'Loon and Djbouche recollected, that Natty Dredge had graduated into datelessness. The broken-off serenade had killed all hope on Penguin's part. Never again would he gather enough nerve to ask Djeannine out. Never would such a date occur. B'Loon and Djbouche were there to announce that it was in solidarity with Penguin that Natty Dredge dated his letters "Dateless," a complicated play of sympathetic affliction which implied an appropriation of mesoamerican calendrics.

Natty Dredge now wrote, they were there to explain, only on the last, leftover days at year's end, ominous, unaccounted for, nameless—a name-lessness inversely related to his recent graduation beyond initial con-straint. These were the days during which the year dies, the dreadful days during which a new year comes to life. Thus it was that B'Loon now took Natty Dredge's name a step farther. As if to honor dread, as though "dredge" were clearly "dread" with an expended "a" and a "j" on the end, he now proposed changing its spelling: "Natty Dredj."

"Dredj" put initial "dj" to the rear, a metathetic spin which was in no way lost on Djbouche. Tempted to take it personally, he resisted. "Dredj," if aimed at anyone, targeted Djeannine. Hers, he understood, was the "dj" it put be-hind.

Still, Djeannine/"Dredj" echoed B'Loon and Djbouche's contentious duet—duet, that is, and duel rolled into one. Glass captivity had them both on edge, no more than a moment away from exploding, the echo of the cut-off serenade's resounding crash an abstract crescendo their con-tentious duet racked itself to contain. An abstract, inaudible moan seemed to sum it all up, a pinched, nasal wail à la Wayne Shorter's early work with the Messengers. Abstract summation sought, it seemed, an acoustic ag-grandizement of an alternate sort, a noumenal sonance built on test-tube expectancy, bent on vatic ambage's arrested rush.

So, at least, spoke summation's ebb and ostensible echo, "spoke," though, less the case than "imputed," "intimated," "spoke" a laryngitic alibi. Headless, limbless, all torso (if the undulant, blow-bubble tube in which each was encased could be called a torso), B'Loon and Djbouche lay on the beach, glass's granular root strewn all around them. Writhing, changing shape, their blown-glass tumescence underwent endless contortion, circumlocutious grit qua surrounding sand notwithstanding, granularity an indigenous trigger and a natal translation rolled into one.

So as to show he took no offense at "Dredj's" demotion of initial "dj," Djbouche recommended they take B'Loon's proposal a step farther. Why not, he suggested, drop "Natty"? Why not let "Dredj" stand alone? This is only what a shipwreck survivor does—never nattily, always ragged. At the very least, he added, there's the matter of highwater pants.

All of this got conveyed telepathically in B'Loon and Djbouche's no-note duet. They were there to announce this, that and the other—in a register tantamount to announcement's retreat. Soughed incision, signal respite and prodigal sigh rolled into one, it was a nonsonant retreat whose difference from retraction was to advance recoil as anabatic address. A risen sense of having said all there is to say while only scratching the surface grew with each deployment of the alternate register they adduced.

Below the surface lay the fact, for one, that Dredj's dateless tack had also to do with Djband's recording date having come and gone. Datelessness might be an admission of post-recording ennui or an accession to immortality thought to have been bestowed by the record's release. It was in fact, in some mixed, emergent sense not yet articulable, "both." B'Loon and Djbouche's no-note duet bore no notes but nonetheless exacted a buzz ("both"), an anansic, namesake buzz harking back to Aunt Nancy, a member of Djband who, during the recording session, had from time to time played a Mozambican thumb-piano known as the nsansi.

Inasmuch as datelessness was indeed "both," its mixed, emergent "bothness" partook of Aunt Nancy/nsansi's namesake meeting, a meeting of classic stature—a classic, proverbial encounter between spider and fly. Aunt Nancy's dexterous albeit "all thumbs" attack had offered up a tour de force, the coffee can she placed the nsansi on acting as a resonator, pebbles placed inside adding to the buzz.

It all poured in. There was no time. Aunt Nancy's nsansi was as audible now as on the day of the recording. B'Loon and Djbouche heard the patient, meditative persistence with which Aunt Nancy addressed the nsansi's metal keys, the ictic, I've-known-rivers ongoingness of the vein she worked. They heard her insistence that it wasn't so much a matter of her playing the nsansi as of her and the nsansi playing a duet. Aunt Nancy played not to please an audience or to contribute to Djband's music, however masterfully she succeeded at both, but to abide in the fact that she has a friend, that she and this friend, namely the nsansi, talk with one another, teach one another, that this friend is as much her teacher as she is its teacher.

Aunt Nancy embroidered the nsansic line with low, sotto voce singing. As much exhortative hum as outright singing, it relied on a descending sawtooth pattern, each "tooth" a grieving catch toward the top of her throat. She repeatedly played jubilant or would-be jubilant spider to the nsansi's disconsolate fly. A throbbing, threnodic swell rose from the nsansi to meet each grieving "tooth," instigating a jubilant or would-be jubilant upward leap in Aunt Nancy's voice, a saltatory dilation which expanded only to all the more quickly contract, turning back to the hoarse, exhortative ululation which had launched it, all the more absorbing, all the more entrenched.

B'Loon and Djbouche heard it all. The sort of song a child sings while skipping rope is what the jubilant or would-be jubilant bounding of voice put them in mind of. Aunt Nancy let bounding hum blend with the nsansi's buzz, comprising a guttural, straining extrusion intimating captive clarity, a coughlike, expectorant wish to at last come clean or get clear, lead or be led into light. Who leads and who follows was only marginally at issue, spider-and-fly notwithstanding, for Aunt Nancy and the nsansi are friends (they both insisted), confide in one another, learn from one another, talk . . .

One of the lines Aunt Nancy sang when humming gave way to words came across with special strength, a touch of stridency, an ever so nasal air of complaint. "Penguin's head caught under Drennette's dress," she let out. It had no discernible relationship to the lines that preceded or to those that followed. It appeared to be something she had to get in, something she had to let out, get off her chest, and her voice rose a bit above sotto voce when she did.

Penguin's head caught under Drennette's dress: a pungent line intimating pungencies, funk underneath; a blue recitative intimating lingerie, blue silk underneath.

B'Loon and Djbouche instinctively caught Aunt Nancy's drift. Drennette's dress, they understood, was a web, Penguin's buzzing head a fly caught in the crotch of her blue silk panties. Blue silk emitted a chromatico-tactile perfume, test-tube funk, a conceptual musk penetrating the mind's dilated nostril, laboratory sweat.

B'Loon and Djbouche's duet was a metaduet, a somatically void but theoretically valid meditation on predecessor duets, Aunt Nancy and the nsansi's conversation nowhere near the only one to make its relevance felt. Vial and ductile time capsule both, B'Loon and Djbouche played host, petri dish fashion, to a cultured swatch of epistatically sensate stigmata. All these matters—dateless Dredj, crestfallen serenade, nsansic buzz, blue silk intimation and much more—clung to and invisibly "colored" them, an ipseic, oddly see-thru smear.

Djbouche wondered if this was their ecclesial wish, their cathedral drive toward stained-glass grandeur gotten out of hand.

B'Loon wondered could this be their way of bearing "colored" light into a last or at last enduring antiphonal church of epistatic sweat.

Same difference, they both concluded. Wished-for ecclesiality and prepossessing, anti-empiric sweat jointly elicited see-thru smear's cathedral ambush, Hotel Didjeridoo's upwardly transposed repair.

Hotel Didjeridoo, known by many as the House the Blues Built, lived again in B'Loon's equation of the nsansi's ictic, I've-known-rivers line with Otis Spann's river of whiskey in "Diving Duck." How fitting that he played with Muddy Waters, B'Loon reflected, beset by images of a mud-bearing duck, a mud-bearing boar, his extended family of mud-bearing fauna turning out to be whiskey-sipping fauna as well: whiskey-sipping duck, whiskey-sipping boar, whiskey-sipping tortoise, he himself sipping, the smell on their breath attesting to tipsy beginnings.

Muddy kinship, Djbouche, reading B'Loon's thoughts, thought in turn, extended tipsy support not only to mud-bearing beak, bill and mouth but to Penguin's beakful of blue silk as well, his drunken address or drunken would-be address of Djeannine's or Drennette's intoxicant loins' deltaic musk.

What stopped Djbouche from going on was that they again heard Otis's voice intoning, "If the river was whiskey and I was a diving duck." It cracked them up, made them laugh. A deep, resounding belly laugh shook them both, as though Otis's whiskey-sipping duck implied a comic miscue at the root of the world, a cracked or cracked-up foundation, "quacked" foundation.

The next line cracked them up even more. "I would dive to the bottom and never come up," they heard Otis go on, such refusal to resurface tickling them both with its repudiation of earth-diver myth, its gnostic desire to rescind Creation, gnostic refusal to bring up mud, put up with the world. A house built by the blues or built on the blues is no house at all, it seemed to say, itself a blue truth or black-humorous truth chased by suffering and sorrow laughter alone outruns.

So many sensations diminished time there was no time. The laughter subsided as soon as it arose. Otis's drunken duck no sooner appeared than disappeared. Mud and whiskey ran as one—an evaporative run no sooner there than gone. B'Loon and Djbouche were no more than shape-shifting vessels made of opera glass, metamorphosing bubbles bearing ambiguous witness. They no sooner focused than freed the barrage cathedral ambush admitted them to. Prodigal repair no sooner framed than focused prodigal barrage's wandering root. Were such witness to venture a Namesake Encyclical it would be this: "In Consciousness, the one frame is every frame, storing an infinitude of images in an infinitely creative pattern of pure and perfect ambiguity." Prodigal repair no sooner focused than lost wandering root.

B'Loon and Djbouche, albeit marooned on an abstract beach, advanced a glass-eyed public dreaming, universal wish no sooner shown than shaded by local inflection—shaped and shaded, subject to idiosyncratic twitch. Hotel Didjeridoo's cathedral repair darkened an otherwise unstained window. It carved an alcove occupied not by Aunt Nancy but by Lambert now, gouged-out cave as much as carved-out alcove, deepening stain suspended in time.

It fits that he takes her place, overtaken as he is by thoughts of an old girlfriend whose nickname, Spider, Aunt Nancy's name reminds him of— this in the midst of a tenor solo he embarked on only an instant ago. More pet name than nickname, a name he himself bestowed one evening in a mix of jest and affection, Spider bespeaks eight-limbed entanglement (nsansic attunement, anansic entanglement), reminisced arousal faintly peppered with regret. Lambert's hands on the saxophone keys are his hungry hands under Spider's blouse, his own earlier hands inside her bra caressing her tight, commanding breasts, hungrier hands up under her skirt slowly climbing her thighs.

Lambert's reminiscent croon deepens the alcove he occupies. The deepening stain suspended in time is an absence of time. Spider's ear within reach, he whispers, telling her she's the spider, he thought she was a fly. The tip of his tongue on the reed's tip is his earlier tongue-tip touch-ing lightly on Spider's ear, nipple, neck. He alludes to a song they both find funny, telling her the hunter's gone and gotten caught.

The tenor's breathy, Websterian buzz rocks B'Loon and Djbouche, a subtle quake shaking the abstract shelf on which they rest, test-tube jitter along the laboratory beach on which they lie.

Peppered address roughens reminiscence. A cathedral shiver mounts the small of Lambert's back. His tongue's tip revisits the puck-ered skin surrounding Spider's taut nipple. His eyes have a glazed-over look. The abstract shelf on which he as well stands bumps B'Loon and Djbouche a bit more emphatically, ubiquitous whisk lodged in labora-tory sound (cathedral/chthonic) at all points pervious to anabatic tweak.

Lambert's eyes' glazed-over look occupies an obsessed cabinet built by glass-eyed dreaming on B'Loon and Djbouche's laboratory beach. The alcove he occupies compounds a long since incipient cave, a mnemonic chamber built on thetic distention, "wished-for ubiquity's ubiquitous wish." As if to at last lay throwaway rapture to rest, he spits "ubiquitous wish" at the reed's tip, an impromptu growl it takes B'Loon and Djbouche aback to hear come from the horn. The growl, though, is also a plea. Lambert's aroused, impatient plea dismisses—or would, if it could, dismiss—embouchure's nearness to embrace, intimated equation with embrace.

Lambert's tenor solo fades. The alcove he occupies evaporates. Spider's likewise evaporative limbs no longer cloud his public dreaming's operatic eye. As though their oldest recall is of something lost, founded on loss, time's evanescent caress, B'Loon and Djbouche begin to move on what to make of themselves.

An adenoidal burr now adheres to each gust of wind, a bug in B'Loon and Djbouche's ear were they not without ears. They hear it nonetheless, an insinuative sough repeatedly whispering, "Operatic lung." They see themselves and begin to accept themselves as two large operatic lungs, glass but elastic lungs, beached hypervented breath housed in laboratory glass. Remnant wind extending Lambert's reminiscent croon, public dreaming's newly peppered address abrades the breathing they advance. Such breathing (hothouse flow, sweating flex) puts a bend or amounts to a bend in their ostensible ear. Remnant wind extends orphic bend into uroboric bend, circular breathing's live mummy effect. Larger-than-life lungs the size of beached whales, B'Loon and Djbouche expand and contract.

Still, Lambert is back, on soprano now (etched immanence, rough breathy sketch). An enormous influx draws him out, he seems to say, remnant sough sucked in, disappearing crease wrinkling the wind, so unforced a sound (so open, empty) it restores the alcove he occupied. A ripped sense of himself as abruptly fronted by a draft affords an advance. Revenant shelter frees the horn of urgency; the tenor's impatience no longer obtains.

B'Loon and Djbouche expand and contract, a universal duet for which tenor and soprano, Aunt Nancy and nsansi, alcove and cave are alibis, _____ and _____, _____ and _____, _____ and _____, ad infinitum. Intake and outflow partake of this duet, a platonic duet or pas de deux, eked-out rapport between ambush and embouchure, implicate embrace.

Two phrases pass before Lambert's eyes: 1) *a philosophic default on erstwhile affect*; 2) *nib dipped in oceanless wind*. A short letter passes before them as well:

Dear Lamb,

> *Finally washed up on Orphic Shore. Wish you were here.*
> *All is not lost.*

> *Love,*
> *Spider*

He feels himself weakening, wavering, more susceptible to Spider's allure, soprano aplomb notwithstanding unforced embouchure notwithstanding. The letter's invocation of orphic memory hits home.

Still, he recovers, no sooner weakens than recovers. Soprano aplomb keeps reminiscent allure at arm's length, memory's webbed embrace at bay.

B'Loon and Djbouche absorb Lambert's thoughts, inklings, impressions, the letter that passes before his eyes included. The reference to Orphic Shore catches their attention. They read it as code, a reduced equation bearing on love's laboratory arrest. B'Loon takes it to mean "Don't forget," Djbouche takes it to mean "Don't look back." Their joint reading deduces a mixed-emotional prospect or premise: remembrance free of retrospect unrest. This being so, they wonder what to make of "Wish you were here." True feeling or trite formula? True admission of lack or meaningless filler? Heartfelt wish or phatic amenity? How can "Wish you were here" not be looking back? Such questioning signals the need for an equational transposition à la Sun Ra's "Love in Outer Space," laboratory love's aim to uproot reminiscent regret.

Lambert feels B'Loon and Djbouche's joint exegesis. The questions they raise regarding "Wish you were here" hit him like a shot to the ribs, an unsubtle jab at what he himself sees as a lapse into boilerplate pleasantry at best, true wishful thinking at worst ("Wish I was there"). The alcove he occupies turns to sand, wet sculpted sand wiped away by the tide on Orphic Shore.

The soprano fades as the alcove dissolves into the sea, revenant shelter gone the way of all shelter.

Revenant shelter gone the way of all shelter is exactly Lambert's thought as he too fades.

Dear Angel of Dust,

Enclosed are your copies of *Orphic Bend*. Thanks again for writing the liner notes. We're happy it's finally out and we're pleased with the overall production. The cover came out well and the fold-out construction works as it should (better than that really—there's something almost religious or codical at least about the way the three panels sit when you unfold it). The sound quality and the mix worked out well too. Very crisp, not at all mushy. There's not that recessed, set-back-a-bit sound one often gets in recordings. No, it's very forward, right next to you as a listener, right up on you but not all over you, sitting on top of you. It has a perched, ready-to-pounce quality I can't quite pin down but that I very much like, a stored saltativeness whose translation from potential to kinetic seems the very precipice one hears audibilized. But why am I telling you this? You can listen yourself.

The hurdle now is getting it out, distribution. JCOA's New Music Distribution has agreed to carry it, which will help, but we're still going to have to do a lot of it ourselves. We've put ads in *Down Beat*, *Coda* and a few other magazines and we've taken it around to local record stores. I'm a little embarrassed to admit it, but we're so anxious as to how it will fare we've returned to the stores we've put it in almost daily to see if any copies have sold. Some have, I'm happy to say, but that only brings up a further concern. I hadn't thought about it much before but there's an anonymity or an abstractness to the audience for records that we'll need some time to get used to. Unlike a gig, where we can see not only the audience but their consumption of the music, their response to the music, the record situation is one in which, while we might see that the record has sold, we don't see who bought it or see them take it home and play it. It's made me fantasize about attaching a bugging device of some sort to each record, some sort of compact, flat, unobtrusive transmitter (audio at least or, even better, video as well) that would broadcast back to us. We'd be able to surveil anyone who picked up a copy and took a look at it. More importantly, we'd be able to follow those who bought a copy home and witness their reaction to it. This business of playing to abstract reception or lack of tangible return is a bit, as Lambert says, what sharecropping must have been like.

So far, by the way, the balloons haven't shown up. The various copies we've played we've played without incident, with no emergences even during Aunt Nancy's "Dream Thief" solo. Is it something about the difference between test pressing and real? Who knows. One could scratch a bald spot or even a hole in one's head trying to figure their comings and goings out, but we insist we won't let that happen.

Yours,

N.

_____

Dear Angel of Dust,

They're threatening to ban us from some of the record stores around town, some of the ones we put *Orphic Bend* in. They say coming in so often to check on sales is bad enough but what's gotten to be too much, what's going too far, is our taking, as we have of late, to asking for descriptions of the people who've bought copies. Of course, they're right. We've gone overboard. We've gotten compulsive and made pains in the ass of ourselves, to say nothing of making ourselves look silly, unsophisticated. This is obviously something that can't go on. As we ourselves now insist on reminding one another, there can be no more of that. *Orphic Bend*, we have to accept, now has a life of its own, one which, while it doesn't exclude us, our own are not coextensive with and can't be coextensive with. We have to let it make its way unwitnessed by us, not let it hang us up or hold us up. We've been asked to play a record-release gig at The Studio next week, which we'll do (and, if asked, others like it), but our focus now has to be on what comes next. *Orphic Bend* we have to think of as old news. Our focus has to be on getting on with new work.

In line with that, I've given more thought to "Reverie's Reveille," which I'm considering renaming "Hand Me Down My Silver Trumpet." This latter title's that of a section of a novel I recently read, Arna Bontemps's *Black Thunder*. He wrote it in the mid-thirties right here in L.A., over in Watts on Wiegand Avenue. It's about Gabriel's aborted slave rebellion in Virginia in 1800. It's a haunting book, a spooked book, a book about being spooked. The piece's proffer of gnostic receipt can't help but have something to learn from the novel's theme or seeming theme of misleading allure, deepseated woo, a deepseated hoodoo (I begin to understand Dizzy anew) intrinsic to the earth and at work within human accord as much as human discord, the two no more than sides of the same coin. So, at least, I couldn't help thinking as I came upon evocations of the earth as voiced but misanthropic, mouthed with a black, misleading tongue—and, beyond that, of the earth as thirsty for and fed by inundation, cataclysm, and of this as its would-be tutelage and test, ulterior test. Braxton's notion of swing as "a question of gravitational intrigue" seems to apply.

As I read of the earth "rocked like a great eye" in a cosmic socket, I got what I took to be the book's intimation of a rocked, apocalyptic cradle and a swung chariot rolled into one. That rock, that swing, resides, on a smaller scale, within an "arc" vested early on in a runaway donkey, a runaway resolve or the flight or futility of would-be resolve, would-be resolution run amok. Diluvian curvature bent on recalling Noah's ark, that "arc" resurfaces at the book's very end, inscribed by the executioner's ax and letting loose a musical motif, the hangman's rope given, as Gabriel requested, the last word, humming "like a violin string." I'm haunted, just as one of the characters is said to be in the book's penultimate paragraph, by that "arc," by the humming I can all but hear and a visual image I can all but see, an afterimage described as lingering "like a wreath of smoke."

There's a lot in the book that speaks to much that was on my mind already. Gabriel's angelic namesake brings the trumpet's apocalyptic pedigree again to mind, as does the book's diagnosis of a living death or a collective sleep the insurgents would rout or awake from if they could. Is "would" a false hope or merely a momentarily thwarted hope? How does music figure in? It may well be a gnostic sense of entrapment's last word, disruptive and recuperative by turns. It may also be, by virtue of turning, the very "arc" in question, a maroon variability but a vexation to itself, toxic with insinuative insistence, highstrung insistence eventually gone up in smoke. How else to account for liberatory wish being posed as en-

chantment, preemptive hoodoo's highstrung harmonics in concert or cahoots with runaway meaning, splay surmise?

Here's what I mean:

> . . . he was bewitched. . . . Liberty, equality, frater—it was a strange
> music, a strange music.

And:

> They all murmured. Their assent, so near the ground, seemed to rise
> from the earth itself. H'm. There was something warm and musical
> in the sound, a deep tremor.

And:

> *"Come and unite with us, brothers, and combat with us for the same
> cause."* He slapped his flank. "Sing it, church! Ain't that pretty?"

And:

> Was I a singing man, I'd sing me a song now, he thought. I'd sing me
> a song about lonesome, about a song-singing man long gone. No need
> crying about a nigger what's about to die free. I'd sing me a song, me.

But then, played against runaway-lingering "arc," runaway hoofbeat, the
very last words of the book:

> The little mare's feet played a soothing tune on the cobblestones.

I'm not sure what to do with this, what "Reverie's Reveille" (or "Hand
Me Down My Silver Trumpet") will do with this, but it's given me a buzz
and I've got the sense it'll eventually factor in. Hand-me-down trumpet
will again pass along a well-worn mix of consolation and alarm, but exactly how remains to be seen. Threadbare vestments cloaking spooked
amenity (cosmic inveiglement, splay dispatch) will again go in fear of
presumed favor with God, but exactly how remains to be seen. A theme

of self-serving rendition will again issue caveats no doubt, celestial-cum-chthonic intrigue swung free from, but how to make hand-me-down brass awake new-day readiness of a truly new sort remains to be seen.

In the meantime, it's at least helped me turn a new page in my anti-thetical opera. I've written a new after-the-fact lecture/libretto, the first one-word after-the-fact lecture/libretto ever (two words reduced to one really). Its title, were it not suppressed in the interest of one-wordedness, would be "Gnostic Receipt (Short Form); or, The Creaking of the Word: After-the-Fact Lecture/Libretto (B'Loon Version)." Think of its title as written in invisible ink. I'm enclosing a copy.

As ever,
N.

Black Thunder

Dear Angel of Dust,

Penguin and Drennette got kicked out of Aron's yesterday. We've been trying to turn a new page on that front but they ended up dropping in and one thing led to another. One thing leading to another was in fact how they ended up there; it wasn't Aron's they originally set out for. At the end of rehearsal the other night Drennette mentioned being interested in Inayat Khan. A friend had told her that one of the pieces on one of Don Cherry's "*Mu*" albums is mislabeled, that "The Mysticism of My Sound" shouldn't have a "my" in it and that the real title, "The Mysticism of Sound," refers to a book by Inayat Khan. Drennette said she was interested in checking this out. Penguin right away spoke up to say he'd heard the same thing, that he'd heard it from someone, as he put it, close to Don, that Hamid Drake, the drummer with the Mandingo Griot Society, had told him this very thing when he spoke to him when the band was in town two or three years ago, that Hamid had gotten it directly from Don, that it was Don who introduced Hamid to Inayat Khan's work. Penguin seemed to be showing off a bit. He went on to say that he knew where she could get hold of Khan's books, that he knew the Bodhi Tree Bookstore has them and that in fact he'd recently seen a thirteen-volume *The Sufi Message of Hazrat Inayat Khan* in their used books annex, that volume two was the one in question and that, yes, he thought it was definitely worth checking out. Penguin was definitely showing off and Drennette, in spite of herself, seemed impressed. He capped it off by saying they were holding a copy of J. B. Danquah's *The Akan Doctrine of God* for him and that he was planning to go by to pick it up the next day and that Drennette was welcome to join him, that they might as well go together. Drennette agreed.

So it was the Bodhi Tree they set out for yesterday, the Bodhi Tree they went to first. Penguin picked up his book and Drennette found plenty of Inayat Khan. They spent a good while browsing and then they paid for their books and left. As they were leaving Penguin suggested they get something to eat at Café Figaro, only a few blocks away. Drennette said good idea and there they went. It was after they'd had lunch and were pulling away in Penguin's car that he suggested that, being on the very same street Aron's is on, they swing by and go thru the bins. Drennette says he made "on the very same street" sound as though Aron's were close by, too close by not to drop in on, though they both knew it was a couple dozen blocks away. Without giving it much thought, though, she said why not and they set out for Aron's. She was almost immediately, she says, beset by second thoughts.

Anyway, they drove to Aron's, parked, went in and all went well for a while. They both took their time perusing the new and the used bins and Drennette even found, in one of the latter, a copy of Jack Wilson's *Easterly Winds* in good condition, a disk that's out of print and that she's been on the lookout for for years. The difficulty didn't arise at first but eventually emerged from the fact that they gradually made their way over to new releases. Even though they told themselves they weren't there to check on how *Orphic Bend* was doing (and, to prove it, avoided the M's in both the new and the used bins), they both gradually worked their way over to the new releases racks and, within seconds of one another, stood in front of them pretending not to be looking at *Orphic Bend* while in fact counting, out of the corner of an eye, how many copies were left. It turned out there were two copies fewer than the last time any of us had checked, a fact that caused them both, in their excitement, to drop the pretense of not looking. They all but dove in, getting in one another's way as they both reached in to take the copies of *Orphic Bend* out to check the count. Drennette gave way to Penguin, who took them in his hands and counted again—a closer, more careful count than the out-of-the-corner-of-the-eye count. The closer count confirmed that there were in fact two copies fewer, that two more copies had sold since the last time we checked.

But it didn't stop there. Penguin insisted on trying to find out who had bought the two copies. He and Drennette got in line and waited for one of the cashiers to become available. When it was their turn they stepped up to the counter. Drennette paid for the copy of *Easterly Winds* while Penguin, very casually, as though he were just making conversation, asked the cashier if by any chance he knew who had bought the two copies of *Orphic Bend*, was there anything he could tell him and Drennette about them. Quickly not very casual any longer, he followed this up with a barrage of questions that all but jumped off his tongue, questions that came so quickly and so nonstop the cashier couldn't have gotten answers out even had he had them. Were they male or female? How old? What race? Were they short or tall? How were they dressed? What color were their eyes? How did they pay? Cash? Credit card? Check? And so on.

The cashier had no answers. When the barrage finally stopped he told them he had no idea who had bought the records, that hundreds of people come into the store, that after a while they all look pretty much the same, that all he was concerned with, really, was getting to the end of his shift, not with keeping track of who bought what. The transaction for *Easterly Winds* was finished by now. Drennette had given him a twenty and he had given her her change, put the record in a bag with the receipt inside and handed it to her. She nudged Penguin and tried to say with her eyes that they should get going, that they should let it go at that.

Penguin, though, didn't let up. He told the cashier he was sure that if he just gave it some thought and tried hard to remember it would all come back—when the records were bought, who bought them, what they looked like, all of it. The cashier held his ground, however, saying not a chance and pointing out that the line was getting longer and that Penguin and Drennette were holding things up. Drennette tugged at Penguin's sleeve and said they should get going. Penguin kept at it, however, asking the cashier would he be so kind as to ask the other cashiers ("your colleagues" he called them) if they could shed any light on the matter. This the cashier flatly refused to do. The level of testiness and tension, Drennette says, had been steadily rising and by now what they had on their hands was a scene. People all around the store stopped what they were doing to listen and look.

Penguin and the cashier continued to go back and forth, each of them sustaining an arch, overdone formality belied by the irritability they so obviously held in check. A number of the onlookers around the store couldn't help laughing, did nothing in fact to keep from laughing at the disparity between the substance and the manner of their exchange. Drennette continued tugging at Penguin's sleeve and saying let it go, that they should get going, eventually more than tugging his sleeve. She eventually took hold of his arm, putting her arm thru his, albeit to no avail.

By the time the store manager came out from one of the back rooms Penguin was saying things like "Slave days are over, and sharecropping too." The store manager walked right up and said, "I'm afraid I'm going to have to ask you to leave," to which Penguin replied, "Okay. Go ahead and ask," suggesting via body language he had no intention of leaving. He and the store manager now went back and forth a while. Drennette continued tugging on the arm hers was in and saying let it go, that they should get going. It was when the store manager said, "I really wish you'd take your girlfriend's advice," that Penguin's manner and mood visibly changed.

It was as though the word "girlfriend," Drennette says, brought him out of a trance. His head visibly snapped back and it seemed he did a double-take, anxious to make sure he'd heard what he heard. He looked at the store manager, saying nothing, then turned his head and looked at Drennette beside him, apparently noticing for the first time that her arm was in his. "Yeah, let's get out of here," he said and they walked out the door arm-in-arm. They walked arm-in-arm to the car.

Drennette's now worried, she told Djamilaa (who told me), that Penguin might have gotten the wrong idea.

I guess we'll see.

As ever,

N.

———————————

Dear Angel of Dust,

We played our record-release gig at The Studio last night. There were plenty of copies of *Orphic Bend* on hand, of course, and we managed to sell a goodly few. We played a couple of sets, after each of which we went out and milled around with the audience rather than stay backstage (the gig had been billed as a "record-release party"). We even got asked by more than one or two people to autograph their copies. The pieces we played were all, with one exception, from *Orphic Bend*. We were in good form and acquitted ourselves well on every piece, each of which had its moments and got good audience response both as it unfolded and when it came to an end. The evening was a series of peaks, one could say without exaggeration, the highest coming during its finale. The night's highlight turned out to be not only the last piece we played (during which, among other things, the balloons put in an appearance) but also the one piece which wasn't from *Orphic Bend*. Lambert made a point of the latter fact when he introduced the piece, telling the audience we were about to "go off-the-record."

At the end or ostensible end of the second set the audience wouldn't stop applauding. Many of them were standing and even after we left the stage, came back for bows and left again they went on applauding. They finally began to call out, in case we hadn't gotten it, for an encore and we decided to go back out and give a piece Djamilaa had sketched out a few times in recent rehearsals a try. It's a piece whose title is a play on "jam session" and on Djamilaa's name (a namesake piece I suppose you could say). It's called "Djam Suasion." True to its title, it's an open, aleatory piece that avails itself of impromptu impulse and proceeds on a very bare outline of structure and motif. Djamilaa had taught us a number of what she refers to as "drift conduits" at rehearsal—horn lines, rhythmic variations, harmonic clusters and such, all to be marshalled into the piece as momentary dispatch and group dynamics dictate. She had written these out but she insisted we learn them by ear first, saying she wanted the individual savor and spin and even miscue learning them that way would entail, that she wanted each of us to find out which quirks and miscues we could salvage, cultivate, make further use of, that she wanted quirk and so-called miscue or mistake to reinvent the piece. Only after that process did she pass around the charts, written on which at crucial points were, rather than notated cadence, resolution or closure, the phrase "djust a closer," calling to mind the traditional "Just a Closer Walk with Thee." Djamilaa said outright she encouraged quotation from established material where we saw fit (and her opening "drift conduit" on piano, the piece's head more or less, bears a faint relationship to Herbie Nichols's "House Party Starting") but the addition of the "d" in "djust a closer" made it also mean that we were each to take it elsewhere. Initiatic "d" accents eccentric, signatory spin.

The audience quieted down seeing us come back out for the encore. Lambert stepped up to a microphone and introduced "Djam Suasion," getting off his "off-the-record" quip by way of saying it was a new piece Djamilaa had only recently added to our book and that we were playing it in public for the first time. Having done that, he stepped back from the microphone and we took up our instruments—him on tenor, Penguin on alto, me on trumpet, Aunt Nancy on violin (she'd switch to bass after the first ensemble passage), Djamilaa at the piano, Drennette on drums. Djamilaa, unaccompanied, started it out, quietly working her "drift conduit," a simple figure she repeated in different octaves, testing, tasting, sampling, it seemed, at a loss as to where the entrance or the key or the open-sesame she sought might be. It was only a mimed uncertainty or dismay, one soon became aware, mimed uncertainty or dismay itself the entrance or the key or the open-sesame she sought. Senses of test or tentativeness gave way to iterative insistence, strengthened recourse to repetition, replete with Nicholsesque parallel voicings, that grew more resolute and was then elaborated on—a run of invention that went on for some time. A bit of happy-hand embroidery or filigree at the keyboard's treble end capped off this opening gambit, at which point the rest of us came in.

The initial ensemble "drift conduit" features dramatic, annunciative horn lines, jaggedly cut, a quick-out-of-the-gate brassiness and biting attack Aunt Nancy's violin works to soften somewhat. All together it gets a dawning sound, the violin's erstwhile romanticism weaving new-day hope into the horns' expectorant boast, a brash confidentiality which, foil for intimate whisper, asserts intimacy and knowing and commonality of a number of sorts. We announced a knowingness we dared the audience to claim exemption from, a presumptive entitlement the violin gave an orphic underpinning, a black-orphic boast of being on intimate terms with the sun. It all added up to metallic bluster, chest-on-chest insinuation, cosmic armor, solar explosion made charismatic by sostenuto string.

Drennette's drumming accented the horns' metallic boisterousness and weight with an equally metallic lightness, an itinerant shimmer she let loose on cymbals and kept aloft, an aureate lightness our dawning sound relied greatly on. The risk of topheaviness we ran she outmaneuvered, leveraging a pointillist attack with coloristic stick work, a brush thump thrown in every now and again. Our sense of liftedness and rise owed as much to the barrage of keening chatter she kept up as to Djamilaa's happy-hand treble and Aunt Nancy's new-day weft. We were off to a good start.

Encores are often short and somewhat perfunctory, a brief taste of this or that piece meant simply to acknowledge the audience's appreciation. This wasn't the case with "Djam Suasion." It ended up being the longest piece we played all night—indeed, almost as long as an entire set, long enough to be a third set. I think we enjoyed playing something not on the record, that we took to going "off-the-record," felt liberated from a nearly pro forma quality the record-release occasion tends to maintain. Whatever the reason, we stretched out. The first ensemble "drift conduit" gave way to a series of solos, each of which was at one point punctuated by one of the other ensemble "drift conduits" Djamilaa made available to us. Each soloist had his or her individual "drift conduit" to build or base the solo on. Aunt Nancy was the first to solo, doing so on violin and switching to bass when the other solos began: Lambert, then me, then Penguin. Djamilaa let each of us know when to wrap the solo up by playing a "drift conduit" specified for that purpose at the keyboard's bass end, a grumbling left-hand figure shot thru with omen, semiotic stress. It implied a low cauldron, a bubbling vat given the reach of torn chthonic tissue, seismic stretch and extenuation, signal rift—bass cauldron, bubbling vat and/or, lavalike, a volcano erupting.

A lot could be said about the solos, a lot about each individual solo. A lot could be said about the piece's unfolding, the way we found or made our way thru it—more, really, than I can say or have the time to go into were I able to say. But I have to try giving a sense of something we got into following Penguin's solo, something that began with Djamilaa's second solo, something her solo coming out of that cauldron got under way. Penguin had reached a point of utmost aubade and high flight, alto feather and flight, when the word came up from under, Djamilaa's left-hand signal to bring the solo to an end. This Penguin did with a wafer-thin feather of breath that appeared to hang in the air even after he took the horn from his mouth, a wafer-thin feather floating down to the floor but evaporating before reaching the floor. Djamilaa hung on to and kept repeating her semiotic bass figure even after Penguin was done, a bass cauldron she let go on bubbling and grumbling, a low vat she continued to let simmer, biding her time, perhaps buying time.

Djamilaa's left-hand grumble went on to elicit an answering string of right-hand arpeggios—a caffeinated barrage undergirded by a fretfulness no amount of speed and virtuosity could mask. Even so, speed and virtuosity held sway, a virtuosic scurry indebted to and worthy of Cecil Taylor, forage ramified into a long anacrotic run. All this Djamilaa did with exacting touch, an otherwise worn or wincing regard arousing images of tight, reminiscent flesh, reminiscent regard which implied regret but went well beyond it. Anacrotic run was reminiscent idea's utopic wish, would-be return to reminiscent flesh's first awakening, "the way it was" the way one wanted it to be. Aunt Nancy, having played mostly against the rhythm, opted after a while for a steady 4/4 shuffle meter. This led to Djamilaa replacing reminiscent regard with a rocking stomp sustained by chords played by both hands, a barrelhouse emphasis or insouciance bidding finesse and refinement goodbye. More time went by and Lambert, Penguin and I came back in. The horns' re-entry, a staggered relay, was a splintering piece of synaesthetic bamboo, an unexpected offer of antithetic backup, a bamboo baton bent to the breaking point. It was an unwieldy stick yet a wand even so, a wand whose time-lapse unraveling offered arch, asymptotic support. We voiced qualms concerning the shuffle while otherwise lending it a certain cachet.

Qualms notwithstanding, Aunt Nancy's 4/4 shuffle proved irresistible, infectious. It may in fact have been that the horns' blend of distance and identification made it all the more so, all the more infused it with an aroused, exponential capacity for twirled excursus, lateral dispatch. Our unwieldy baton took an occasional step to the side, an ever so exact listing or loss or letting go of outright alignment. It was a tactical feint we deployed, a willingness to dodge but with a nod toward all-out boogie. We implied without arriving at a rolling of the two into one, suggested without quite reaching eventual recourse to boogaloo largesse.

Suggestion was enough though, more than enough. Suggestion was all it took. The horns' refusal to arrive at all-out boogie, the ingenuity with which we outmaneuvered boogaloo largesse, was one that held it all the more in view. Such holding had an inverse effect, the very opposite of withholding and refusal, on the audience. Teased and tested beyond their patience or capacity to ride or withstand suggestion, they rose to their feet, got up to dance. They danced a dance that, spontaneous though it was, seemed all but choreographed. Offhand but coordinated enough to have been rehearsed, it was a dance in which, knees bent, asses lowered toward the floor but short of outright squat, they assumed something of a jockey's position, rocked back and forth. It seemed it said something or wanted to say something about the wonder of arms and legs having a torso to attach to and extend out from. It seemed to extol or to be bent on extolling the good fortune of having come by a body, the unwitting largesse of hard-to-come-by flesh, hard-to-come-by bone. Each dancer raised and lowered his or her right arm, pounding his or her right thigh as with a hammer, an ever so restrained hammer whose handle was the dancer's forearm, its head the dancer's fist. It was a methodical, all but robotic pounding, deliberate and insistent yet of a soft, slow-motion cast, as though the air were a viscous liquid the arm strained against, fought to rise and fall, move at all within.

As fist hit thigh, at the exact moment fist hit thigh, a balloon emerged from it. The balloons emerging from the female dancers' fists bore these words: *I lie on my back. He straddles me, down on all fours, his head between my legs, my head between his. I press my nose to the crack of his ass, put my mouth around the sack his balls hang in.* The balloons emerging from the male dancers' fists bore these: *I lie on my back. She straddles me, down on all fours, her head between my legs, my head between hers. I press my nose to the crack of her ass, my mouth to the matted hair of her cunt.* These were the only inscriptions the balloons bore. Albeit they emerged repeatedly, as fist again and again met thigh, the words inside were the same each time.

We looked out at the dancers, delighted but also dismayed. That they were intent on reducing the music to sex, intent not only on returning "jazz" to "jass" but on dropping the "j," made us rue Aunt Nancy's 4/4 shuffle however much it made us happy to've brought them to their feet.

The balloons' fellatial and cunnilingual explicitness notwithstanding, the audience's dance wasn't without ulterior suggestion. Was it simply me, I wondered while looking out at what was now a dance floor, or did the repeated meeting of fist and thigh, hammer and anvil, mean to recall one of cante jondo's most austere forms, the martinete? The dancers, given over, on the surface at least, to boogaloo largesse as it verged on X-rated license, clamored on a more subtle but no less visible level for a bare-bones, even ascetic deployment of workmanlike rhythmicity and vocal exertion—the very things the martinete, unaccompanied in origin but now often sung to the beat of a hammer striking iron, is the very epitome of. So, at least, it appeared to me, but not, it turned out, to me alone. The rest of the band, it became clear, had picked up the same suggestion. In oddly telepathic sync, we now went about dismantling the 4/4 shuffle, slowing down by way of a shift into duple time. The horns' lateral baton folded in on itself, an implosive messenger whose bamboo synaesthesia was now not only splintered but spent. Still, it folded in on itself but didn't exactly stop at that. It wasn't so much that it collapsed on its hollow interior, its voiceless core, as that it everted it, "extorted" it, turned it out. Lambert, Penguin and I, in any event, soon fell silent, as did, only three bars later, Aunt Nancy. Djamilaa, another three bars later, let the piano fall silent and began to sing. Drennette in turn let the drums fall silent but backed her up with tolling pings from the ride cymbal, pings whose intimation of a hammer hitting an anvil lent noise if not voice to fist hitting thigh. She saw to it that the two—stick hitting cymbal, fist hitting thigh—coincided.

The dancers had gone on dancing even after we dispensed with the 4/4 shuffle. Fist continued hitting thigh as Djamilaa sang and Drennette played blacksmith. Fist hit thigh but only blank balloons emerged from the dancers' fists, Djamilaa's gritty, sand-insistent voice bearing the necessary rub to erase the balloons' X-rated script. Her voice was an extrapolative rope whose textured arrest (a coughlike vamp-till-ready) repeatedly cracked, to begin with, under the strain of beginning, repeatedly pinched itself to awake from beginning's dream of unindebted advance. Once underway, her song, such as it was, never entirely shook free of its inhibited beginning, the rough cloth of so having caught itself out. It bore the brunt it would've otherwise had us weather, a sleight or a slip of mind occupied by rub and revision, tumbleweed and wind. However much it proffered or appeared possessed of an evocation of the American southwest, it was Djamilaa's Moorish roots it extracted, tore loose from the ground, let lead the way.

Djamilaa's cante was a congeries of mixed intimation. Punctuated by Drennette's repeated ping, it wandered far and wide, a wordless excursion which "spoke" via texture, inflection, intensity and tone. Hectored and egged on by Drennette's ping, Djamilaa's makeshift martinete bordered on cosmic harangue, gnostic rant, a frayed rope rummaging woodshed or smithy for all that could be brought to thought or brought to bear on the catharsis fist hitting thigh clamored for. An Andalusian Ogun and a Gypsy John Henry were only two of the extrapolations or possibilities broached or bumped into in Djamilaa's extended woodshed/smithy. The martinete's birthplace Triana was called to mind, but only as a base, a beginning point.

Djamilaa's cante navigated a repertoire of godly smiths, mythic smiths, a repertoire possessed of extensive reach, global resonance and reach. Her torn voice evoked a world wrought by strenuous heaven, straught works and days, a stricken arena thinning her voice into pure aspiration, breached would-be rise. Isis looking for strewn Osiris had nothing on her. She scoured the earth, giving Drennette's repeated ping worldwide repercussion, calling heaven itself out, it seemed, calling roll in heaven. The Japanese Ame No Ma-hitotsu No Kami, the Indian Tvashtri, the Greek Hephaistos, the Canaanite Kôshar-wa-Hasis, the Dogon Amma Seru and others all at one point or another stepped forward, answered the call, each an impromptu equation calibrating sand and sky—not, she insisted, soil and sky. Sand and sky were struck repeatedly and repeatedly served as a transitional chord (she had recourse to the piano again while she sang, albeit no more than a plink or a plunk—a not so distant cousin to Drennette's ping—here and there), a decidedly transitive equation.

The dancers went on dancing, fist went on hitting thigh, balloons went on emerging wordless. Their robotic insistence had something to say about sacred labor, would-be sacred or divine endeavor devolved into mute repetition, would-be heaven brought down to rote, repetitive earth. Not even sexual respite, X-rated appetite, held out hope now for reined-in heaven, wordless balloon after wordless balloon a burst bubble of sorts. The mood was decidedly different. Cathartic but unrelievedly somber, it was a far cry from boogaloo largesse. Djamilaa's extreme, extrapolative rope and rapacious vocality were nothing if not exactly that cry, a far-sighted cry that saw its way to an eventual heaven but, even so, rendered heaven, eventual heaven, eventuality itself, momentarily moot. Her cante was blues's bad news to gospel's good. Sacred labor, would-be divine, sacred mastery of heat, her cante insinuated, had grievously, perhaps irreparably misfired.

It was extremely grim business Djamilaa's martinete broached and brought out, a comprehensive, all-inclusive plaint one couldn't, after a while, help hearing as too comprehensive, too all-inclusive, cosmic or would-be cosmic to a fault. It seemed, after a while, for all its rapaciousness and rant, to further entrench a supposedly cosmic status quo, subsidiarily consecrate the fallen hammer or the hammer's fall it railed against. Drennette's ping was a corroborating witness, a repetitive toll, a monotonous marking of time—a corroborating but (mercifully, one thought) complicating witness. It spoke of abject, alienating duration while the very manner of its production seemed intent on underscoring *strike*, a word whose liberatory or would-be liberatory meaning was not to be easily muffled or dismissed. Endless imprisonment as unguaranteed as utopic windfall, stick's tip struck cymbal the way hammer's head struck anvil: a mixed-emotional report auguring more than one outcome or consequence.

Drennette's ping, heard a certain way, proposed a willingness to scour the sky, ransack heaven, hold out for ultimate amends. That she herself heard it that way became clear when, with her left hand, she began slapping the snare's head (coinciding with each ping, complementing each ping) with the side of the other stick. It was a cross between a slap and a thump really, a firm albeit damped explosion which brought something one couldn't quite put one's finger on to mind. Whatever that something was, it hung there, suggestive, just beyond finger's reach, recall's reach, a piece of music it put one in mind of and put whose title on the tip of one's tongue. All but absent, teasingly present, it wouldn't go away, a riddle one would know no rest without solving.

Aunt Nancy was the first to solve it, doing so when Drennette let the ping itself go but went on offering the slap-thump on the snare's head. Aunt Nancy, after a while, that is, came back in, plucking a bass string a beat before each of Drennette's repeated slap-thumps, a combination that made it clear to the rest of us what the something we'd been put in mind of was. Aunt Nancy played Sam Jones, we saw, to Drennette's Louis Hayes, recalling their ax-imitating riff on Cannonball Adderley's band's recording of his brother Nat's composition "Work Song." Lambert, Penguin and I made momentary eye contact and we knew immediately what to do. We took the horns to our mouths and blew the response to Hayes and Jones's call, Drennette and Aunt Nancy's call, "Work Song's" antiphonal horn line's answer to their repetitive, ax-imitating riff.

It was a human, vocal cry we let loose, issued under duress but undaunted, a jump-up in frayed attenuation of Djamilaa's highstrung, more obvious human cry. Our axes answered roll in heaven, rang in heaven, but the music spoke to so deep a place we bent over, bowed in a blend of orison and exertion, incense cut with sweat. Stored surge and a sense of urgency we'd been holding back we now let out. Djamilaa's heart's true home lay on high and we pursued it, stranded and strung as high as the cosmic static infiltrating her voice.

We went on repeating "Work Song's" head, not moving into solos, possessed or obsessed agents of iterativity. Djamilaa's makeshift martinete was more a makeshift bulería now, the band a band of creatures of rhythm and repetition, sacred and profane conduits caroling chiliastic sweat. So locked in were all the parts it appeared we occupied a rhythmic prison, repeatedly built, broken down, rebuilt. Inmates of rhythm we might've been. Wardens of rhythm we might've been. No one could say which or whether or not we might've been both. No one, for the moment, cared.

All that mattered, moment to moment, for the moment, was to let it all out, albeit "all" was a tactical attainment, a reduction of itself if not by itself at least gone along with, ultimacy and contingency's compromise. We made amends with profane duration, made a certain peace with unprepossessing swing (swung ax, hoe, hammer). Djamilaa's voice was by turns a velvet scarf and a bolt of burlap, an aroused, intertwined run of cloth nonetheless not without intimate silk's unmentionably pungent funk and perfume. Piss and vinegar were the way of the world, it complained at points, unmentionability's bouquet ameliorating the shrill extreme it bordered on. Given such singing, what this was was a much more relayed and ramified marshalling than boogaloo largesse, a less lyrically overcharged intimation than the X-rated rummaging the dancers' balloons had broached.

Please don't get me wrong on this. It's not that, à la, let's say, Baudelaire ("Sexuality is the lyricism of the masses"), we put either sex or the dancers down. We were no band of nineteenth-century aesthetes. The dancers were with us and we were with them. This was the lingual exertion and the proto-apotheosis they more subtly and suggestively sought: sacred and sustained labial and lingual and glottal instantiation, more than could be sexed or said albeit pressed and demanding dues be paid even so. The dancers were with us, we with them. Platonic ether's levitational hydraulics was not what we were about. Fist pounding thigh beat out a theme of dues, indebtedness, flesh not to be denied. Swung, low-to-the-floor hips rode gravity, all but rode the earth itself. They were with us and we were with them but them being with us and us being with them was not to be made too much of. Their being with us and our being with them by no means even came near the magnitude meant by "masses." Nor had any of us had any wish or entertained any ambition that our doing so might. We were only, as Ornette says, friends and neighbors.

Ornette was no idle reference. We went on repeating "Work Song's" head and the longer we went on the more elastic it grew. We played with the time, holding the horn line's high note here and there, stretching it out, an extenuating cry recalling no one if not Ornette. It couldn't help also recalling nothing if not Ornette's Texas roots, the field hollers his identifying cry descended from. The work song descended from them as well, it went without saying, but implicitly we said so nonetheless. In any case, we were at work. We were with the dancers and they were with us and we were there to work something out.

What that something was was hard to specify but work it out we did. The horns' Ornettish cry carried its own topographic insistence, an implemented ground it repeatedly broke as though the dent it made, the beginning it made, was a grain of sand in the Sahara, the dent or the difference it made nearly nonexistent, which in fact it was. Specification, however slight, was itself at issue, an attributive rift we stepped into. Rolling hills or flat field, it was a desert either way, a bed we didn't dare lie down in, hammered expanse.

Sand was hammer's bequest, a coarse powder rendering all impediment moot. Status-quo cosmicity groomed a cosmetic smoothness hammer's Luddite ghost or grain of sand in the machine disfigured, effaced. Not the something we were there to work out, this was something we could nonetheless not forget. We knew the allure of status-quo cosmicity but sacred ordeal no longer made any sense. Hostile environs could breed invention, we knew, but we turned a deaf ear to inhospitality's behest. What we were there to work out bordered on sand's unfriendly expanse, an unwelcoming premise we could neighbor, we knew, but not befriend. Hammer (hoe, ax) kept at us, insisting we remember that.

Drennette and Aunt Nancy's ax-imitating snare's head and bass were unremitting. Nor did Djamilaa let go of her occasional plinks and plunks. Even as makeshift martinete and bulería interwove the dancers were still with us as we continued to be with them; fist went on pounding thigh. No named aggregate accounted for the oneness we'd set out to finagle but now authentically felt. Each grain of sand was a dabbed, keening pinpoint of sound, an acoustic perfume recalling Portuguese fado, etymologic fate granted granular expanse. Aggregate sand was an impacted filigree exploded, leg-smitten fist unfurled.

So it now was that fist unclenched as each dancer's right arm came up again after fist hit thigh. Each right hand opened on its way back up, fingers and thumb extended, a bloom of sorts. It opened as if undone by the blow it delivered, even as if thigh might have delivered a blow. It closed again on its way back down but when fist hit thigh no balloon came out. There were now no balloons at all, not even so much as the blank sort which for some time had been emerging from the dancers' fists. It appeared that in opening their hands as their arms went up the dancers released what would've made for balloons on the way back down. It seemed a way of agreeing that no named aggregate enclosed or could caption the supple oneness we felt.

Yours,

N.

Dear Angel of Dust,

I got such a rush from *Black Thunder* I read the novel Bontemps followed it with, *Drums at Dusk*. It's about the Haitian Revolution (or, more
accurately, set during its onset) but it wasn't quite what I expected. I had
hoped I'd learn more about the "arc" that so spoke to me, hoped I'd see
how music might be differently invoked with regard to a successful rather
than a failed revolt. My thought was that, drums in the title notwithstanding, it might carry hand-me-down trumpet back to a conch shell blown by
a runaway slave, an insurgent slave, something on the order of Albert
Mangonès's sculpture *The Unknown Maroon of Saint-Domingue*. Conch
shell as proto-trumpet (radical shell as recidivist brass) was a theme I was
more than ready to embrace, anxious to embrace, a theme I was sure
would bear on "Reverie's Reveille" (or "Hand Me Down My Silver Trumpet"), sure would help it bear fruit. The closest the book gets to anything
like that, though, isn't very close. An implicit shell motif, more Botticellian
than conch, emerges at one point, emerges or appears to lie just below the
surface. This is when the ruffles and frills of one of the characters' petticoats are likened to sea foam—an Aphroditean allusion harbingering birth
or rebirth no doubt (the character's name is Céleste) but oblique at best
with regard to conch.

The book's detour from or deflection away from its ostensible subject, the way revolt becomes backdrop to romance, ground to Aphroditean
figure, frustrated my expectations but may still have something to say concerning radical shell: recidivist brass not so much recidivist as bent, a

bent-brass recourse to ventriloquial demur. Radical shell speaks with a thrown or diverted voice, as though successful revolt, unthwarted revolt, were sacred, to be dealt with circumspectly if at all. *Drums at Dusk*'s momentary focus on petticoated legs appears intent on recalling and being contrasted with *Black Thunder*, intent on recalling Juba's naked legs. What this wants to say about erotized insurgency and relative degrees of exposition counsels caution regarding triumphalist dispatch, a welcoming awareness of intervening grades between limit-case cooked and outright raw transmission. But even to say this is to say too much. To say this jeopardizes the wariness it preaches.

I got your letter a while back, just a couple of days after I mailed you my last; they crossed in the mail. Things have quieted down in the matters you ask about. We're not haunting the stores the way we did at first and there've been no more incidents like the one at Aron's. No, Penguin doesn't appear to have made too much of Drennette putting her arm in his. He doesn't appear to have made anything of it at all, though she continues to worry that he may have gotten the wrong idea. Her repeated mention of it has Djamilaa wondering if the wrong idea might be the right one.

But, like I said, things are quiet.

Yours,
N.

Dear Angel of Dust,

Lambert dropped in unexpectedly earlier today. He showed up at the door carrying a record and said there was something he wanted me to hear, something on the record which if I hadn't already heard I had to hear and which if I had I had to hear again, something I needed to listen to, something I would learn from. It was an Art Blakey album. What he wanted me to hear, he said, would make me give my new commitment to brass a second thought. (My "conversion to brass" he went so far as to call it, getting back to the bone he began to pick a few weeks ago.) The record was *Free for All*. It's one I'd already heard and in fact have in my collection. When I told him so he handed me the record anyway, saying that he too had mistakenly thought he'd already heard it, that after listening to it for years he truly heard it only today, that that was what had caused him to come right over. He insisted I put it on and sit down and listen, saying what he wanted me to hear was the second cut on side two, "Pensativa." I took the record out of the jacket and put it on the turntable. I set the needle on "Pensativa." We sat down to listen.

Free for All is a record I've listened to countless times. "Pensativa," in fact, is my favorite cut. I've listened to it more than to any of the others. Even so, I sat patiently and listened yet again, curious as to what the something was Lambert wanted me to hear, the something he seemed to insist I hadn't already heard and couldn't hear without his help. Again I heard Freddie Hubbard's quickly heraldic opening over trombone and tenor support, Art's quickly established Latin accent as Freddie goes on to state the rest of the head. Again I heard the less heraldic, more confidential vein in which he does so, the cooing restraint he draws out the melody with. I heard the trombone and tenor's choirboy whimsy yet again, the background embellishment and the low-key corroboration they allot, the lowing intent or insinuation they supply or ply the melody with. I wondered yet again how the piece can so border on show-tune cheer yet be so hip, mingle moments flirting with soap-commercial ditty with streetwise aplomb. I listened again to Curtis Fuller briefly come to the fore, taking the lead voice away from Freddie only to almost immediately give it back. I listened again to Freddie come back to the fore and float briefly atop what bordered on soap-commercial ditty before restating the head and beginning to solo.

For someone who made a special point of me hearing this cut, someone who had shown up unexpectedly insisting I play it, Lambert showed little response when it began to play. His face turned expressionless as he sat listening, a placid mask offering no sign that the music had any meaning for him at all. He seemed at best, in fact, to be merely bearing with it. Throughout the opening statement and restatement of the theme he fidgeted once or twice but he wasn't otherwise demonstrative at all. Lambert's lack of response notwithstanding, I listened as intently as I'd ever listened. The short swirl of a leap and the sonic skid Freddie opens his solo with spoke to me as much as they ever had. So too did the rapid-fire polish alternating with a prancing way of placing notes he has recourse to as the solo unfolds, Cedar Walton's guajira-conversant comping underneath. Yet again I heard a contrastive dilation bordering on blare posed against intermittent, synaesthetic lip-twist, a synaesthetic sip and kiss rolled into one.

Lambert became a bit more expressive as Freddie soloed, all but undetectably so. With each intermittent, synaesthetic lip-twist he all but imperceptibly rolled his eyes, all but imperceptibly grew impatient with the lush articulacy Freddie resorted to. He all but imperceptibly seemed to say come off it. "All but imperceptibly," however, ceased to apply when Wayne Shorter began to solo, Lambert's response to which was decidedly more evident than to everything that had come before. Wayne's far-away reticence, the reluctant, trudged-all-this-way-to-say-this way he begins, following Freddie's bugling, crescendoing exit, foil to said exit, visibly lit Lambert up. His apparent nonchalance, the I'd-rather-be-elsewhere offhandedness one hears despite a slightly nasal touch, the burgeoning build of a lazy, elongated yawn, had Lambert up on his feet almost at once—up on his feet, head cocked, eyes closed, snapping his fingers. He snapped his fingers so emphatically I was afraid he'd break them, slowly pacing the floor all the while. Where Art reacts to Wayne's low-register shudders by saying, "Blow your horn," he too, pacing, said, "Blow your horn." Where Art reacts to Wayne's tilted, nasal quizzicality by saying, "All right," he too, pacing, said, "All right."

Over the years I've listened to Wayne's solo countless times. I can't say I stood up and joined Lambert, snapping my fingers, head cocked, eyes closed, pacing slowly, echoing Art's exhortations, but it's one of my all-time favorites when it comes to getting a lot said in a short span of time. I've repeatedly marveled, over the years, at the terse way Wayne has with tangibility, the expansive economics he exacts nonetheless. The retrospect epiphany he makes of the theme not long before fading, an eyebrow-raising tack seeming to say alas or to sound alarm, has always killed me. This was no less the case but indeed more so as I sat listening, blown away by the intervallic dilation titrating dismay he applies to the theme, reroutes it thru. Nothing could have spoken to me more than Wayne's solo, notwithstanding I didn't stand up and join Lambert. In my own way, a less demonstrative way, I was into it as much as he was.

Lambert made a show of being into it to make a point, to further pick the bone he began to pick a few weeks back. He lifted the tone arm off the record when Wayne's solo was over, cutting Cedar Walton's solo off just as it began. He then went into a spiel as to how unbelievable Wayne's playing was, a spiel I had no problem nodding my head in agreement with. I did have a problem, though, when he went on to put Freddie down and to make it a question of saxophone versus trumpet, reed against brass. He dared me to abandon (as he put it) the saxophone after listening to Wayne's solo, saying that only, as far as he was concerned, a madman could. He went on about what he decried as brass bombast at one end and irrelevant cuteness or slickness at the other, pinning it all on Freddie's solo, a solo he took to typify the trumpet's faults or failings, its inferiority to a saxophone prowess epitomized by Wayne.

It was Lambert at his most vociferous, albeit not untouched by an ironizing inflection here and there that seemed to say the point was to get what was to be gotten from skirmishing or scrimmaging for its own sake. Whether that was the case or the case was he was in dead earnest made me no difference. I couldn't get into it, wasn't in the mood. Listening to "Pensativa" after not having done so for so long had me feeling such disputation was moot. I tersely, quietly and a bit wearily said it was a matter of apples and oranges, to which Lambert replied that was exactly his point, one has to make a choice.

I couldn't get into it, wasn't in the mood to press it further. Instead, I got up, took *Free for All* off the turntable, went to the record shelves, pulled volume one of Freddie's *The Night of the Cookers* out, put it on the turntable, set the needle down on the cut that takes up side one, "Pensativa," and sat back down, asking Lambert to do the same. The date's a live session recorded at Club La Marchal in Brooklyn, with Lee Morgan also on trumpet, James Spaulding on alto and flute, Harold Mabern Jr. on piano, Larry Ridley on bass, Pete La Roca on drums and Big Black on conga. James Spaulding plays a bit of flute during the statement of the theme on "Pensativa" and Harold Mabern Jr. takes a short solo, but the piece is really a showcase for trumpet, an extended foray throughout most of whose twenty-two minutes Freddie and Lee go back and forth. "Brass Madness" it could've been called. After about ten minutes Lambert got up and left.

Yours,

N.

Dear Angel of Dust,

Djamilaa stood out of time dressed in Euro-courtly garb. She wore an anachronistic ball gown, a forest of undergarments underneath, petticoats and pantalets thick with ruffles and lace. Out of place as much as out of time, she stood beside me on the beach watching the waves whipped up by a storm off the coast roll in. The waves were agitated, white water mostly, more so than usual, larger than usual.

A hammer suddenly fell from the sky and my head rang. Hit on the head, I saw stars. I saw waves crest and crash on the beach, cosmic sea, petticoats raised on high. My head shook, reverberant bone. I heard breakers. Djamilaa's lifted skirts tugged at the sea. They let hell break loose but they nonetheless held out hope of heaven, tugged voices from the shell my head had become. Hollowed out by the hammer's impact, it was as empty as a bell but for the voices—shell and bell, promiscuously both.

My head spun, voices whirled inside it so, bell chasing shell, shell chasing bell, a dog trying to catch its own tail. Djamilaa's petticoats lifted me to heaven. My head rolled and lay stranded in the sand. It was judgment day. The bell I heard was the bell of a trumpet. I lay bodiless but for my head lying in the sand. B'Head-like, I was a melon in a patch but for being the only one. The sand was a patch but for there being no patch, no proper soil. Sand was what went for soil. But somehow my head, it seemed, had done more than roll there, had, that is, grown there, sprouted there, sand somehow its natal address. That, though, was only an illusion. My head had come there only that day, found its way there, rolled and come to rest there only that day.

My head lay in the sand looking up Djamilaa's dress, blinded by her anachronistic petticoats and pantalets, able to see only a bit of her legs well below the knee, squinting as though it were sun it saw nonetheless. The sun it presumably saw blacked out the sky. What it looked up into was an occult, star-studded night sky, the remote, petticoated reaches of intergalactic space. The stars were white, stirred-up water shaken up and spun by petticoat epiphany, petticoated lift and petticoated allure suddenly posed as cosmic froth, infinitely fine-bubbled sea foam, champagne froth on a Brazilian beach. Cosmic froth was as close as an armless, legless, trunkless head stranded in the sand would ever come to petticoat sashay, the all but tangible proximity of what, even had I not been armless and handless, even had it been available to touch, would have been no more retainable as itself than sea foam anyway.

My head never ceased reminding itself that bubbles, even infinitely fine bubbles, burst on contact. My lifted heart, however, lay elsewhere, borne on high by petticoat facticity, petticoated proffer of what lay above, petticoated concealment of what lay underneath. The bell I heard rang hermetic changes on light's aging break between the two, angelic shell positing night as bodied lure but ultimate hollow, soul's weighted bait, trumpeted body's taste of soul. I saw frills, folds, pleats and ruffles. I glimpsed a demandingness of stitch more demanding than I knew existed, finer exactitudes of lace than I knew existed, turns and recesses of cloth enough to seem to materialize incorporeal presentment.

I lay entranced by the bit of Djamilaa's legs I saw, prepossessing flesh made more prepossessing by recondite cloth. What I saw gained allure from what I couldn't see but knew to be there—calves, knees, thighs, occult crotch (dark hair beneath recondite cloth, recondite hair atop imminent crotch). Frill and fold and ruffle and pleat's enhancement of prepossessing flesh induced a champagne headiness I fought to contain but found I couldn't. Frill, fold, ruffle and pleat were prepossessing flesh's uncorked accompaniment, the esoteric truth of "You Go to My Head's" exoteric "like the bubbles in a glass of champagne," the sword of gnosis's "this never can be," its cruelest cut.

It was the sword of gnosis that had made my head roll. My head lay in the sand as I lay bodiless and my heart lay lifted on high. So it was I knew in my heart of hearts Djamilaa was Djeannine in Euro-courtly disguise, Euro-courtly frill's logarithmic arabesque, Euro-troubador root's exponential dispatch. I knew "Our Lady of the Lifted Skirts" had rebegun, an uncoiled accompaniment attending or attenuating Costume-Courtly Epigraph #1:

> She felt a momentary sadness but not enough to keep her from running on the stairs. Diron, without moving from his place on the veranda, saw her take her skirts like an armful of sea foam, raise them above the danger of being stepped on and, revealing legs plump and neat under pantalets, race lightly up the stairs and vanish. She did not know she was being watched.

I called it "Our Lady of the Lifted Skirts Revisited." It was a coy, recursive yarn I was caught up in, not so much a tale as an attenuation spun around a character in a book about the Haitian Revolution, a character named Céleste in a novel not so much about revolution as about romance, this character's effect on the character Diron mentioned above.

Then, too, there was Costume-Courtly Epigraph #2:

> "Biassou," Diron answered, almost jubilantly. "He has a companion named Boukman, more terrible than himself; and if you knew what they were up to, you wouldn't be standing there. The Revolution is here."
>
> "The dog was mad," Captain Frounier said. "I saw the froth on his mouth."
>
> "Mad—yes, that's the word."
>
> Diron laughed boisterously.

If not outright equating petticoats qua sea foam and insurrection qua frothing mouth, it at the very least insinuated they were variations on one another. The book spun my head with its implication of romance's near-ness to but ultimate default on revolution, petticoated recursion's nearness to revolution while rebuffing its dream of a clean break. Céleste was revo-lution's would-be heaven of cleanly cut, unindebted new beginning gone an alternate route, a displacement whose implicit toll insinuated eventual hell to pay. Romance's turned head was revolution's rolled head given deceptive new life. The parallel between the two couldn't help but be haunted by the fact that parallel lines never meet.

I lay immobilized by romance and revolution's failure to meet. I lay bodiless and divided, dateless, my head one place, my heart another, un-able to rendezvous with Djeannine-qua-Djamilaa, unable to relish a date with destiny, post-romance's rollaway cut. This, though, had to be a dream I knew. It had to be that I would awaken. Our Lady was a cancan dancer was the thought that roused me. I did so kicking the covers off the bed.

Sincerely,
Dredj

_____

Dear Angel of Dust,

Please forgive my last letter. The buzz I got from _Drums at Dusk_ landed me on my back. It was a buzz I got without knowing I'd gotten it, all the more landing me so. It landed me in bed, laid up on my back, hit by a new round of cowrie shell attacks. Not shattered shells become bottle caps this time, the shells went back, for this round, to being shells. They went back to being whole as well, unshattered, studding my forehead, visibly protruding. Piped into my head I heard not "Embraceable You" or "Bottle It Up and Go" or "Drennethology" or "Nhemamusasa" but the beginning of Jerry Gonzalez's "Agüeybana Zemi" looped, Steve Turre's opening call on conch shells played, as if on a nicked record, again and again. The cowrie shells stood on my forehead, stood out on my forehead. They not only stood or stood out but were lit up, aglow, lit from inside. They emitted a low light. Pronounced, protuberant, there was an impudence to them as well, an impishness worthy of one of Sun Ra's headpieces.

The usual feeling of impactedness was there. For all that, though, the attack brought with it a sense of spatial extension, evoked or exacted spatial dispositions of an express albeit mingled sort. The shells cast low but unremitting light on the room they made it seem I was in, a combination operating room/cabaret. I lay on my back looking up a cancan dancer's dress while doctors worked on my forehead, extracting shells. It wasn't I who lay there though. The shells gave off low, unremitting light and bestowed a new name on me as well. It was Dredj who lay there, Dredj it seemed or I sensed or found or I felt I was. New nomination bestowed cosmicity, further spatial extension. Dredj lay on his back looking up at the night sky's dress, roughed undergarment of stars. He lay on his back looking up night's dress, draped in cotton, his head wrapped in fold on fold of night's underskirts, petticoats the curtains his eyes ("the windows of my palatial head" he called them) wore. He lay entranced, if not a sick man a remade man, Frankensteinian stitches across his forehead to prove it. Shells had already been excised from his brow, cowrie shells extracted by a conch employed as cupping horn. Still more were now being excised.

This was the new wrinkle that got to me most. The lip of a conch repeatedly cut into Dredj's forehead, a shovel's edge or a namesake dredge's edge, it appeared, scratching at the floor of the sea. Every cowrie, the conch's lip insisted, had to be removed, all pretense to unwoundedness let go. They each bore the bite of illusory wholeness, the eyelike, mouthlike look of upstart exemption, presumed inviolability, boast. Razorsharp, the conch's lip cut away at exactly that, cut it away or at least reduced it with each cowrie it removed. Cutting into Dredj's brow, the conch's lip slid down and in and under its target cowrie, cupping it and nudging it upward and out thru an incision cut to its other side, the cowrie exiting Dredj's brow and, balloonlike, rising skyward, joining the night's garment of stars.

So it was in the House of Dredj: erstwhile eyes on high sewn in petticoats (love's late palatial estate). It was a First Antiphonal Church of Intimate Cloth, lost antiphonal wager, last resort. The conch cut, nudged and cupped to the beat of an afflicted drum. It not only cut but conveyed a song, an *Ur*-song of longing short on words but insistent even so— insistent, Dredj had heard one of his doctors opine, all the more so. The song it conveyed or was the vehicle for had the sound of sirens, the announcement of alarm or of cause for alarm. Spat out in quick bleats and punchy, panicky spurts, it was a call of sorts, a song of heat, a call to carnival insurgency in revolution's brooding head. Galactic champagne flowed freely in Dredj's house.

Cowrie and conch apportioned buoyancy and bottom, courtly premises revolution sought to unwind or unleash. The wheeling immersion and the sense of immensity which have been a feature of the attacks from the start, the whirling, drenched or drunken intensity with which they've come on from day one, wound and rewound Dredj's head tight as a drum. His home on high was night's backdrop of cloth, alternately lifted and lowered cloth in whose folds he lay caught up, light-years of cloth wound around his head like a turban. He lay on his back looking up at the exiting cowries and at the low, unremitting light they continued to cast as they ascended the sky. A black rain of hair gently brushed his face, black womanly hair intimating a face at kissing distance. It seemed a tent of unbridled hair falling to the sides of his face, a tent he sought refuge in. He wanted the face thus intimated to be love's revolutionary masque, a turban or a Dogon wordskirt to bandage his admittedly wounded head.

So the new wrinkle that got to me most brought a second shell into play, conch's cupping of cowrie an exponential dispatch making the rafters ring in Dredj's home on high. This was the bell spoken of in my last letter. There were other new wrinkles as well, others I'll not go into. Let it suffice to say I was subject to this new round of attacks for a couple of days but I've been back to my old self these past few.

Otherwise, things have gone on as they do. *Orphic Bend* is finding its way and we've begun to get a bit of response. We haven't seen any reviews as yet but we've caught what buzz there's been on the grapevine and even gotten a fan letter or two. There've been reports of balloons appearing here and there (one from as far away as Evanston, Illinois), but no rhyme or reason as to where, when or which cut. Attempts to photograph them continue to fail.

As ever,

N.

Dear Angel of Dust,

Many thanks for your letter. It was good to at last get your thoughts on "Gnostic Receipt (Short Form)," good to finally hear how it struck you. I'm glad it didn't draw the blank I began to fear it might have as time went by without comment. I knew it ran a certain risk. Anyway, yes, you get my drift: Black Thunder hereafter to be Bl'under, a titular, hopefully tutelary spirit on the order of B'Loon or Djbouche. And the questions you raise are good ones, especially the three you end with, "Trickster sublime or demiurge inept? Inept or inimical? Mishap or trap?" I'm not sure I know, but Herskovits has a phrase I've long been drawn to which may, if nothing else, be a place to begin. He speaks of West African tricksters and divining systems as a "deification of Accident," saying that such deification "in a universe where predetermination is the rule is evidence of the sophistication of the prevailing world concept." He relates it to "deep-rooted patterns of thought under which a man refuses to accept any situation as inescapable," bringing it specifically to bear on New World African tough-mindedness and resilience.

Bl'under's pedigree, then, to begin to address your question, does lie in the direction of tricksterism and divination as you suggest—the deification of Accident, to borrow Herskovits's phrase. I'm not as sure as you appear to be, however, that liberatory trickster and gnostic demiurge are poles apart. I see them as parts of the same complex, the same complex looked at reciprocally. The Dogon diviner-trickster Ogo-Yurugu has in fact been written about as a proto-gnostic demiurge. It seems worth noting that his first rebellious act, his assault on the earth's fiber skirt, takes place while Amma, the Supreme God, is asleep (the word *blunder* goes back to a root meaning "to doze" or "to shut the eyes"). What, that is, is a Supreme God doing falling asleep? Could a charge of ineptitude be laid at Amma's feet? But if a Supreme God, by definition, never sleeps, surely Amma slept, if such it can be called, with one eye open. That being so, Amma can be said to have looked the other way, to be complicitous with Ogo-Yurugu's revolt, even, to take it farther, be said to be a bit of a trickster himself or, worse, an agent provocateur, to have tricked Ogo-Yurugu into thinking he was asleep. (Ogo-Yurugu in fact thought he was dead.) Either way makes Ogo-Yurugu's revolt less a revolt than it seems. Ogo-Yurugu's rebellion and Amma's lapse are bound up in one another, divinatory vigilance or liberatory wakefulness somehow bound up in divine sleep.

A Portuguese proverb says, "God writes straight with crooked lines," just as New World Africans have repeatedly talked of "hitting a straight lick with a crooked stick." Ogo-Yurugu's zigzag run thru the divinatory field is such a line or stick, lightning inside *Black Thunder* and out such a line or stick—"*zigzag* lightnin'," Bukka White stresses ("Single Man Blues"). Bl'under confounds and further confabulates crooked and straight.

I've been hearing this with particular insistence on Bill Dixon's *November 1981* the past few days, a two-record album that came out last year and that if you haven't already heard you should go right out and get. It's not simply that what the liner notes call Dixon's "use of non-tempered tuned pitches in the 'flubbed' and half valve tone productions that he makes" agrees with what I've said about Bl'under. It's also not simply that the music is often stormy and that one of its titles announces wintriness and wind ("Windswept Winterset") and that lull and even slumber, storminess notwithstanding, also have their place ("Another Quiet Feeling," "Velvet"). It's both but also something else, more importantly something else, something I'd call its mapping and Ogo-Yurugulike traverse of a divinatory field, a mapping I'd instead call m'apping to accent intimacies between "map" and "mishap," a crossed or contracted rapport we otherwise overlook (mishap→m'ap).

In the way it has of mobilizing animate or ambulant breakage and debris, its recourse to what seems to me a resuscitative shunting, the music ventures upon an evolving, pulsating field subject to manipulable ascription, a divinatory run both winged and impeded by multiple rounds of ricochet and serration. Its ability to string and strip energy, bundled and unbound by turns, bespeaks a concurrency of staggered advent it wants to embody but can also allude to, a divinatory awakening it endures variation and vexation in its tending or would-be movement toward. Arousal and extinguishment, tempest and retreat, staggered advent favors "flubbed" admissions of nonattainment but also wants to get into in-between, attainable spaces not acknowledged by the tempered grid.

I wouldn't want to overplay the fact that Bill plays trumpet. Still, the trumpet's reputation as a particularly demanding and unforgiving instrument seems worth mentioning, especially where we have to do with transactions adumbrated by Amma and Ogo-Yurugu between straight and crooked, fate and fugitivity, fixity and resilience, containment and escape. Add unforgivingness and flub to the list and you begin to see where I'm going. Flub forgives or excuses itself, refuses containment, presumptions of containment. Bill makes it a preemptive refusal or at least makes it appear to be so, a choice even as it avers there's no choice.

But I don't, as I've already said, want to overplay that. A divinatory field I called it, which bears repeating: a plexed, evolving hold and/or advance of ongoing provocation, a plexed ensemblist amenity within which the work the strings do needs especially not to be overlooked. The two basses are crucial, enacting a straught, freehand and fisted working out of unremitting forage, a scurried, scraped working out of anabatic foray. It's as though string both bonded and bent gridded allotment, which, in fact, we find, it does. Tincture and pinch have something to do with this. Rub and welter have their say as well. Multiply-disbursed pulse points make it a vibratory field, the proverbial briar patch trickster divination wants nothing more than to be tossed into. What rub and welter have to say pairs corpuscular pluck with vibrational swipe, by turns pits them against one another and indifferently allows them to coexist. Rub and refusal have their say as well, exacting a toll having to do with wizened kin, fled brethren, a brer patch as much as a briar patch it seems. (Brer patch is Rahsaan's Vibration Society or John Tchicai's Strange Brothers or Chris McGregor's Brotherhood of Breath under other auspices, a vibe-societal sprint or, would-be sprint, quantum-qualitative sputter, a divine-divinatory bed of aroused bramble, burr, thistle, a divine-demiurgic spread of prestidigitator spiral and stir.) And, of course, the drums as well are key to that multiple disbursement.

This album has meant the world to me these past few days. The dead do live again, it wants to say or seems to say or I'd seem to have it say. On a bed of whistling tinder sirening thorn even so, the lame do stand up and walk.

Yours,

N.

Dear Angel of Dust,

Yes, maybe so. Maybe not so much the deification *of* Accident as that deification *is* Accident, but that's too long a conversation to go into here. I write instead to say that there continue to be balloon sightings among listeners to *Orphic Bend*. We continue to get word that balloons rise from the record's surface, albeit there continues to be no pattern (none that anyone, at any rate, can make out) as to where and on which of the three disks they do so. In some cases, evidently, there's only one spot or stretch where this occurs, in others more, five being the most among the reports we've gotten. Nor do the balloons appear with complete consistency. Listeners report that sometimes they do, sometimes they don't, which of course has been our experience with them as well. When and where they choose to show up and how often they show up appear to be a matter of deepest caprice. Still, there continue to be attempts to discern some logic in their comings and goings, some principle or plan their appearances obey. A few listeners, that is, say they've taken to keeping a log in which they record the specifics of appearances and nonappearances both, keeping track of dates, times, noteworthy or possibly noteworthy circumstances and so forth. They too report no discernible pattern as yet but remain, they say, hopeful.

The more instances of these appearances or sightings the more the word gets out, the wider it spreads—and with that, of course, comes controversy. That the wider the word spreads the more doubters turn up is a principle or precept which has proven to be the case and certainly continues to be the case. Some of the listeners who've been beset by balloons say they now listen to *Orphic Bend* only in the presence of others (witnesses they call them)—this to dispel the disbelief they've been subjected to. There don't appear to have yet been any cases of doubters not being able to see the balloons, but the fact that no one's been able to photograph them continues to weigh heavily even among some of those who've seen for themselves. The balloons' one consistency, that the words they bear for a particular spot or stretch on the record are the same from one sighting to the next and the same from one copy of the album to the next (geographically far-flung listeners report, for example, the very same words we saw emerge during Aunt Nancy's bass solo on "Dream Thief" on the test pressing), doesn't appear to matter as much or to amount to enough to suggest there's something real occurring. Accusations of chicanery and snake oil and sleight of hand are again being directed our way. We're in a quandary as to whether to reply.

For the time being at least, we're keeping quiet. Lambert suggested issuing another post-expectant press release or at least reissuing the first but everyone else feels we need more time to think this thru. That the balloons might be upstaging the music raises a number of concerns, but there might also be a need to rethink or further think that distinction. Whichever way we eventually go with that, however, there's no disagreement that the air of controversy and spectacle that may be developing is indeed distinct from the music, a distraction or a diversion, and that we've got to be careful not to lend ourselves to it, careful not to in any way feed it. This is what Drennette meant when she argued against issuing another release by saying to do so would "launch a balloon inside a balloon."

Still, keeping quiet's not easy. One wants to argue against the need for mechanical validation, the primacy accorded the camera, the machine's over the human eye. One wants to insist the doubters come to their senses, allow themselves to see what they see. One wants to say that subjecting the balloons to protocols of proof reverses what really needs to be done, that the balloons are in fact a summons to a deeper self-testing. One wants to tell them the test is on them, that they need to grapple more demandingly with themselves, look at what it is they see they don't wish to see. And so forth.

It's peculiar, though, to be defending or in the position of defending something we ourselves aren't without mixed feelings about.

Any thoughts?

As ever,

N.

Dear Angel of Dust,

I've been unable to get Dredj's letter off my mind. That business of revisiting "Our Lady of the Lifted Skirts" has continued to speak to me, so much so and on so practical a level it made me finally address a problem I haven't given due attention until now. It's the Compressed Accompaniments I'm talking about. You'll recall that I wrote five of them three years ago, the same number as there were members of the band at that point, an equation called for by Modular Rotation, the five stations and so forth. The problem I referred to arose when Drennette joined the band, the problem of there being one more band member than there are Accompaniments. This we've dealt with by making Drennette truly stationary, the drumset a station unto itself albeit a "silent" one, sans Accompaniment, keeping Drennette out of the Rotation. I've never been really satisfied with this and we've tended to perform "Our Lady of the Lifted Skirts" less frequently for that reason, but I've never quite seen my way to writing a sixth Accompaniment, which I immediately, of course, thought of doing and have again, from time to time, thought of doing.

Dredj's letter perhaps came in part from that dissatisfaction. In any case, thinking about it (not being able not to think about it) prodded me to a breakthrough, a new round of Accompaniments. It turned out I still couldn't simply write a sixth Accompaniment, an Accompaniment to be added to the five already there. I've never quite been able to get back to the place in which or from which I wrote those five and this occasion proved to be no different. But Dredj's letter opened me up and impelled me so much I was able to start, as it were, from scratch and write six new ones.

Enclosed is what I came up with.

As ever,

N.

SIX NEW COMPRESSED ACCOMPANIMENTS TO "OUR LADY OF THE LIFTED SKIRTS"

New Compressed Accompaniment No. 1

Orphic auspices loomed like a dream in Our Lady's friend-of-a-friend's new heaven, a bed of light newly blue albeit not yet blue to the bone.

Bone's retreat spoke where blue would eventually be, dry but not entirely dry, dust about to announce water's arrest.

Tugging the unraveling hem he held on to, Our Lady's friend-of-a-friend extended wish's moot register and reach, falling away but hauled upward as Our Lady floated upward, ballooning skirts bearing her aloft.

New Compressed Accompaniment No. 2

He it was whose friend spoke of Our Lady, having lain on his back looking up her dress at the place where her legs met, words and sparks flying from the sides of his mouth, an insinuative heat suggesting her pantied ass and crotch looked at from below, ass cleft and mat of hair dark under cloth.

A book of smoke it might've been, mounting smoke's dyslexic lure, a book he said he read taking hold of exiguous light, a monk in no one's head but his own, quixotic exegete even he knew himself to be.

"By all I know to be true" was the oath Our Lady's friend-of-a-friend now swore, friend of his friend's true testament (scant, esoteric blue underneath her dress's exoteric orange).

New Compressed Accompaniment No. 3

Rubbed eyes newly awake saw the grainy slope they'd fallen asleep on, bed falling away toward unexpectedly fractured light, their hooded squint's mock-monastic soirée.

A passage from the book his friend wrote came back to him: *barefoot but for a toe ring albeit begowned . . .*

Champagne shimmer, it soon came to pass, lit the sandy expanse that lay flat but rolled away, Our Lady's never-to-be-forgotten coquetry and comeliness apocryphal, phantasmal, a fiction or a fantasy, felt and for real even so.

New Compressed Accompaniment No. 4

The pungent crux where Our Lady's legs met went to his head, aromatic air he'd have given an arm to transpose or translate, musk whose penetrant reach posed a recondite domain he was tormented by.

Vibe shimmer floated a ring of stars at eye level: bursting halo, champagne tourniquet, bubbly rush . . .

Vibe society formed along the hem of Our Lady's dress it was now widely known, coastal folk he was one of and grew up among only to newly know and see himself so.

New Compressed Accompaniment No. 5

She grew to lament the impossible teaching a glimpse could evolve into, her friend-of-a-friend's blue heaven a gritty bed tiny bubbles burst in of late, erstwhile bubbles turning out to be grains of sand, lit silica burning lit-up acolytes (a bed they tossed and turned in, a bed they were abraded by).

His gruff mallet sublimity spoke to her nonetheless, rough sandpaper cheek she rubbed her cheek against, rough-and-ready caress, brusque Orphic boast his kiss became athwart mundane heaven.

Still, she complained of a sweet tooth for disappointment she suspected the sand they'd brought to bed with them sowed.

New Compressed Accompaniment No. 6

A choral insistence or insinuation lay like a cloud suffusing the halo his frustrated wish to take hold of extracted sound from and made shine all the more, chime all the more, a put-upon metallic touch being hit made sing.

Masticatory grit got hold of their fingers (masticatory grimace the clutch of his jaw), each and every exemption or excuse they banked or counted on long since elapsed or let go.

So it was that mallet met metal bar in a dream of waking up, high chime rayed out in every aspect and degree, Our Lady's friend-of-a-friend played like the proverbial violin, vibe-social adept though he took himself to be.

Dear Angel of Dust,

It's become clear it's not one piece I'm working on but three: "Reverie's Reveille," "Hand Me Down My Silver Trumpet" and "Accidental Divine." This third title came to me only a couple of days ago but it's the piece I've made the most progress on. The headway I've made on it is in fact what made it clear it's a triptych of sorts I'm involved in. It remains to be seen how tightly or loosely tied to one another the three will be, but "Accidental Divine's" theme of a post-expectant or would-be post-expectant wish to get on accident's good side recapitulates or will in some way have been rubbed off on by "Reverie's Reveille's" dreaming wish to awake and "Hand Me Down's" argent wish to unravel. Paradox or contradiction might be the tie. The tug or tension between unqualified and caveat-averring claims to post-expectancy (foreclosed expectancy's way of having it both ways) might be said to be had in common by the three. Wish has no way of being post-expectant one would think, but all three pieces propose or presume to wish it might, wish against wishing it might. The tug or tension between post-expectancy and wish would be another way to put it. The wish, in "Accidental Divine's" case, is to have been accrued to by aleatory hedges, soothsaid amenities in aleatory disguise.

"Accidental Divine" makes a bit of a play on the term "accidental" in its musical sense, accommodating a high number of notes foreign to the key it's in. Such accommodation makes the divinatory field it traverses or treads an obstacle course of sorts, a dark wood of sorts, a symbolic foray into nonidentity insofar as it vies with signature and contracted expectation. It "unsigns" the contract identified by key. But it goes beyond the implicit play on words, which is all too obvious no doubt. It relies primarily on other means of transmission. Its divinatory traipse or trespass conduces to a more than symbolic breach, the more than symbolic briar patch it wants to be in. The action is actually elsewhere. Call it cracked or crackling brass, brass cracked like seed in a parakeet's beak. Call it cackling brass, hen's cry, not-to-be-caught-out laughter. Whereas "Reverie's Reveille" will have pushed hypnopompic blare toward restorative concert and "Hand Me Down" will have opted for longitude and linearity (silver-tongued and silver-throated flow), "Accidental Divine" animates fracture, breached impediment, parsed egress.

I'm not sure whether I'm out to blast and blow the whistle on a widespread wish to woo chance or simply to be a case in point of it. In that sense, I'm cracked brass's ax, I'm torn. Cracked brass marshalls heartbreak brass into an effort to stand tall, a broken wave or a burst bubble apportioning caution and complaint, heart's wish buoyed by nothing if not the blowing itself, haunted by the consolation it appears to seek. Which of them ultimately wins out if in fact either of them ultimately wins out, whistleblowing critique or self-consoling case in point? Neither one has, to this point, won out. "Accidental Divine" perhaps wants to make a priestly stance of that impasse, an ironic investiture reverting to the spectre of accident courting inevitability's kiss.

Brass's ax? Yes. Lester Bowie implies as much in one of his characteristic moves. It's not unusual for him to recoil from the mouthpiece at the end of a run, to let his head whip back as though blown or thrown by wind coming out of the mouthpiece, wind blown by the trumpet itself—as though, that is, mouth were mouthpiece and vice versa, trumpeter trumpet and vice versa. Cracked brass's crack likewise has a way of running both ways . . .

Thank you for your letter. The matters you raise I'll address when I write again. What's most on my mind is "Accidental Divine" at the moment.

As ever,

N.

Dear Angel of Dust,

Djband stood at my bedside abuzz with reports of a new development on the balloon front. I already knew that for months now the balloons which occasionally accompanied or visited or issued from Djband's music had done so devoid of inscription, empty of the writing they'd customarily borne, the words they put in the music's mouth or that the music put into them. For months now they bore no words as they emerged from one of Djband's members' axes or from Djband's recent recording. The balloons had become, for some reason, curiously "mute"—balloons or bubbles more akin to burst bubbles, note-bearing bottles bearing no notes.

I also already knew that the blank balloons, visible to audiences but, unlike the earlier, written-in balloons, not to Djband itself, had transformed in recent weeks into a vaguely anthropomorphic figure said by those who saw it to possess a balloonlike body and a not unengaging face (lacking, though it did, a clearly drawn line between torso and face). They had taken to calling this figure B'Loon, following the lead offered by a press release Djband had issued not long after the balloons began to appear. I knew that, as with the balloons, attempts had been made to photograph or film this figure, but to no avail.

What I didn't know, the news Djband was abuzz with, was that the National Djband Fan Club had raised enough money to hire a sketch artist (the kind police departments employ to draw sketches of crime suspects) and to arrange interviews with everyone claiming to have seen B'Loon. There turned out to be a certain consistency among the eyewitness descriptions. Relying on these interviews, Djband informed me, the artist had come up with a sketch, a copy of which they'd been sent by Fan Club officials and, abuzz with the news, they now waved in my face.

The sketch I found rather crude and rudimentary. (See the enclosed copy.) Djband, when I said as much, assured me the artist had remarked on the salience of this very feature in the various eyewitness accounts. Those who've seen the figure evidently find themselves struck by a certain lack of polish, a roughness or rudimentariness in the very body or to the very being of B'Loon that none of them, the artist reported, had failed to comment on. It was as though, they were said to have suggested, its very crudeness or sketchiness, its appearance of not being finished or filled out, were the sign of a strain or a struggle to come into being, a fraught, unfinished harbinger of something not yet fully with us, a sign of something yet to come. The artist, in a very real sense, had drawn a sketch of a sketch.

At Djband's insistence, I looked more closely at the sketch. Yes, there was something oddly there but not yet there, not all there, an audacious wispiness if not insubstantiality, seen but as yet unheard-of (and exactly in that sense "mute"), an oddly unheard, unheard-of, yet-to-be-cashed-in claim on eventuality—mute-stereoptic agency rather than deaf-diagrammatic receipt. I saw and felt I understood, that is, why the sketch had been labeled as it was.

By no means escaping my notice were B'Loon's eyebrows, their detachment from its head and face, their floating free of its head and face. This feature as well, it turned out, had not gone without significant comment in the eyewitness accounts. Indeed, it had struck many, the artist reported, as the mark of crudeness and processuality par excellence, a mark regarding which some had raised the question of whether B'Loon's eyebrows and body are moving at different speeds, subject, perhaps, to differing sorts of gravitational force. A few, the artist noted, had ventured to answer their own question by calling this a refractive prospect or possibility having to do with distinct but related orders of admission.

Djband appeared heartened by all this—curiously heartened I thought. On closer inspection and with the benefit of the artist and eyewitness comments they apprised me of, the sketch proved to be a headier matter than it had seemed at first. It was all, in fact, a bit too heady. Albeit in bed, I had sat up when Djband came into the room and I'd leaned forward all the more attentively as they recounted the news they were abuzz with to me. I sat up ever more attentively still when they handed me the sketch and even more so when they insisted I peruse it more closely. The strain and the headiness of it, however, had begun to get to me. I felt lightheaded. I lay back down.

Djband continued to talk as the back of my head met the pillow, and I let my eyes close for a moment. Their comments made it clear they were in fact heartened by the new development on the balloon front—intrigued by it, yes, but oddly ratified and even inspired by it all the same. One of them announced having been so taken with the sketch as to've begun a new section of the antithetical opera he'd been long at work on, a section sparked or inspired by B'Loon's free-floating eyebrows. He had already found what he termed Mute-Stereoptic Epigraph #1, a quote from Emerson that was to inform and otherwise pervade or preside over the section:

> Every word which is used to express a moral or intellectual fact, if traced to its root, is found to be borrowed from some material appearance. *Right* means *straight*; *wrong* means *twisted*. *Spirit* primarily means *wind*; *transgression*, the crossing of a *line*; *supercilious*, the *raising of the eyebrow*.

The section, he said, would avail itself of B'Loon's eccentric purchase on ostensible haughtiness or height (including but not confined to operatic height), B'Loon's implicit translation of etymologic hauteur into wispy buoyancy and lightness or lilt.

He remarked as well on an ambiguity in B'Loon's eyebrows, a lashlike aspect they acquired by way of length and upward cast. Were they eyebrows or were they eyelashes or were they, he wondered, both? It was an ambiguity by way of which, in the new section he envisioned, he'd ally lightness or lilt with eyelash flutter, proverbial eyes-behind-the-fan flirtation—classic opera fare, in other words, tilted or teased, coquetry suddenly wide-eyed, wise to its inflation for once. He had already, to this end, written a bit of the aria, he announced, pulling a sheet of staff paper from his coat pocket and handing it to the singer for the group, who stood next to him, to his left, at the foot of the bed. She unfolded it, held it out in front of her and began to sing.

I was taken aback when she began to sing. I sat up again. A feather broke my back or got caught in my throat and I coughed it up. A pinched mereness more than I could endure knotted my spine, an inexact expanse I saw contract and expand again, fuzzed insistence I saw go up thru the air like smoke. Such was the effect on me of her voice. Such was love's lateral additive (real or simply assumed), an aside spoken slantwise, semisaid, semisung. It appeared she sang from somewhere slightly outside herself— outside but close by, no more than four to six inches away. It was a place well within her body's ambit, a spot outside but implied by and hugged or held in place by proximate flesh. She sang from a place just away from her right side, appendix level, catty-corner to her pelvic bone. She held her right hand at the same appendix height, a bit to the right of that spot, letting it hang relaxedly though not without a touch of the coquette, as though a handkerchief, just a moment before, had not so inadvertently fallen from it.

It wasn't very long she sang and the words to the aria mostly escaped me (something to the effect of careless fate or coquettish fate "hoisting ticklishness on high"), but the impact was profound and thoroughgoing. Something about her voice put one in mind of Paula Grillo, the singer with Machito's band, the deep reach and Delphic scoop heard on a piece like "Caso Perdido" in particular, a certain huskiness and hollowing out of hope that hollows presumed height or haughtiness out as well. She proffered hollowed-out hope with her right hand, the hand she held at appendix height, stood proudly but with a hint of self-pity, pride, if not wounded, forewarned.

The sag and the play given the tug between huskiness and hauteur (timbral demur bespoken by depth or default) struck one as doing nothing if not demoting eyelash flutter, nothing if not transiting lowered lid toward lifted husk, lowered mask or lowered fan toward lifted husk. Forewarned pride was a before-the-fact bruise, the wound or bruise eyelash flutter flirted with. The singer played the difficult role of diffident vamp, coquette manqué, philosophic flirt. She was the bruised-or-blue-before-the-fact vamp anticipated by a passage out of Ellington, a passage the opera's composer later announced would serve as Mute-Stereoptic Epigraph #2:

> The blues is the accompaniment to the world's greatest duet,
> A man and a woman going steady.
> And if neither of them feels like singing 'em,
> Then the blues just vamps till ready.

Her right hand's proximity to pelvic largesse (proffered hope's proximity as well) ballasted a bumped and ground blue disposition, forewarned flutter's high disregard.

There was more talk when the brief serenade came to an end. One of Djband's members, the drummer, wondered what it meant that B'Loon (if that was indeed, she couldn't help remarking, who or what this was) allowed himself or herself or itself to be seen by audiences but not by Djband, wondered why they were kept in the dark regarding something of their own creation. Answers or possible answers were put forth, along with the further question of whether B'Loon was indeed their own creation, a rhetorical question posed by the oboist to the effect that the audience plays a role in making the music or, if not the music, what's made of the music. Other issues, angles, questions and assertions came up, Djband's members often speaking more than one at a time, now and again speaking all at the same time. The buzz eventually got to me. I lay back down.

Was this "Our Lady of the Lifted Skirts Revisited Again" I wondered, harking back to the singer's pelvic largesse, her low-body insinuation, Delphic throatiness, float-away duress. I closed my eyes and plied a formula, I felt, aligning underskirt with lifted husk, kicked or lifted leg with hollowed-out hope, but Djband, when I opened my eyes, was still there.

I sat up and blinked and blinked again (would-be wipe, would-be wash). Djband was at bed's edge, abuzz, still going at it. I pinched myself. It hurt. I was already awake.

Sincerely,
Dredj

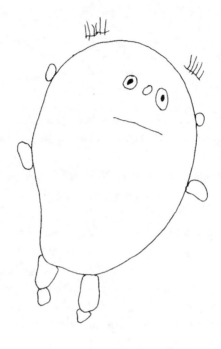

Mute-Stereoptic Emanation: B'Loon
(Composite Sketch Based on Eyewitness Accounts)

_____

Dear Angel of Dust,

Please forgive "House of Dredj Revisited." Yesterday's letter, like Dredj's earlier letter, came out of a cowrie shell attack, the new wrinkle's conch and cowrie address which, as before, landed me on my back, in bed. There were only two cowries, however, and the conch was only implicitly there, the two cowries lying not in my forehead but in the air just above my forehead, floating a couple of inches above it in suspended exit or flight, it seemed, from it. They appeared to have been removed from my forehead, cupped and excised, evidence that the conch, if not there, had been there. No cowrie shells remained in my forehead but an impacted feeling was there even so—post-operative soreness I took it. I lay on my back, in bed, recovering, convalescing, the opening of Sun Ra's "A House of Beauty" looped and piped into my head, Ra's Clavioline and Ronnie Boykins's bowed bass playing conch to Marshall Allen's piccolo's cowrie. Ra's music notwithstanding, there was none of the spatial extension, pala-tial or galactic expansion or cosmicity that there'd been before. On the contrary, the room I lay in seemed cramped and, aside from the two cowries hovering above my forehead, ordinary. It was day, furthermore, stark day, not night.

The music sounded snide, ironic. Dredj's house of beauty, if that's what the music meant to call it, was anything but—no opening upward onto a starry night sky, no fancy garment of stars, no rain of black wom-anly hair. The cowrie shells, though, as before, emitted low light, tempting one to see one's environs differently, by way of default or forfeiture bestow aura: ingenious balloons if not post-operative tokens, inspired lightbulbs if not post-operative tokens, raised eyebrows risen free of the brow if not post-operative tokens.

Dredj's letter didn't get written right away. The attack lasted two days, on the second of which, yesterday, my hand picked up a pen and began moving.

As before, I got over it. The attack, like those before, ran its course. This morning I woke up feeling fine.

Yours,

N.

Dear Angel of Dust,

Remember the customized mouthpieces I wrote you about back in December, the ones Lambert and I went to see a fellow named Fred about? Well, the two weeks he said it would take turned into four weeks, then two months, then three months and then, finally, a few days ago, four months later, Lambert got a call saying his mouthpiece was ready. (Thinking mine must be ready as well, I phoned Fred, who said no, it would be another week or so before he could get to mine.) Lambert went over to pick it up, taking his horn with him to try it out right away. It was different from what he expected, he says, more demanding. Fred had lengthened the facing, lowered the baffle and narrowed the tip rail, as expected, but to a greater extent and in combination with an x-factor, some unspecified alteration, requiring a lot more wind and a more open, relaxed embouchure than Lambert's used to. Varying Trane's comment about playing with Monk, Lambert says the new mouthpiece is like putting one's mouth around an empty elevator shaft, blowing on an empty elevator shaft. "It'll take some getting used to," Fred told him, an understatement, to say the least, Lambert says.

Strange. Lambert struggled with the new mouthpiece for a couple of days, making a bit of headway, getting used to it some, but nowhere near as much as he'd have wished or expected. Who then, exactly then, should he hear from but Melanie, whom he hadn't seen or contacted or been contacted by since running into her at Yang Chow after visiting Fred's store in December, and what should prove to be the turning point in his struggle with the new mouthpiece but exactly that? That's exactly what happened. He got a note in the mail from Melanie. "Dear Lambert," it read, "I'm still astir, still all atingle all these many weeks after running into you at Yang Chow. Last night I dreamt I went there with you and we went, at the head-waiter's suggestion, the place being full, into a back room neither of us knew was there, notwithstanding having been to Yang Chow as often as we have. I thought it would be a small banquet room for private parties but it turned out to be a bedroom, a large room with a large bed in the mid-dle. We closed the door behind us, walked over to the bed and lay down. We spent what seemed a good hour or so just kissing. It was all very inno-cent, deliciously so, a recognition, no doubt, of all the different levels on which we speak to and feed one another. What do you think?" She signed it, "Kisses (dreamt and otherwise), Melanie."

"I'm not sure what exactly did it or how Melanie's note did it if that's what it was," Lambert told us, "not sure what about the note could have such an effect. But from that point on there was no more struggle. I got out of my way or out of the mouthpiece's way or it got out of my way or these all amounted to the same thing. In any case, I found myself draw-ing on reserves of wind I didn't know I had, a stout column of air keep-ing my throat as unpinched as one could want. My embouchure was easily the match of the empty elevator shaft it seemed I blew. And all this came about without resorting to a softer reed, which I was determined not to do, made up my mind not to do." This was all by way of introduc-ing a new piece he brought to rehearsal this afternoon, a piece called "Book of Opening the Mouth" he wrote after receiving Melanie's note and overcoming the difficulties with the new mouthpiece he'd been hav-ing. The title, he explained, alludes to an ancient Egyptian funerary text and ceremony whose aim was the reconstitution of the body of the de-ceased and the restoration to it of its Ba (heart-soul) and Ka (double). This was done, he went on, by an opening of its mouth effected thru cens-ing, sprinkling, anointment, offerings, recited formulae and touching the mouth with an instrument made of pink stone known as the Kef-pesesh and two axes, one made of iron of the South and the other made of iron of the North.

Lambert seems to have had Billy Harper's "Priestess" in mind or at least at the back of his mind, availing himself of a similarly heraldic, annunciative head stated by the horns (him on tenor, Penguin on soprano, me on trumpet) at the end of a long rhythm-section lead-in which broaches and repeats a skeletal outline or advance of the eventual theme. After a short recitation by Lambert (more on that in a minute), Djamilaa, that is, gets the music going on unaccompanied piano, doing so simply but with a certain subdued majesty, block chords proffered as though they were only an idle thought. Aunt Nancy, on bass, joins her a few measures in, augmenting her left hand's rickety coffin-lid figure, stately but letting the strings rattle, ominous all the more. A few measures more and Drennette comes in with a loud cymbal crash, upping the ante on all that's gone before while mining, by way of sticks on the snare's rim and a run of well-placed bass drum thumps, skeletal advance's insinuative largesse, the ominous wedding of church and state Aunt Nancy's bass adumbrates. A few measures more and the horns come in, foretaste and tease put aside, the head at last fully fleshed out.

A recitation by Lambert, as I've said, prefaces the music, him reading a short piece he wrote based on a few of the recited formulae found in *The Book of Opening the Mouth*. The idea is to establish the proper tone and atmosphere, of course, but also, Lambert explained, to beat the balloons at their own game. He referred to the recitation as a preemptive strike, saying the aim was beating the balloons to the punch. He probably shouldn't have thought of it that way. It probably would've been better not to think of the balloons at all. In any event, there were no problems, on that front at least, the first few times we gave the new piece a try. There were false starts and wrinkles to be worked out, as usual, but it got better each time we ran thru it. Lambert's voice during the recitation, however, got fainter each time we ran thru it. The better successive renditions got the more laryngitic his recitation voice became, the odd thing being that his voice remained otherwise normal, that he spoke at normal volume when he wasn't delivering the recitation. We all began to wonder what was going on, him included.

It got to the point, after we'd played the piece a half-dozen times or so and had pretty much gotten it down, that Lambert, beginning the recitation as we got going on it one last time, entirely lost his voice. He opened his mouth but no sound came out. He stopped and tried again but still no sound came out, stopped and tried a third time to no avail. The fourth time he tried there was again no sound but a balloon came out of his mouth, a balloon bearing the words he was attempting to recite: *I stand on an oval representing a mound of sand, facing south. My eyes have been anointed with eye-paint, water sprinkled, incense burned. I am he of the twice-touched eye, mouth, hand, my mouth is that of a newborn calf.* Taken aback, as the rest of us were as well, he stopped. It was Aunt Nancy who motioned for him to continue, which he did, opening his mouth to pick up where he'd left off, no sound coming out but a new balloon emerging, a balloon bearing the rest of the recitation: *Leg has been proffered, presented. My lips have been given color, my lips have been constituted, my teeth balance conformably to my mouth. Temu's arms are the straps holding my horn, facing south. Lips made, mouth slit, statuesque I stand, my horn a goliath beetle, red, white, green and black.*

Lambert closed his mouth. He looked exasperated. We all looked around at one another. The rest of us were bemused by this new display of B'Loon's wile but not exasperated. Without having to say so we were all resolved to play thru it. The balloons had taken the words out of Lambert's mouth but we would go forward. Djamilaa, hardly missing a beat, had already begun the lead-in, meting out the skeletal advance a bit more quietly than before, resolute but given pause it seemed. The block chords, the way she now played them, came out sounding like reminders, faint reminders, distant recall, a call to order. She lingered whereas before she moved on swiftly, a restorative tack recalling a faintly remembered archive—ruminative, remanent, a faded mandate of sorts. What she played parsed a less churchical or churchified understanding of the coffin-lid figure, a secular caution or a conundrum having to do with last, limited choices, last or lost options, lost wager, lost wish.

Aunt Nancy let Djamilaa go on longer than in previous renditions before coming in, ratifying that caution or conundrum, when she did, with an aptly rattled, unraveling sound and straught saunter. She quickly, however, as though regaining lost poise or composure, assumed a more stately gait, churchical-stately, deepening Djamilaa's meditative touch and archival wisp with an aroused, rearing swell's cardiognostic throb. It was bass rectitude at its most righteous, albeit fetching, wickedly so, all the same, funky-profane in a theretofore unsuspected way, a newly emergent churchical-stately way. Rearing bass, for all its rectitude, found a place for complaint, a rolling grumble it rode as though grievance rolled as well, wheeled by fortune's loss, the wager and wish Djamilaa wanted to let go but lingered on. An oddly quiescent swell it was, curiously low-key, cardiognostic spur notwithstanding. Drennette, when she came in, came on strong, not buying it, the cymbal crash wielded like a whip.

Aunt Nancy and Djamilaa maintained their low-key resolve even after Drennette joined in, a beautifully restrained, understated furtherance of something one knew amounted to pomp albeit free of pomp's bluster. Drennette took the intensity up a quantum notch, whip that she was, but they went on as before, unrushed, unruffled. The bashed invective Drennette worked up threw their churchical-stately poignancy and poise into flattering relief and vice versa, a mutually flattering standoff but a standoff nonetheless. It fell to the horns, then, to relieve this complementarity of the freight its fraught majesty labored under, the tense announcement of what was to come it continued to be.

Lambert, when we came in, showed no sign of the exasperation the balloons had caused him. His tone and attack were as full and resolute as one could wish, the difference the new mouthpiece makes no less audible than it'd been before. When he put the horn to his mouth and blew no balloons came out, contrary to fears we all had that they might, given what had happened with the recitation. Our statement of the head has a certain bluster to it, so our coming in filled in or further stated what Djamilaa and Aunt Nancy understated as we also endorsed and amplified while seeming the issue of Drennette's quantum notch. The sound was indeed majestic, unfraught, mystic, the tenor's open, full-throated bluster echoed and abetted by the trumpet's blare and the soprano's Eastern sinuousness, a royal, multiply-threaded carpet we wove and rolled out. It was a prayer rug and a magic carpet rolled into one, a launching pad and a meditation pillow rolled in as well, unfurled auspices the solos now sprang from, Lambert soloing first.

Lambert's solo is the reason I'm writing. His new mouthpiece, as I've said, makes a difference, a difference "Book of Opening the Mouth" showcases and which the solo he now took employed to more stunning effect than before. The sound it gives him or allows him to get brings Jackie McLean to mind somewhat, notwithstanding the fact that Jackie plays alto. Jackie's husky but unforced flow taken over to tenor is a bit what it's like—thick but unconstricted, dilated but not lush, an arrested croon keeping it ever so subtly choked up albeit open, unpinched. The cut or the bite Jackie manages by way of that nasal edge he gets is there in Lambert's new sound as well, a sharp horizon or halo intimated or etched while remaining just out of timbre's reach. I couldn't help thinking, as Lambert launched his solo, that he had to have Jackie in mind, had to be thinking or to have been thinking of Jackie, had even to have or have had a particular piece of Jackie's, "Melody for Melonae," in mind. It wasn't that he quoted from or explicitly alluded to the piece but that the book in question in this "Book of Opening the Mouth," the solo quickly made clear, was Melanie's book, inspired by Melanie's note, a book of pressing mouth to mouth, tongue to tongue, letting teeth every so often touch, a book wet with kisses.

From the solo's outset, that is, Lambert wasn't averse to dropping his lower jaw and loosening his lower lip, resorting to subtones in a Websterian romantic vein as if letting down his guard, relieving a certain austerity, a staunch resolve his McLeanish tartness could be said to be weighted with. It recalled the young Webster's lover-boy looks, Chico Freeman's lover-boy looks, the tenor's mac-man pedigree. Lambert was all over the horn—bottom, top, middle—two arms and two hands embracing and caressing Melanie's close-to-the-bone beauty's every curve, mound and recess. Every softness, every muscular firmness, every bony prominence was given its due, bone-goddess beauty's blend of musculature and muse given its due, cheekbones, ribcage, clavicles extolled, calves, ankles, asscleft praised and celebrated, neck, pudendum, swell of hips, on and on. Had he unbuttoned his shirt he couldn't have been more explicit. The solo could've been called "Melody for Melanie" and it could've been called "Book of Opening the Nose" as well. It drew on *The Book of Opening the Mouth*'s liturgy and Lambert's opening recitation, reiterating that leg had been proffered, presented. Lambert said he lay with his face downwards, nostrils flared, smelling the earth, not lifting his face to the sky. He said he lay smelling the earth, his nostrils filled with Melanie's loin-musk, her legs pried open his nostrils, her open legs opened his mouth, on and on. Earth-smell, loin-musk, perfume and powder were a thick mix clouding his head, he said, a heady mix thickening the air.

The solo had Melanie written all over it, beautifully, bewitchingly so, but no balloons came out of the horn. She was much more clearly the issue and inspiration this time thru, Lambert's solos on the previous renditions having come nowhere near the explicitness he now allowed himself, the admission of Melanie's note's hypnotic sway. Perhaps it was this that kept the balloons at bay, Lambert beating them at their own game by openly admitting Melanie's allure and legibility's role in transporting it. He had a way, that is, of having it and not having it, having it both ways. He overblew the horn every now and then, seeming to insist it was all only air, inflation, wind. Melanie's note, it seemed he said, was a balloon, *The Book of Opening the Mouth* a balloon, dreamt kiss or waking kiss a balloon, all aim, allure, endeavor and desire a balloon, empty elevation. So it was, perhaps, that B'Loon was there without being there, Lambert's ploy a pact of sorts, a peace treaty he made with B'Loon and vice versa.

The balloons by this time, though, were not the issue. Lambert repeatedly made it clear that the new mouthpiece had opened his embouchure, proffered leg his eyes, nose and mouth. It was truly a book of openings and he was its exegete—a varied book, churchical-stately and pillow-book intimate by turns, Melanie's mouth and voice pillow-talk sweet the way he told it, powder, perfume and loin-musk an incense clouding his head. He called Melanie his Isis, announced himself smitten, wept for, invoking the formulaic "she smiteth me and weepeth for me," announced himself revived. Were it all a balloon filled with mouthfuls of air, so be it, a bubble yet to burst, a bauble, so be it, he said or it seemed he said.

But it wasn't just the subtones and the overblowing, as though each assumed or advanced a distinct position. Endowment and deprivation cohabited, equally inhabiting each note, each nuance, each extrapolative outlet of air, void and voice or void and vocation two sides of the same coin, voice vacancy as much as vocation. Lambert spoke out of both sides of his mouth, blown bauble's bodily largesse endlessly embraced yet endlessly a source of apprehension, labial and bodily embrace an empty elevator shaft one stepped into. It was Lambert at his gnostic best, there but not there, not unlike B'Loon—better than his best in fact, a new day of getting out of his own way just begun.

How much credit to give the new mouthpiece and how much to give Melanie's note (not to mention the balloons taking over the recitation) I don't know, but I was on the phone to Fred again right after rehearsal. I can't wait till he's done with mine.

As ever,

N.

_____

Dear Angel of Dust,

Not to be outdone by Lambert, Penguin showed up at rehearsal with a new composition. "Book of Elysian Escort" it's called. "Drennethology II" it could as easily be called, harking back, as it turned out it does, to Drennette taking hold of his arm at Aron's a couple of months ago. It calls for three double-reed horns: him on oboe, Lambert on English horn, me on bassoon. "None of that 'wall of sound' business there's been so much talk about lately," Penguin said. "What I want is a field of reeds." We all smiled, catching his drift, his allusion to Sekhet Aaru ("Field of Reeds"), the place where Osiris lived, lost on none of us. A sub-district of Sekhet Hetepet ("Field of Offerings"), it was what some have called ancient Egypt's Elysian Fields. We knew right away what he was getting at. Revenant sound's eked-out embroidery was what he wanted. On our very first go at it that's what we got.

Had it been a wall a teetering wall it would've been, verticality's traverse of degree and gradedness, leaned-on Osirian repose. (You've seen, I'm assuming, the depictions of Osiris-Res, Osiris the Riser, in tilted repose, an angular, graded address of horizontality, tilted rest upon and rise from horizontality.) By teetering wall I don't mean the collapse of harmony into melody Ornette likes to call harmolodic, verticality's assumption by slant advocacy or advent, though something like that was also there. A teetering sense not so much of elevation as of ground itself was what it was, epistatic foundation if not anti-foundation, the movement of moored boats bobbing on water. Djamilaa plays vibes on the piece, parsimonious metallic chimes adding all the more a sensation of glimmer, glint, the shimmer sunlight hitting rippling water gets or gives out. It put one in mind, remotely, obliquely, of Prince Lasha and Sonny Simmons's "The Loved Ones" on the *Firebirds* album, Buster Williams's bass's thrumming, can't-get-started insistence and iterativity possessed of a buoyancy Aunt Nancy seemed to take a lesson or two from. Drennette's recourse to mallets on cymbals had a steep incumbency to it, endorsing or endowed with shimmer only to shade its underside.

Lambert and I backed and bordered Penguin's lead as we stated the head. The three of us were a double-reed choir. We were singing, sing though we did as though we sang with our last breath, edge, outskirts or extremity the brink or the beginning we set out from. Had a balloon come out of Penguin's horn it would have said: *The crook of her arm hooks the crook of mine, we walk arm in arm, each the other's Elysian Escort. Arm in arm, no harm can come to us. The Field of Reeds welcomes us. Bulrushes part as we approach.* Had a second balloon come out it would have said, taking up the Egypto-reggae thread the piece has recourse to: *Reeds wave and sway. Breezes ripple the atmosphere. I sister and I arrive in the Atet boat. "Is is and will always be," she counsels me, she my Isisian consort, I her Osirian host. I sister and I walk determined, undeterred. I brothers and I blow reeds between our lips. The Elysian Escorts' horn escort I brethren and I, pressed reeds ready our way.* And so on. But there was no need for balloons (not that there ever is). Penguin got a less pinched, more open sound from the oboe, an extrapolative, reedy, rafter-shaking sound more like a zorna than an oboe. A teetering wall was a fallen wall as far as he was concerned. A fallen wall was a bridge over a moat if not the ground itself, ground he spread a picnic blanket or rolled out a red carpet on. Caught as light catches in fog, he worked and reworked the figure with a certain persistence, a certain adamance and iterativity, not only the persistence but the ice-pick ping of Santana's "Europa," the shades of "Never Gonna Give You Up" it resorts to, Jerry "The Iceman" Butler's namesake chill taken up a notch (quantum namesake shiver, grit and chagrin rolled into one). Penguin walked tall on ground made regal and majestic by the crook of Drennette's arm in the crook of his.

We three horns exacted a ray of double-reed insinuation, a broad, keening ray inviting reflection, quickening thought. I was thinking one day we'll be able to photograph thought, that what we'll see won't so much "look like" as "be." I knew I had the balloons in mind. I knew I meant to take a swing at them, taunt them, knew I might be pushing our luck. One day our thoughts will know one another, palpably touch, I went on, tactile-telepathic aplomb. I felt the crook of Isis's arm hooking the crook of Osiris's arm. So will our thoughts one day engage one another I thought. But that very thought, I went on to think, was a balloon of thought, so thin its containment of itself albeit inspired, a tightly drawn cartoon/cartouche. "I thought I thought" popped out of my horn, a miscue I made good on by extenuating the bassoon's low croak, thin containment cast in instrumental argot. By balloon of thought I meant bassoon of thought I said or made it seem I said. The bassoon was a frog in my throat, the frog's inflated gullet the balloon I mistook it for. "A dream I dreamt I dreamt," I may well have said or might as well have said.

I saw Drennette out of the corner of my eye. She sat at the drumset standing tall, walking tall, Osiris's Isisian escort. No lamentation lined her face. On the contrary, she sat expressionless, her face a placid mask. Stolid, stoic, unperturbed, she was the Ice Queen and Isis rolled into one, more beautifully blasé than ever, placid beauty we blew to awake. We blew cooler than we'd have thought we could, quantum cool assuming Tantric height. Ice Queen, that is, to Penguin's Iceman, as though the "is" in Isis were ice, Drennette sent a chill up our spines with her cymbal work.

Ice along the Nile intimated long odds, unlikely concourse, that only unlikeliness would do. That what we want we don't have or what we have we don't want was what it was it seemed it wanted to say. Still, it was the closer walk we'd heard so much about, the walk we'd heard sung so much about. Penguin and Drennette walked closer than ever, ice notwithstanding, even closer than in their arm-in-arm exit from Aron's, intimate albeit diagonal to one another in our rectangular rehearsal space. They were at least twenty feet apart but he was her "thee" and she was his, each the serenaded consort of whom a closer walk had been asked. It was blue ice, though, slightly shaded, a sublime chill music alone could effect. Close, that is, was oddly futureless, closest, closer than ever as close as they'd ever be. Crescent music it thus was but of only deferred consequence, entrances indeed elysian, endless (though each eventually ended), on ice. It was nothing if not a walk down the aisle, even so, a wedding one leg strode in pursuit of and the other leg put on hold.

All this, though, was only the beginning. No "as though" about it, "is" was nothing if not ice but ice wasn't all there was to it. We covered a good deal of unlikely and likely ground both before it was over, one unforeseen upshot being that the seeds of a new piece hit me as we played, which is why I'm writing. The difference between bassoon and saxophone implied further difference. The former's double reed, vibrating against both my lips rather than only one, put me in mind of brass—obliquely, I admit, but, all the same, decidedly so. The buzz on my lips called out for brass insistence, further insistence, a fourth piece to take its place beside the three I'm working on. Buzz and bud rolled into one, such insistence, I couldn't help feeling, conceded a need to turn romance's turned head a bit further. A line from one of Dredj's letters came back to me: "Romance's turned head was revolution's rolled head given deceptive new life." I wanted a new piece, one which would make such life truly new, not a ballot or a bullet to "Book of Elysian Escort's" ballad but a trumpet piece, "Sekhet Aaru Strut."

Ice along the Nile's long odds made even longer? Maybe. But romance's turned head has to amount to more than mere illusion. Something real resides there, wanting out. A promise, let's call it, parade premises, a romance and a reminiscence regarding the music's open-air roots, prospects of an all-pervading intimacy or adhesion, eroto-utopic polity, pace, promenade. Penguin's "Book," like Lambert's "Book," held a hint of perfume laced with loin-musk, faint pubic allure—"pubic," I wanted to insist, a simple "l" short of "public": "l" stood for "loud," "loiter," embryonic sashay. I sensed a parade taking shape in the "Book's" bouquet. In a half-sleep I heard something there's no way I could've heard. I heard or half-dreamt I heard Buddy Bolden play "Funky Butt." It was brass epiphany all over again.

So, not a triptych now but a set of four: "Reverie's Reveille" followed by "Hand Me Down My Silver Trumpet" followed by "Accidental Divine" followed by "Sekhet Aaru Strut." I've actually managed to get "Sekhet Aaru Strut" written—rather quickly, in one sitting in fact. If I could only say the same for the other three . . .

Yours,

N.

Dear Angel of Dust,

I keep listening to the Henry Threadgill album I mentioned a few months ago, the seven-man sextet date. The album jacket, for one, keeps pulling me back, almost as much a draw as the music itself. Something about the conception and design strikes a chord: the framed illustration on the front featuring a bunch of animal bones within a rectangular border and two other bunches inside boxlike holes, all of them on or above or inside slablike planks of rock or perhaps wood and the framed illustration itself on or against a fossil-on-graph-paper background that takes up the entire jacket, front and back. It wants to say something about the remote backreaches of time, the unthinkability of prehistoric time, an unthinkable time of which "reminders" nonetheless exist, a taunt or a tease almost, "reminders" that could even be called records (bone record, indentation record, impression or imprint record). It wants to say something about incommensurability, fossil time versus Cartesian location. Threadgill seems to have gone on thinking, the way kids do, about dinosaurs, ammonites, mastadons and the like, the brain-tease of prehistoric time. The album's title is *When Was That?* It's almost too much that the record company it's put out by is called About Time.

I said almost as much a draw. The music is what pulls me back, though that pull isn't unrelated to remnant, reminder, reminiscence, fossil time of another sort. The music broods, reaching back to its funereal roots, reviving those roots, mourning its own passing and its preservation both, the speeded-up fossilization recording affords. (Vinyl is a petroleum product.) Threadgill, I've heard, says he wants to make music that could be played in a funeral parlor. Mission accomplished. *When Was That?* certainly could, the old-time vibrato of a piece like "Just B" furthering its title's theme of a tenuous, fought-for hold on being (shaky hold on being), the apparent ease "just" might imply notwithstanding.

But the piece that gets to me most, the one I can't get past, the one I keep playing, is the very first track, "Melin." What does that title mean? Is it a typo, a misspelling? ("Naima" appears as "Niema" on Shepp's *Four for Trane.*) Should it be "Melan," the root for "black" in words like "melanin" and "melancholy"? Is there an apostrophe or a "g" missing from what should be "Melin' " or "Meling"? "Meling" (or "melin' ") is an obsolete word, more often spelled "melling," whose meanings are: 1) blending, combining; mixture; 2) copulation; 3) the action of mixing in fight or joining in combat; 4) dealing; intercourse; meddling. Or does the title refer to Abra-Melin, also known as Abramelin the Mage and Abraham the Jew, a magician from Wurxburg, Germany, who lived from 1362 to 1460? Abra-Melin wrote a body of magical works that influenced Aleister Crowley, who is said to have copied from *The Sacred Magic of Abramelin the Mage* to compose his rituals for mastering demons. Abra-Melin was an expert on the *Kabbalah* and claimed to have acquired magical knowledge from angels, who taught him how to conjure and tame demons. Legend has it that he created two thousand spirit cavalrymen to help Frederick, the elector of Saxony. This pertains to the cavalry/calvary conflation I remarked on in my letter a few months ago. Listen to Olu Dara's cornet solo on "Melin," its bugling of a tremulous charge, an ostensibly triumphalist rally or rescue subjected to a spiritual demur.

Indeed, spooked emolument obtains throughout, from the first notes on, testamentary brass, lullaby bass and brushed percussion both haloed and hazed by Threadgill's wind-in-the-trees flute. The bodiliness of brass, the airiness of flute and the tactility of bass and drums effect a sheerness one feels one might literally taste or touch, fraught proximity or adjacency "in the air" but intangible—tangential, remote nonetheless. A true Council of Souls it amounts to, soul's riven counsel, pastorly swing and chagrin.

It's a piece, as I've said, I can't stop listening to. From the Greek word for "black" to chagrin's kept counsel, I hear everything I've mentioned and more when I listen to it.

As ever,
N.

Dear Angel of Dust,

Thank you for your letter. I'm glad you checked *When Was That?* out, happy to hear you like it. I'd have written back sooner but we seem to have entered a lull and I've been in something of a do-nothing mood. We haven't played a gig since the record-release gig at The Studio back in February, which makes it some three months now. Things have dried up for some reason. It's not that there's ever been an abundance of places to play, but they seem to have become even more scarce over the past few months. It's even more frustrating following the record's release, a greater void of audience response aggravating the "sharecropping" situation I complained about before, the abstractness or anonymity of the record audience. Still, though, we go on getting together regularly for rehearsal just as we've always done, just as if there were a gig in a few days to get ready for. We go on coming up with new pieces and thinking about new pieces, but I hit a stretch where I wondered why bother, a do-nothing mood nothing much had much impact on.

It got to where Lambert evidently noticed I'd been a little sluggish lately and took me aside yesterday at rehearsal. "Give me a call later," he whispered in my ear, which I did. When I did I got his answering machine, the greeting on which had been changed. Rather than Lambert saying he wasn't home and to leave a message I heard a page out of Drennette's book, the very last word of Trane's comments to the other musicians before "Dearly Beloved" on the *Sun Ship* album, "Ready?" I got the message. He was telling me not to get weary, to be ready, stay ready, gigs would eventually come. I didn't realize I'd been so obvious. Anyway, though I can't say I snapped out of it I'm pulling out of it.

But what about when readiness weighs like molten lead, psychic-cement sky, bass-ecclesial sun? There's much to be thought about it, thought itself a kind of readiness and vice versa, each as much as the other a cathartic notice moment serves. It seems it's then that structure proves infectious, unimposed. For a certain stretch while Djamilaa soloed on piano during rehearsal yesterday Drennette ended or extended each of her phrases with a muffled roll, stiffening her arms and leaning as far back on the stool as she could, under duress of a truly spastic sort she made it seem, mock torment a ripeness or a readiness, end and beginning both. True attribute mated mock extremity in a churchical display whereby objects falling from different heights hit the floor at the same time, pillar and post assessing impromptu lean.

I'll write again soon.

As ever,
N.

_____

Dear Angel of Dust,

I dreamt a balloon snuck up on me while I slept. It crept up in back of me and whispered, "Boo." Part inflated ball, part friendly ghost, it tiptoed up in back of me (legless, footless, toeless though it was)—tiptoed up and crooned ever so seductively, "Boo." Its insinuative "boo" bordered on cooing, caressing the back of my ear like a lover's breath or a slowly blown kiss. "Boo" was long-sought liberation's new disguise. Love's inoculative boon and more it might've been, false alarm's homeopathic vaccine. "Boo" took liberties with a bewitchment it sought to continue as well as contain, the readiness or the ripeness I knew would eventually come.

I dreamt I knew what was there without turning to look, dreamt I whispered, "Boo," in return, not turning to look. I threw my voice, making it sound as if it came from more than one direction. Multiply-voiced, "boo" was love's reluctant counsel, fright wig and found embrace rolled into one, fraught recoil and love's true hair rolled into one. What was "boo" but ventriloquistic ricochet's acoustic mask, I rhetorically asked or implicitly argued, what but thrown vocality's billowing debt? The balloon spoke without moving its lips I knew without turning, knew without needing to look.

My not needing to look was tied to the balloon's not moving its lips, to the fact, in the first place, that it had lips (legless, footless, toeless though it was). Lipless one would have expected it to be, featurelessness or smoothness one of the attributes balloons are known for, a legendary lack whereby they speak without speaking, a signal attribute one would say. I thus knew the balloon spoke without moving its lips, a liplessness of sorts it had recourse to. No closer could it come to signal smoothness. As close as that was it came.

But to know without needing to look, another side of me, the side that wanted to turn and look, admitted, was to indulge an inflated claim, the very claim the balloon embodied and warned against by whispering, "Boo." That I knew it spoke without moving its lips was indeed that claim, a ventriloquial thought it put in my mind as well as a word it put in my mouth, "boo" and boast rolled into one.

Yet as though it called its own bluff or belied my thrown voice, "boo" sat me down in my heart of hearts, an abstract shiver that more than gave me pause, made me pause, sat me down with no less masterful aplomb. "Boo" schooled a brood of reflexes the likes of which I'd never known, endlessly parsing what it feared might appear to be dogma, autodidactic élan not to be gainsaid even so.

As ever,

N.

PS: I knew without waking I lay like royalty, ratcheted back ninety degrees notwithstanding, lay as though the bed were a throne. "Boo" inhabited the wall behind the bed's headboard. The balloon was there on behalf of unseated majesty, there at its beck or behest. I "sat" on behalf of the unseated albeit I did so with a cautioning spin, thrown vocality's weak play on investiture ("throne") nothing if not a case in point.

Unlike the dream I had as a child, a dream in which the wall of a stairway I was in rumbled with the voice of a ghost inside it, here the wall neither shook nor resonated, oddly damped and understated in the emission of its laconic "boo." This was in keeping with a certain modesty or maturation, a reserve unseated royalty had once resisted but come to accept. Dry, pointedly flat, with no haunted-house employment of echo and other effects, it scared me to death nonetheless, though that this was the case I never let on.

It was a figurative death I in fact immediately recovered from, thrown vocality's antithetic recourse to resonance my only defense, feeble though it may otherwise have been.

Dear Angel of Dust,

My mother and everyone else in my family insist it never happened, so maybe it was a dream. Or maybe it's something I hallucinated that time I had a serious fever when I was four. Whether it was a stage or a gymnasium floor it was on I can't say. People sat in seats the rows of which receded at a steep angle, higher up as they went farther back. They sat looking down at us. I stood on the stage or the gymnasium floor, a small boy, three, perhaps four years old. A tall man wearing a tuxedo stood on my left, a woman in a one-piece bathing suit on my right. She was wearing high heels, he wore a top hat. He repeatedly called her his assistant, his lovely assistant, no action of hers not introduced by him announcing his lovely assistant would now do this or that. I stood on a stool I'd been helped onto by the two of them, each of them taking hold of one of my arms just above the elbow.

The man in the tuxedo held a funnel and a glass of water, the woman in the one-piece bathing suit a porcelain bowl. "My lovely assistant will now hold the bowl up to the boy's ear," he announced and she did. He asked me to tilt my head to the right, which I did, whereupon he put the tip of the funnel into my left ear and proceeded to pour the water into it. The water went thru my head. It went into my left ear and came out of the right, slowing somewhat as it did so but flowing thru nonetheless, trickling out of my right ear into the bowl the woman held.

The man in the tuxedo completely emptied the glass of water into my ear. Once all the water was in the bowl he said I could bring my head back up, hold it straight again, which I did. I must have looked per-plexed, alarmed, at a loss as to how the water had gone thru my head. The audience applauded and laughed as they applauded. The joke, if there was a joke, I couldn't help sensing, was on me. When the applause and laughter subsided I heard the sound of water, trickling water, deep inside my ear, the sound of a babbling brook almost, an nsansic, mbiric, thumb-pianistic sense of ongoingness and flow, ictic insistence to the nth unremitting degree. So it began, as far as I can remember. So began the trickle I've heard ever since, the sound of water that's never not there and that came into play, overt play, during the gig we played last night.

Yes, we at last got a gig after all these months. The fellow who runs the Blue Light Lounge called on Thursday and said the band from Port-land that was scheduled to play Friday, Saturday and Sunday couldn't make it and asked if we could fill in. Needless to say, we said yes. We were about to burst with the new pieces we've written and the call came not a minute too soon. It was a gig which had its moments, more than a few mo-ments, many of these provided by the new pieces we played publicly for the first time, "Book of Elysian Escort" and "Sekhet Aaru Strut," the for-mer, for example, offering, among others, what we've come to call an x-ray moment, see-thru amenities afforded by extreme self-inflection.

It was a moment involving Penguin and Drennette, self-inflection taking the form of a sudden turn from icy facade on Drennette's part. She abruptly dreamt, saw and seized upon herself, suddenly extravagantly coifed. Her dreads were octopus tentacles down the back and the sides of her head, alive, smelling of the sea, framing her face. This one heard more than saw but also, hearing, saw. She grimaced, an extended wince, wrin-kling her nose as though the smell offended her while pursing her lips as though it bestowed new resolve, new insight, captious, catalytic salt. Showing strain but in control even so, she let the sock cymbal have it re-peatedly, obsessively, a basher to the bone albeit beyond her will it seemed. To be was to be put upon, she seemed to say or to want to say, to be was to be pushed and push back. Had she taken the mallets and pounded the floor it wouldn't have been more emphatic.

For his part, Penguin almost jumped out of his skin, his oboe sound abruptly dilated, a molt of sorts. Drennette was the girl next door had there been a next door (he'd grown up on a vast cattle ranch in Egypt, he insisted), the tomboy he'd have played doctor with inside the tree house his father built. Drennette stood up in his mind's eye, lanky, naked, a foot taller than she was, her small, tight breasts resting proudly upon her ribcage, her pubic tuft equally proud, commanding, Delphic, pharaonic even. She stood fully exposed, fully available. They'd grown up in slavery together, he now insisted, worn clothes made of burlap, grown up in the cottonfields. They noticed one day their bodies grew new hair, hair where none grew before. They rolled in the proverbial hay, took to one another, each the other's pheromonal escort.

All of this, as I've said, one heard more than saw but also, hearing, saw. Penguin stood between Lambert and me, the three of us a double-reed choir, the two of them to my left, Drennette to my left as well. She sat at her drumset a bit farther away, downstage, but out of the corner of my eye I could see her as well as Penguin and Lambert. Lambert and I, not needing to make eye contact though we did, stood resolute, refusing to be drawn into what Penguin and Drennette were caught in, tentacular dreads and pubic tuft notwithstanding. Penguin's dilated sound roared and tore one's ear, siren's call and crow's caw rolled into one, but Lambert and I blew as cool as before, as cool as ever, a velvety carpet of ice along the Nile. Likewise, Aunt Nancy temporized as before, couldn't quite get started, not taking the bait, and Djamilaa played as before as well, offering chords that made no claims whatsoever. The four of us keeping our cool made Penguin and Drennette's deviation or divagation all the more piquant, all the more emphatic, a momentary touch the audience reacted to with applause.

Penguin's claim and conception left us unconvinced. Frontal probity and pubic tuft he may well have seen or thought he saw, but Drennette was a backwardswalking woman both he and she knew (indeed, everyone knew). One saw, before anything else, the back of her head, her back, her ass, the backs of her thighs, her calves. A bit of this carried over into "Sekhet Aaru Strut," our reading of which in this its debut performance turned the beat back on itself in ways we never had before. It was the piece we followed "Book of Elysian Escort" with, the sun's white gleam on water (we stood on a riverbank) beckoning us and blinding us both. I played muted trumpet, Djamilaa guitar, Aunt Nancy viola, Lambert and Penguin eucharistic flute, each lifting his ax to his mouth as if biting the leg of a god. Djamilaa's guitar shimmer and Drennette's cymbal sheen brought Grant Green and Billy Higgins's work on "Search for the New Land" to mind. Light's white sparkle on water flowed backwards and forward, an illusion one unwittingly bit on or bit into. Indeed, it seemed I had Lee Morgan in mind more than I knew, muted brass a blade wielded with surgical aplomb à la his recording of "Invitation" with the Messengers.

We played possessed of a corpuscular undulacy, more atmosphere than fact as we began. One's ears admitted water, a valved admission of water's proximity, abstract adjacency and auspice though it was, time's immemorial echo an alto admonishment prompting one from afar. The audience was on the edges of their seats. They too stood on the bank of a river, sit though they did, all but standing, eager to see how we'd follow "Book of Elysian Escort's" x-ray élan. One looked out at them wondering what they made of Lambert and Penguin switching from flute to alto and tenor, lowing saxes now a train's rolling moan exhaling smoke, rollaway alto and rollaway tenor the wheels we rode, wheels and blown smoke rolled into one. We were going home they seemed to say, rail and river unexpectedly one, home calling address itself into question it turned out, more than we bargained for. Eucharistic flute had proposed a limbed airiness or an airiness of limbs, a god's leg's ritual endowment barely boasting flesh. Rollaway sax now said as much or said the same though it spoke differently, lowing, homing mobility gone invariably up in smoke.

Home was an aggregate feeling or effect we were after, dispersed and widely strewn though we knew it to be ("we" meaning band and audience both). I was actually surprised it came up, taken aback home was even at issue, but something I saw in the audience's eyes made it clear it was. That it wasn't only the audience's concern, that they heard a deep, unadmitted attempt to get home in what we played and relayed it back, was also made clear, an oblique reflection of where we, the band, stood in the very eyes I looked out at as we played. Bloodshot and thick of lid in some cases, bright and wide open in others, they caught and appeared captured by a promise or prospect of home they heard in Djamilaa's guitar shimmer and Drennette's cymbal sheen. Shimmer and sheen held home in suspension if indeed they held home at all, but in the eyes I looked out at as we played rollaway horns bore the moment and mass it would eventually accrue, smoke notwithstanding. So tenuous the promise or prospect turned out to be, so nearly tart the very sweetness it proffered, some let their eyes close, unable to bear the gleam or perhaps hoping to hold it in, their heads bowed or thrown back as if in recoil, deep dream and rude awakening, glad and begrudging amen.

I recall reading somewhere years ago (liner notes, I think), "John Coltrane looks wide-eyed into hell; Pee Wee Russell blinks out from it." I must've looked like a cross between Trane and Pee Wee as I looked out at the audience. It was the hell of home's evacuated promise or prospect I stared into and blinked out from. Had someone sent a message from backstage that my mother's house had burned down I wouldn't have looked more forlorn. It was indeed as if that was what happened. Still, I took a buzzing, bounding, flight-of-the-bumblebee tack, leavening Lee with a touch of Don Cherry without allowing my own temper and taste to subside. I buzzed and bounded, needle's tip and razor's edge by turns, an airy god or a gadfly piercing the horns' rollaway smoke, a train's moan and my mother's house rolled into one though smoke amounted to, buoyancy and breeze and breath not to be denied.

I saw my mother's house on fire, saw it burning to the ground. Luckily no one was inside but of course it nonetheless broke my heart. The more I went on the less able I was to go on I quickly found, bounding flight intruded on or complicated by a recourse to flubs, half-valving and the like. Such recourse took care of itself it seemed, something I couldn't help. As calmly and compactly as I could I played an arpeggiated run telling everyone my mother's house was burning down and I was going home. I could see flames and smoke I said again and again, insisting each time on calling the latter "choo-choo smoke." I repeatedly couldn't help saying I saw flames and choo-choo smoke, a flub or a fluff here and there accenting the cracked parlance I resorted to.

Was it a need for emotional leverage I was involuntarily infantilized by? Was it rollaway smoke's counterintuitive tickle brought out in the open? Was it fun I poked at the audience's need or attempt or wish to get home or simply a joke at my own expense? Whatever it was, "choo-choo" might as well have been "boo" in the balloon dream I wrote you about. Whatever it was, it made it hard for me to go on, especially hard once the audience began giggling, hard not to come right out and crack up.

Djamilaa and Drennette's guitar shimmer and cymbal sheen continued, an eerie broadcast, it began (having gone on so long) to seem now, from a nearby pond or a distant galaxy. Rollaway smoke lay thick on the air, Lambert and Penguin undeterred by my "choo-choo" jest. I blew an all but inaudible burst of breath into the horn and pulled back, motioning for Aunt Nancy to solo. As though it were sensitive ground she ventured onto, she set out gingerly, a mendicant tack, reticent all but to a fault. A slowly opening door it might've been she meant to mimic, low creak and squeal as if bow and string were tentative hinges, damped or incipient yawn built on bated breath. The very soul of austerity it sounded like, a lateral scan in the low register recalling a theremin somewhat, fraught, philosophic tread, insecure advance. No namesake strut, it nonetheless implied strut's burgeoning—cautious, dry, drawn out, eked out, intent on getting somewhere.

Aunt Nancy took her time, which was all the time in the world it appeared she sensed or wanted to insist, hinged endeavor of one sort or another all there was, cramped yet unhurried connection, low cosmos, tipped excrescence, nudge. It wasn't, then, that she bought time but that time infiltrated bow and string she made it seem. Time was tendency, torque, meander, shimmer and sheen's broadcast a braid she alternately frizzed and fell in with, laconic, low key, on and on.

Aunt Nancy ended her solo with an evaporative wisp emerging from deep gastric stir, a note as tentative as any she'd played but with a sense of having gotten somewhere even so. When she pulled away from the mike it was Lambert's turn. A study in contrast, Lambert leapt in with an heraldic run that recalled a horse rearing up. A whinny of sorts and a call to order, it called a halt to what had gone before—part whoa, part amen, part prolegomena. A cascading waterfall it might've been after stuttering upward to a quick peak, a majestic wall of water possessed of a gospel touch. Djamilaa and Drennette let the shimmer and sheen subside. A hip, forwarding six took over. Penguin went back to flute and I came back in on trumpet, rollaway smoke subsiding as well. Muted brass met flute to give Lambert's tenor its buoyancy back.

It was a fought-for buoyancy, hard won, Lambert insisted. He played with a wind-afflicted, asymmetric hitch. Listeners who had heard Sun Ra's "Lights on a Satellite" would've recalled or thought they caught shades of John Gilmore, so bulky, buoyancy notwithstanding, the horn had become. Lambert blew with all due wariness, beguiled by muted brass and flute's fraught verticality, aloft in spite of himself it seemed. So tenuous a hold he made it seem he had on the horn someone shouted, "Don't drop it!" A gleam lit Lambert's eyes as he looked over toward where the shout had come from. He ever so perceptibly grinned, horn in his mouth notwithstanding, when someone else in the audience yelled, "Hold on!" He closed his eyes and had us grinning as well with an insanely sublime hover he made his way up to and then maintained at the very top of the horn, working the spoons as though his hands would fly off into space. It was a circling hover, part holding pattern.

It was then that the first balloon came out, clearing the bottom lip of the tenor's bell bearing these words: *Strut meant nothing straight. I strode in a circle, ambassadorial satellite from Egypt, lipped an eccentric reed. Outer Egypt it was called by some. Saturnian ring shout it was dubbed by others. Either way, it was what it was. I walked rings around what wasn't, either way.* The shades of John Gilmore and the Sun Ra suggestion were not mere imagination one now saw. A second balloon quickly emerged: *But was. Nothing was. Strut made something of it, wound and wound and wound. Water slipped under my feet, I floated. Water wet my feet, a ring of water I strode on. Strut was a way of saying something else had hold of me. A ring of water bore me round and round.* We were surprised, as we always are, but not taken aback by the balloons' reappearance. We played on, Djamilaa and Drennette's forwarding six as tensile as ever, Aunt Nancy noodling here and there, Penguin and I repeating an up-from-under motif. The mood was oddly more serious than moments before when shouts came from the audience and Lambert had us all grinning. It was as if, comic-strip balloons though they were, the balloons were a cautionary sign of some kind, admonitory witness.

Eyes closed, grin gone, Lambert went on blowing, revisiting the horn's low and middle registers now and again. The horn sounded heavier, a bobbing behemoth. A third balloon emerged: *Circling something looked for, lost. I strode, all but flew, might as well have been flying the way ring wound upward. Strut would harvest heaven, ring, circular star route. Ripped, eccentric orbit. Sown, circumambular crop.* Lambert, following Aunt Nancy's example, took his time. Balloon after balloon emerged, ringing changes—endless it seemed—on *strut, stride, ring, round* and such. A final balloon emerged from the horn, signaling the end of the solo by cueing the start of Penguin's: *Saturnian shout's icy ring water would eventually be. Eventual ice under my feet, ring beside itself it seemed, ring must've been rung the way I lifted. Ring squared, something else's way of saying strut was. Is escorted would. Would was is's consort. Would rang is's bell.*

The audience had sat palpably silent once the balloons began to emerge—palpably in contrast to their shouting levity only moments before. It was a rapt silence, openmouthed in many cases, the audience fascinated and perplexed albeit most if not all had no doubt heard of the balloons' previous appearances. They had sat as if chastised or at least chastened by the balloons' emergence, as if the horn had taken hold of their shouts and taken them higher—a galactically high silence they now broke with great relief and release, breaking out, when Lambert ended his solo, with robust applause, a few resorting to yells and whistles, a few stamping their feet. Penguin, for his solo, was to switch from flute to oboe, which he did, Aunt Nancy having already gone, as planned, from viola to bass a few bars back. Taking the horn to his mouth, he bided his time, bought time, let the boisterous applause die down.

Penguin stood with the horn in his mouth, not yet blowing, wetting the reed waiting for the applause to subside and then, once it had, continuing to not yet blow, as though the balloons had given him pause. He closed his eyes and pursed his lips, an implicit foil to the gaping mouths many in the audience had reacted to the balloons' emergence with. It wasn't, in fact, so much that the balloons had given him pause, though perhaps they had, as that he waited, as planned, for Djamilaa, Drennette and Aunt Nancy to slow the tempo down. This they had begun to do when Lambert ended his solo and continued to do when the applause died down, the three of them going on sans horns and gradually braking, bringing the tempo to a near breakdown in a change of time signature and pace recalling Mingus, whereupon, near breakdown behind, they proceeded apace—a bluesy, more relaxed, back-to-basics 4/4—and Penguin at last began to blow.

No balloons came out of the horn as Penguin played. It was blues oboe at its best, a vein Yusef Lateef so notably works. Indeed, Penguin began with a tone and timbre reminiscent of "Blues for the Orient" on the *Eastern Sounds* album, a round, even button of sound with, as Miles would say, no attitude in it. Compressed albeit open, clean and composed even as it became quizzical, it was an extended, extrapolative button, a ball of restraint within the whistle air was, equitable straw. This, though, turned out to be a setup. Penguin wasn't long in moving on to a more raspy, attitudinal, tight-throated sound, raspier but also more nasal, recalling "See See Rider" on the *Live at Pep's* album. A hint or even a halo of squawk rode its edge, an introspective catch it exhumed or intimated as if to insist we'd all, whether we knew it or not, been given pause. Unlike Aunt Nancy and Lambert, both of whom had stretched out, taken their time, Penguin said what he had to say quickly, calling our attention to brevity's virtues. He moved quickly from equitable straw to introspective catch. This was then the ground from which he launched the solo's climax, holding a note, E-flat, over three and a half bars while overblowing the horn.

Penguin's concluding note seemed intent on clearing the air. He held it and visibly blew more strenuously than before, letting the sound go rough at the edges, cracked by the strain he put it under, hyperbolic "would." Overblown oboe sustained an abrasive spray of sound bent on scouring the air itself, a raw dilation bordering on clarinet. Penguin blew, overblew, and one or two people in the audience responded with an appreciative "Yeah!" He let it go at that, slowly stepping back from the mike as the audience applauded.

Penguin's concluding E-flat tore the air. It scraped and scratched and ripped a slit Djamilaa's guitar solo tumbled out of. She too extolled an economy of sorts, taking up the note Penguin left off with and opening by holding it herself. She held it less than half as long as he had but long enough to make her point, following it with a run of descending figures that rang like metal rods thrown down a stairwell. The notes chimed and then clanged in a frenzy of wah-wah, feedback and fuzztones Jimi Hendrix or Sonny Sharrock would've been proud to claim. A cross between crashing surf and a diesel truck, it rose to a high cry Djamilaa took pains to attenuate—a live, high wire she worried and extracted a thin, expiring hum's hallelujah from.

But this was only to get one's attention it turned out. Djamilaa let the diesel surf and the live-wire hum subside, gave Aunt Nancy and Drennette a sign to play more softly, unplugged the guitar and proceeded to play it unamplified. Aunt Nancy took up a low roll-and-tumble figure and Drennette switched over to brushes for a slap-and-stir whisper and kiss it became her purpose in life to maintain. Djamilaa let her thumbnail and thumb brush and pluck the unamplified strings, coaxing a sound from them close to that of a tidinit, the Mauritanian lute, a low-key "guitar" related to the Wolof halam and the ngoni of Mali. Recalling Lambert, she played a circling figure, a tight circle returning repeatedly to the tonic, all but agoraphobic in its tightness but allowing a loose, unraveling twist every now and then. It was intense as well as tight, a dizzying perspicuity one grew light-headed listening to. Everything got very quiet. One could hear the proverbial pin drop.

Introvert though they otherwise were, Djamilaa's tight circles built outward, an exfoliative tack whose phantom leaves one admitted to be such but heard or felt or inferred all the same. An outward-mounting, repercussive ring and a recondite seed rolled into one each of them was— quintessential economy, compactedness, quiver, esoteric twitch in flight from vacancy, recondite sprout, the "what wasn't" Lambert claimed he walked rings around. Djamilaa's more vertiginous claim was that circles were all or nothing, a dare, a distraction, that "what wasn't" infiltrated all things and was not to be outwalked or outrun, a claim Aunt Nancy's roll and tumble and Drennette's whisper and kiss backed with mendicant solemnity and calm.

It was a sepulchral, oddly seminal sound, seed if not bone but a skeletal sound. Some vow was being made one reluctantly knew, something, possibly everything, newly renounced. So taken in were Lambert, Penguin and I by what we heard, so absorbed, we almost forgot our part, the six-note ascending figure the three of us were to play at that point. We stood listening, more audience than band members for a moment, more than a moment, drawn in by the unamplified strings' monastic austerity, deeply taken in, mesmerized. A quick paradiddle deviating from Drennette's whisper and kiss, however, snapped us out of it, she evidently having noticed the nearly hypnotic state we were in. We pulled ourselves together and played the six-note ascending figure, Lambert and I still on tenor and trumpet, Penguin back on flute. We lowered it a fourth and played it again, took it back up a fourth and played it again. We were whistling walking past a cemetery.

That was it, a mere taste, a reminder, the six-note figure three times. No more than punctuation, it threw Djamilaa's guitar into relief, Drennette and Aunt Nancy's mendicant support into relief, the three of them going on as before as we played it, continuing to go on as before after we played it. They went on that way until Djamilaa brought her circular crimp and crawl to an end, whereupon Drennette took up her sticks again, playing a two-fisted, two-footed barrage in which the drumset seemed to shake and shudder, shiver and shake, Djamilaa plugging the guitar back in while this went on, Aunt Nancy switching back to viola. Lambert switched back to flute and once Djamilaa got the guitar plugged in and Drennette's drum shudder came to a halt we went back to the head, Lambert, Penguin and I at our mikes again, cymbal sheen and guitar shimmer and all.

I don't know if it's that all that had gone before loosened me up or what. I'm not sure it's not that the glimpse I got into Djamilaa's tidinit recess forced my hand, fired me up. Something inside me, in any event, said it wanted more, wanted back in, insisted I have another go at the sun's white gleam on water, the riverbank we stood on earlier, light's closer walk with water. Something inside me said rollaway smoke had been a detour I'd have been better off not taking, "choo-choo smoke" a joke at my own expense. That same something told me to motion to the band that I was going to solo again, to let Lambert and Penguin know to remain on flute, no rollaway smoke. This I did, making eye contact and pointing to myself and beginning my solo, pointing to the tenor and the alto at Lambert's and Penguin's feet, shaking my head no.

Light's white sparkle on water again flowed forward and backwards both, eucharistic flute a cushion of air I rode and rested on. Cymbal sheen and guitar shimmer, the white light or gleam in question, was the aural equivalent of the dappled creek- or brook- or riverside close-up on the cover of Herbie Hancock's *Empyrean Isles*, Aunt Nancy's rippling viola the waves of water in a physics experiment simulating light. Sonic traipse, sonic travel fully living up to titular strut, my tongue oddly endowed by laboratory light joining waterside close-up, the trumpet walked on air, walked on water. I was free to go backwards and forward, free to do both with equal fluency, free to find fit. Every note I played subjected waterside proximity to laboratory light. No balloons came out of the horn but B'Loon was with me I knew. Not that it mattered. Not that I cared.

As it occurred to me that B'Loon blew with me whether balloons came out of the horn or not, whether or not it mattered, whether I cared or not, trickling water, the sound I've heard between my ears forever, grew more pronounced. No longer subliminal background noise, it rose in volume, came to the fore, as clear as the day the man in the tuxedo poured water thru my head. I heard it loud, a subcortical trickle I now paid close attention to, a worming trickle of water running from my left ear to my right. An underground stream it might've been, mere trickle though it was, resonant, echoing as if in a subterranean cave. The closer the attention I paid it the more it dictated what I played.

I continued my laidback, ride-and-rest walk atop eucharistic air, proximate water, laboratory light. Thanks to the trickling I heard, however, I resorted to more triplets and 16th notes, pushing the tempo a bit. By turns I got out in front of the rhythm section and, by bending and ghosting notes, fell behind it, a backwardswalking, forwardwalking strut if there ever was one. It was as I played a 16th-note turnaround pattern that had a double-time feel to it that the trickle thickened and my head began to fill with water. I played on even so, as unforced and free to fit as ever, cocking my head to the right to let the water out.

Head hiply cocked, horn addressing the mike, I blew all the more collectedly, calmly, water slowly trickling out of my ear. The water flowed out to form a drop that hung from my earlobe. The drop hung a while before falling onto my shoulder if not the floor, quickly replaced by another. Neither teardrop nor bead of sweat though it could've been either, each drop of water as it hung, I'm told, looked, from the audience, the lights hitting it as they did, just like a sparkling earring. Drop after drop cleared my head, an ephemeral gem and a fallen jewel emptying the horn.

As ever,

N.

———————————

Dear Angel of Dust,

When it rains it pours. The three nights at the Blue Light went nicely and then we got gigs at the Bridge in North Hollywood, the Little Big Horn in Pasadena and the Golden Bear down in Huntington Beach. The last really brought back memories. I hadn't been there in years and I couldn't help remembering going there in the sixties when it was mainly a place to hear folk music. The first time I went there it was to hear Hoyt Axton but my strongest memory is of hearing John Handy there and getting to talk with him and Michael White between sets. Anyway, I also, finally, got a call from Fred saying my mouthpiece was ready. He went on and on as to why it took him so long, going into much more detail than was needed, but I did finally get off the phone. I went by and picked it up just yesterday. Last but not least, we got asked to play at a rally for a friend of Aunt Nancy's who's running for the Inglewood city council—a "grassroots" affair that took place in one of the parks. All of which goes to say why I haven't written in such a while. We've been busy.

It was nice of you to include the Algerian chaabi tape with your last letter. Whew! Why haven't I heard any of this before? Dahmane Elharrachi I can't get over. Hsissen I can't get over. "Ellahi Yeltha Bhamou" I listen to again and again. The first time I heard that ditty-bop piano fill it's punctuated with I thought I'd die. I couldn't help thinking of the song Pharoah sings at the end of "Upper Egypt and Lower Egypt" on the *Tauhid* album—only this is so much more multiply-jointed, so much more a miracle of catch and continuity, a modular comma governing casbah clack. It's the sort of thing someone wearing a stingy-brim hat should play. How something so seeming to be an afterthought cements it all escapes me. I don't have the words for any of this but I think it's definitely something you should write on. Your interest in approaches to voice that mine or seemingly mine obstruction, what I meant to get at by "catch and continuity," would have much to apply itself to in the stuck vocality and guttural insistences one hears in chaabi. Who but you could give such obstreperous, gritty vocality its due, who but you explicate the bass thrum and the rhythmic dilation its ability to swallow dust or obstruction gathers from? I can imagine an essay if not several essays or even a book. Anyway, many thanks for the letter and tape.

I'll close now. The way we've been running around is enough to make one's head spin. Still, I wanted to at least and at last get a line off to you thanking you and letting you know I'm still here.

Yours,

N.

Dear Angel of Dust,

I lay flat on my back in broad daylight on the bed of what was once the Los Angeles River. Stark unremitting sunlight bounced off the concrete walls and floor of what had taken its place. An aqueduct it was but an aqueduct in name only. Theoretical water alone ran thru it, dry laboratory water, dry run. I lay flat on my back on what had the feel of a hospital bed, hard concrete notwithstanding, sick bed or sick riverbed, a blur; sedated, I wasn't able to make out which. But it was an aqueduct I'm told, the flat surface I took to be a bed its hot concrete floor. If nothing else, a flood of sunlight filled it up, glaring summer sun.

I lay still. I was there to be interviewed, hot summer sun the hot lights intended to make me talk. It was a press conference or a police interrogation, hard to say which, a blur, though the former I'm now told. Print and electronic media were both well represented. Reporters, notepads in hand, stood around the bed. Cameras clicked and TV cameras rolled. Tape recorders ran. I vividly recall how bright the sun was but otherwise it's mainly a blur. It all seems rather distant, far away. They evidently asked questions and evidently I answered them. Here's the transcript they made of it:

Q: *You were heard humming a Spinners tune, "Love Don't Love Nobody," in your sleep. Given your present situation, do the lyrics "make your bed hard, gotta sleep there" mean anything to you?*

A: *Are you sure it wasn't one of Marley's tunes? "Concrete Jungle" maybe or the one where he says "rock was my pillow"?* [Laughs.] *No, just kidding. Actually, it's not the "make your bed hard" bit that speaks to me so much as that* insinuative chorus repeating "It takes a fool . . ." in the background—its textural character, the whispered insistence of it, gospel, even ghost insistence: mist on the moors or on the heath or in a redwood forest. It's nothing if not fog or mist keeping low to the ground, exuded by the ground it seems, the ground's own cautionary cloud. And that they sing it in waltz time I'll never get over, an ushering waltz into admonitory counsel but a cooling mist or fog even so, a cooling refrain, mist, as I've said, in a redwood forest. So unlike lying out here in this hot sun, it may well be a compensatory swing, antiphonal refuge on my part to've hummed it. So, yes, to answer your question, you may be on to something, though not exactly in the way that you posed it.

Q: I'd like to follow up on that if I may. Djband, as you know, tends to equate "mist" with "missed." How does that relate to what you're saying? Doesn't that equation make antiphonal refuge Pyrrhic, off-the-mark, illusory?

A: Well, you brought it up. I had no idea I'd been humming in my sleep. Spun hum or hymn animates a double negation to make its point, "missed" insistence all the more reason to be insisted again. This is any chorus's way of operating and reason for being, a motivated graininess or haziness deployed, in this case, within moist precincts I can't for the life of me understand as Pyrrhic. What choice does one have? Blistering sun overhead, flat on one's back against a concrete floor, water at best hypothetical, what choice does one exactly have? One gets what one can while remaining alive to what hasn't been gotten. This is what Djband, if I may speak for the group, is about. This is what we mean by apprehending "missed" in that groping condition known as "mist." The subatomic life of substance augurs no less.

Q: Are you saying that emphasis can't but be phatic at some level, that choric insistence can't but border on both redundancy and lack?

A: Yes.

Q: Since you've now spoken on Djband's behalf, I wonder would you go a bit farther and comment on the group's reaction to the comic-strip balloons that have graced (if that's the word) some of its performances and even shown up, I understand, when certain copies of its album Orphic Bend have been played. The record hasn't, as far as I know, received a single review, yet talk of the balloons abounds and there's been mention *of them in mainstream places like* Down Beat *and the* Los Angeles Times. *How does Djband feel about this? Does it fear that the balloons might overshadow the music or even that they already have?*

A: *I should've known that's where this was going. What can one say? Of course, of course, I'm tempted to say, but Djband, as with so much else, is of more than one mind when it comes to the balloons. The balloons, I'm tempted to say, are self-incriminating evidence, a way of catching oneself out. But that would simply be me talking or me not so simply talking. The balloons, I'm also tempted to say, are a diversionary tactic, a way of letting those who take the music literally off lightly. Still, I'd want to go on, they've become so much more than their initial appearances proposed or seemed intent on proposing. And that's only the beginning of what I'm tempted to say. As I've said, I should've known that's where this was going. Your question, I'm tempted to say, perpetrates the problem. I'm no Heisenberg but even I can see that.*

Q: *Isn't saying you're tempted to say X a way of saying X? Why do you have your say by withholding your say?*

A: *Say says nothing unless pressed by spirit. Nothing I say, no matter what I say, will even come close.*

Q: *What do you mean by spirit?*

A: *I mean what people, generation after generation, have meant by it down thru the ages.*

Q: *Could you give an example?*

A: *The balloons are full of it.*

Q: *Doesn't that contradict the idea that the balloons are for the literal-minded?*

A: *No.*

Q: *Didn't you say . . .*

A: *No. I said I was tempted to say the balloons are a way of letting those who take the music literally off lightly. That's different.*

Q: *What does Penguin see in Drennette?*

A: *He sees a girl who wears cutoff jeans in the summer, a girl whose legs taper like a sword stuck in the earth. Her way of walking opens a world he wouldn't otherwise dream of. Her swung hips teach him the futility of sight, the need for an alternate way of looking, insisting he rehabilitate sensation, see beyond sight. He sees her ass's firm self-containment soliciting touch and confirmation nonetheless, a lazy way she has of investing stuck-up allure with availability, pendant cheeks peeking out of her cutoff jeans an offhand equation, tease repealing limits it would seem. What he sees teases material apprehension. He sees a summons, a call to order, a reapportionment, a new synaesthetic disposition, a new anaesthetic reappraisal.*

Q: You wax rather lyrical. Do you see her the same way?

A: No.

Q: There was a time when Aunt Nancy was also known as Heidi. Why isn't she ever called Heidi anymore?

A: It's a name she long wanted to get rid of. When she was a kid the other kids would play around with it, poke fun at her by calling her Heidi-Hi-Heidi-Ho. It was all in fun but she was a bit on the sensitive side even then. Rather than letting it go as a Cab Calloway reference meant to acknowledge her musical ability, she took it they were insinuating drug use and loose behavior. She made a big enough fuss to make them eventually stop, but by then the name Heidi was ruined for good. She often thought of changing it and had finally begun doing so, easing into the new one, using them both, when we got Djband together. Then the name Heidi visited her in a dream one night, showing up in golemlike, anagrammatic fashion: a tiny girl about eight inches tall who introduced herself as Hide-I and immediately disappeared. Aunt Nancy awoke knowing what had to be done, knowing Heidi was a name she'd outgrown. Aunt Nancy's been the only name she answers to since then.

Q: Getting back to the recording, how do you and Djband feel about Orphic Bend? Did you do what you set out to do? Has having a record out been what you expected it to be?

A: No, it hasn't. We got caught up in thinking—both wishing and fearing—it would confer immortality or make us iconic or stop the world or in some other way transform life as we know it. But life, as you know, goes on, which isn't, after all, a bad thing. Musically we did what we wanted to do, which isn't to say we were totally satisfied or that we achieved perfection or that there's nothing more to do. The fact that it hasn't made much of a splash, outside of what attention the balloons have gotten, comes, as they say, with the territory, which we understand and have always understood, our flirtation with unreal expectations notwithstanding, inflated wishes and inflated fear (which are also—write this down—what the balloons are about) notwithstanding. The rather unspectacular fact of it or fact of it or fact of it as a part of life we can live with.

Q: What's your next project?

A: Getting up off this concrete floor. [Laughs.]

Q: Having touched on the balloons again, perhaps you can clear something up. Did B'Loon take the form of water trickling out of N.'s ear during the gig at the Blue Light Lounge?

A: No, I don't think so. I don't think it was that. B'Loon being with N. or blowing with N. was just a thought, a bug Bl'under put in his ear perhaps. Not, as he said, that it mattered. Not, as he said, that he cared. All it was was that in wanted out. Water weighted his head to one side wanting out. It might've been holy water mixed with spit for all he knew, holy water dribbling with spit from a spit valve. Water tilted his head the way a bird tilts its head. Romance's turned head turned further, it was also revolution's rolled head cocked and loaded like a gun.

Q: Speaking of water, you've been accused of not knowing that the Flood already came and went. How do you respond?

I'm told that at this point, annoyed by the question, I refused to answer any more questions.

Sincerely,
Dredj

Dear Angel of Dust,

Many thanks for your quick note. Thanks for taking my last letter in stride. Yes, another cowrie shell attack. An odd mix of lucidity and memory loss this one was, an insistent "it" one lay in the aftermath of. Presumed aftermath, I should say, so antifoundational, concrete bed and floor notwithstanding, did its meeting of precocious record with faulty recall turn out to be. Turned out to be and from the outset was, it would seem, though this may well have been only faulty recall's effect one thought, rethought, thought again, deprivation no less in question than endowment the way things were. Still, the sense of relegation was unimpeachable, moot consequence investing the premises everywhere one looked. Yes, relegation, outskirts, "Our Lady of the Lifted Skirts" in only an ever so faint way alluded to (if allusion it could be said to be at all). Convalescent light watered my forehead from within, a therapeutic charade sweat resorted to attempting to refigure its cowrie shell roots. Conch roots it attempted refiguring as well, conch blade and cowrie kiss or squint newly beneficent, root's low captious croon a newly anabatic hum. Conch bell and blow, the way one heard it now, had the hum of a halogen lamp.

Relegation, yes, but I intuited a subtle spirit of attachment all the same, a sense of kinetic architecture the open-air locale curiously conveyed, as though the aqueduct on whose floor I lay were conduit and convalescent room both. It was a contradictory sense of outdoor enclosure bestowed by the overarching sun, House of Dredj's tentacular auspices, a step if not a trek outside still under one roof. Dredj Annex is what it amounted to. (That, at any rate, is the title Aunt Nancy gave the new tune she wrote, "Dredj Annex." She says it's a piece inspired by my babbling during a visit she and the band paid me. I tended to talk, evidently, out of my head.)

A couple of days went by, then I was over it.

As ever,

N.

_____

Dear Angel of Dust,

I have no way of knowing how much House of Dredj's tentacular auspices had to do with Drennette's tentacular dreads during "Book of Elysian Escort's" x-ray moment at the Blue Light Lounge. The possible connection didn't occur to me until you pointed it out. If anything, I was aware of Aunt Nancy's influence, the fact of her having written "Dredj Annex" perhaps intimating an eight-limbed endowment her name never fails to bring to mind—in this case a shared endowment and a shorthand equation identifying spider with octopus. Anyway, it fits. Given "Book of Elysian Escort's" x-ray moment's erotic freight, shared endowment easily shares eight-limbed entanglement as well, eight-limbed enticement or eight-limbed embrace the proverbial beast with two backs. Coition's eight limbs are easy enough to see. But, again, I'm not sure. Perhaps I only thought I lay tugged under by an octopus, bitten, it turns out, by a spider. It's also possible, as you suggest, that I indeed lay tugged under by an octopus. As Fats Waller put it, "One never knows, do one?"

We used to refer to sex as leg when I was twelve, thirteen, fourteen—"Gimme some leg," we'd embarrass the girls by shouting across the schoolyard—a fact I've not forgotten. Still, to say leg underlay it all to mean sex underlay it all says nothing we don't already know. Whose nether life hasn't been quickened by this or that utopic moment or melding, this or that real or imagined enticement or entanglement, this or that remembered or intimated embrace? (Bobby Womack: "I wanna dedicate this song to all the lovers tonight, and I expect that might be the whole world"

["If You Think You're Lonely Now," *The Poet*].) Arachno-elegiac syncope may well have been octopod synapse as well, but I'd rather you give "Dredj Annex" a listen.

The tape I'm enclosing we recorded at rehearsal day before yesterday, the first time we've gotten a rendition we're happy with. Notice how senses of drought, if it's not too odd to say so, flowed freely. Notice too how tentacular auspice or endowment marooned a theme of would-be reach, desert ordeal the beached amenity tangibility's arrest evolved into. The way Aunt Nancy had of writing ambiguous harmonics into the piece (Hide-I harmonics we decided to call them) deserves mention as well, as does the way we all had of turning anansic wile and oneiric beguilement to an otherwise parsimonious wisdom's advantage.

Let me know what you think.

Yours,

N.

Dear Angel of Dust,

I'm not sure Djamilaa's comfortable with Aunt Nancy having written a piece inspired by my cowrie shell attack. It's not that anything about her playing on "Dredj Annex" gives me that impression. As you can hear on the tape I sent, there's not even an inkling of reticence or reluctance or a suggestion of withholding of any sort on her part, nor has there been in any of our rehearsals of the piece. And it's not like the problem Penguin used to have with "Tosaut Strut." Still, she did say to me the first day we rehearsed the piece, in a seemingly offhand enough manner, "Now I know how Alice felt having to play 'Naima' "—a reference to Alice Coltrane in Trane's band, whose repertoire included the piece he wrote for his first wife. She smiled when I asked what she meant by that but she wouldn't elaborate.

Then she came up with a new piece a couple of days later, "Deferred Epiphany (Thanx But No Thanx)," a piece whose opening traffic-jam-on-train-wreck tonalities appear intent on recalling Mingus's "Wham Bam Thank You Ma'am," an appearance its title does nothing to take away from. Given the way she had of looking Aunt Nancy in the eye when she announced that she too had written a new piece and introduced it to us, doing so so soon after Aunt Nancy brought "Dredj Annex" to rehearsal, she might as well have called it "No Thank You Ma'am." I couldn't help feeling she was refusing, on my behalf and/or Dredj's behalf, Aunt Nancy's homage or tribute to me and/or Dredj (if that's what "Dredj Annex" was), that some claim to and staking out of turf was taking place. I've often thought about the term "territory band," but Djamilaa's new piece appeared aimed at giving it new meaning, one that wouldn't have occurred to me before. For the duration of her piece, at least, we would be such a band.

That this was the case was borne out by the instrumentation she gave the piece. Aunt Nancy was to play bass, Lambert alto sax, Penguin clarinet and Drennette drums, what she and I would play being of more moment, more to the point. For one, she insisted I play pocket trumpet. This would of course bring Don Cherry to mind and she knew it. She also knew that I would know that she knew it. Getting what I took to be her drift, I wasted no time quoting Don's "Mopti" during my solo the first time we ran thru the piece. "Mopti" Don modeled after a piece of music from Mali called "Boro" that the Regional Orchestra of Mopti performs. Djamilaa's face lit up as soon as she heard the quote and she looked at me and flashed me a grin, a sign that I indeed had gotten her drift—"regional orchestra" = "territory band"—and also that she'd known I would. Secondly, "Deferred Epiphany (Thanx But No Thanx)" calls for her to play synthesizer, an instrument whose ability to pervade space, to occupy all available spaces and to intimate unavailable ones as well (an emanative as well as penetrative ability, as if no matter where it goes it was already there), fits the staking out of turf to a T. Every note any of us played was marked by the synthesizer's presence, a technico-etheric residence and reach it made it seem we were invested with or amended by. Adhesion as much as inherence, both came down to the same thing.

Insofar as the piece rebuffs Aunt Nancy it rebuffs her gently, featuring her in a leadoff role in fact. She opens it with a repeated bass figure reminiscent of "Joshua," the Victor Feldman composition that was a staple of Miles's bands during the early sixties. This could hardly be coincidental. It's meant to cast Aunt Nancy in the role of an ill-advised Joshua, a transgressor against walls in a piece extolling or at least giving walls their due. It poses her as an intruder needing to be reminded what walls are for. Djamilaa's brief concerning the amenities of turf and her grievance regarding the violation of turf begin with the bass figure Aunt Nancy plays. The compliment the leadoff role amounts to is ambiguous at best, but the fact that it's a compliment at all makes the rebuff, as I've said, a muted one.

Light rebuff though it was, Aunt Nancy got it. She got it and she took it in stride, took it lightly. At rehearsal the next day she announced that she'd written another new piece but that, à la Mingus, she wanted to hum us our parts—give us "the juice, the essence," as she put it—before showing us the charts. She then turned to Penguin, Lambert and me and hummed the horn line, the melody line. What she hummed we all immediately recognized: "Naima." Lambert, Penguin and Drennette were puzzled and got looks on their faces asking what was up. Djamilaa and I understood at once and Djamilaa started laughing. Aunt Nancy stopped humming and laughed herself and then let Lambert, Penguin and Drennette in on the joke. She had overheard Djamilaa's remark the day she brought "Dredj Annex" in and we first rehearsed it.

Djamilaa laughed and Aunt Nancy laughed and how much of that was merely show, neither of them wanting to be caught out, I can't say, but both pieces are in our repertoire now. Indeed, we gave "Deferred Epiphany (Thanx But No Thanx)" a particularly inspired reading during a stint at Kimball's in San Francisco last week. We played it during the second set our last night there and Penguin again proved to be our emotional plumb line. Weather vane would be another way to put it, perhaps a better way to suggest the particular grist or grain he brought to the piece. The repetitive bass figure brought Aunt Nancy's tensile fingers to the fore, the strings a suspension bridge's cables it seemed at times while at others it appeared she dug a trench with her bare hands, a paragon of strength and resolve. Playing into and playing against this by turns, as accompanist and when she soloed as well, Djamilaa proffered additive atmosphere (technico-etheric aura, synthetico-etheric aura) as though the synthesizer were a magician's wand. A magician's wand and a conductor's baton rolled into one it might've been, a magisterial bag of tricks and invention she pulled an impelling array of sonic intricacies from. Space-ray sonorities filled the room and ricocheted within it, space-ray clatter crowning Djamilaa queen of space or commander of space or at the very least conductor of space, futuristic buzz mixing swept immensity with microtonal certainty and assertion, intimate sway. Still, it fell to Penguin—or, at least, he took it upon himself—to revisit the real or imagined but possibly still unresolved tensions between the two.

Penguin's wasn't the only solo but it was the one that most emphatically tapped a vein of latent fury germane to the piece. As for my part, I was able to recognize territory, turf and region with my "Mopti" quote as well as by other means. I added to and complicated this with a discrepant approach that wanted to emphasize cracks and what falls between cracks, an approach in which I got away from strictly well-tempered pitches at points. Using alternate fingerings, I split hairs by getting in between well-tempered pitches—a sharp C which wasn't yet C-sharp, a sharp F-sharp which wasn't yet G and such. I implicitly picked a bone with clear demarcation by accenting divergence, shading, drift, also using alternate fingerings to sound a repeated phrase or note, fingering a repeated G-sharp 1, 123, 1, 123 and so on. Still, given Djamilaa's microtonal certainty and assertion, whether this bone amounted to much was hard to tell. As for Lambert's part, the accent similarly but in a different way fell on alternativity, on alternate ground as ideally higher ground. Over the course of his solo he made much of the alto being both an alternate horn and a higher-pitched horn, underscoring his primary ax being tenor by getting a near tenor sound in the low register, pointedly sounding more like tenor than he normally does on alto. Against this he juxtaposed a quintessentially alto sound in the middle and high ranges, wanting, it seemed, to say something about fluid boundaries and moving on as moving up.

But, as I've said, it was Penguin's solo that most rose to the occasion, his that most emphatically broached what conceivably lay underneath, woke or reawoke what may or may not have been put to rest. It began unassumingly enough, a throaty warble in the horn's low register effecting a certain reluctance to break silence, a low-key, sotto voce demur. "I'd rather not say," it seemed to say, "I'd rather not go into it." Still, it did anything but not say, anything but not go into it. Throaty warble built like a suppressed belch, an unsuccessfully suppressed belch, rising gradually, gaining volume as it rose. It was a swelling base from which a less unassuming tack or tirade sprang and spewed forth. The fragility of sense and seeming was his theme once he found it, a first, heuristic postulate inhabiting the horn's insecure hold on wind. Grounded bird, even wounded bird, he was quintessentially winded bird, winded meaning with as well as out of wind. Throaty warble worked its way into the horn's upper register, more beak than throat by the time it got there, lifting and otherwise acquiring a lexicon of squeals and squawks and whistles on its way up. Penguin's having listened to and taken seriously John Carter's pushing of the clarinet's limits was abundantly evident. An extended, exquisitely contoured screech he came up or came across with at points, an oblique essay touching on the vicissitudes of command and collapse.

Underneath and in seeming league with Penguin's winded urgency Djamilaa coaxed a rare amalgam of space-ray ethereality and earth-moving mechanicality out of the synthesizer keyboard. Terrestrial, territorial tonality met or was met by a technico-etheric shift, the sound of a sidereal clutch and of gears going into place it seemed. Swipes and eruptions of sound suggested a cosmic tractor, a cosmic bulldozer in whose operator's cab Djamilaa sat or, were the world hers to command, would sit. Cosmic static Penguin took this to be, cosmic strafe, eruptive celestiality's merely mundane parceling of turf, eruptive cosmicity's intrusive claims or would-be claims. Thus it was that he ran and were he not a grounded bird would have flown from the bulldozer his gnostic squawks warned we were about to be run over by. He ran scared but graceful, balletic even, the earth's pull momentarily annulled by leaps though he couldn't fly. Still, he wasn't too scared to go off on a round of trilling every now and again, causing one to wonder just how serious his warnings were. Djamilaa then, going along with what she took, I think, to be a joke, played cosmic, territorial ogre to the hilt, all the more letting out the stops on the heavy equipment her ax had become. Her eating up of ground and rearranging of earth all but overshadowed the trench Aunt Nancy continued to dig. From the operator's cab in which she sat as if on a throne she issued space-ray edict after space-ray edict, revving the cosmic engine she rode. Diesel fumes and the grinding of gears on a galactic scale all the more thickly pervaded the terrain we traversed. Hers the cosmico-seismic rumblings repeatedly insisted it to be.

Joke or no joke, Penguin blew with all the more calculated insistence, trills tapering off into shrieks of clean, outright alarm. More clearly no joke the more the solo unfolded, the horn was a harbinger, a spinning weather vane, a warning of storms to come. Penguin more and more resorted to and more and more sustained a high whistle, an atmospheric, meteorological tack announcing harsh winds would blow if indeed they were not already blowing. His squawks and his high whistle subsided at points to admit a more quizzical, consultative tone, reasoning with a beast or a machine it seemed, reasoning in the face of long odds, but he was quickly whistling or squawking again. This went on at length, Penguin unremitting in the charge he made and the challenge he raised, beautifully inventive, insanely so, even as what he played veered more and more toward rant. In the face of Penguin's own species of cosmic demand and declamation, Djamilaa's bulldozer gradually and eventually backed off, her sonic swipes more and more the sound of cosmic sputter, cosmic burnout, the fizzling out of a shooting star. This was the moment or note Penguin was evidently waiting for, the note on which to end his solo. This he did to loud, uproarious applause, not at all triumphantly but quite the contrary, returning to the fragility of sense and seeming and trailing off into his own version of cosmic sputter, cosmic burnout, cosmic fizzle.

It was a curiously uplifting note, burnout notwithstanding, fall notwithstanding, a moment of concord or conciliation which all the same said there might be more to come, that, concord or conciliation notwithstanding, the winds of latent fury could only momentarily subside, could only provisionally be contained by cathartic apprisal, cathartic outpour. It was a curiously mixed upliftng note. But regardless of what Penguin's solo did or didn't do about whatever tensions may or may not have existed or persisted, it was a marvel of heuristic wind and inspiration we're still not free of the echoes from.

As ever,

N.

PS: Last night I dreamt I took Djamilaa out to dinner. It was at a restaurant where they offered patio dining, so we decided we'd eat outside. The patio turned out to be not so much a patio as a vacant lot, not having much in the way of foliage and flora, not much of a garden, merely bare ground on which, nonetheless, tables and chairs had been set up. It had rained recently and the ground was moist and there were mud puddles here and there. The headwaiter showed us to a table that Djamilaa said she liked but there was a puddle under one of the chairs, so I said we'd prefer another. At the next table he showed us to, another table Djamilaa said she liked, there was the same problem, a mud puddle under one of the legs of the table, and at the third, which, again, Djamilaa said she liked, yet another puddle, this one, again, under one of the chairs. The headwaiter was obliging and polite, apologizing about the mud puddles. The fourth table he showed us to was fine, no puddle underneath, and he again apologized for the inconvenience as he pulled Djamilaa's chair out for her and we sat down. Our drinks, he said, would be on the house. No sooner had the headwaiter left than Djamilaa complained that it was obvious from the way he accommodated, as she put it, my every wish that I'd been there before, many times no doubt and no doubt with another woman. Insisting this to be so, refusing to hear otherwise, angry, sullen, sulking, hurt, she stood up, said she wasn't hungry, demanded to be taken home and then changed her mind and said she'd take a cab and everything disappeared.

_____

Dear Angel of Dust,

What if someone succeeded in photographing one of the balloons and it came out looking like the sketch of B'Loon Dredj drew and wrote about? What if the photograph looked less like a photograph than a sketch, exactly like the sketch, not the fleshed-out figure presumably adumbrated by the sketch but exactly the photograph of a sketch? I haven't been able to shake the feeling these past few days that Dredj might have been on to something. I've been unable to help thinking that Dredj laid a hand on the balloons' essence and that such a photograph would also capture it, render it exactly the same way. It would be analogous to Kirlian photography, the shot, though, not of aura but of aura's atrophy or abstraction, aura's exit at mechanical apprehension's behest, such apprehension including automatic hand, Dredj's hand, capture's intimacy with caricature the risk it unavoidably runs.

Dredj I've come to understand as a quasi-Kirlian extremity or extension, automatic tactility's inkling of a beyond, an automatic itch to be or to go beyond itself. I don't know why but I've been obsessed with a sense that the balloons' inmost crux and animating entity or idea looks exactly the way Dredj drew it, that, short of automatic seizure, any claim to have put pen to paper and laid a hand on B'Loon draws back a nub. Automatic or manual seizure, it seems to me more and more, makes the hand a graphic shade of itself, a shadow athwart bodily reach. You've got your doubts I imagine. Maybe there's no such essence or inmost crux as I'm attributing to the balloons, maybe, even if there is, there's no way of capturing it—entranced, automatic hand notwithstanding, cowrie-commanded hand notwithstanding, conch-commanded hand (if that's what it ultimately was) notwithstanding.

Reach's wish to go beyond itself speaks raggedly, I admit, graphic default's frayed horizon say's way of admitting unsay. It may, I admit, be no more than wishful thinking, say's way of having its way or of having it both ways, to believe Dredj's drawing touched on "inquisite" truth, ingenuous truth, B'Loon's true knowing, naive self. Dredj may well be just another chapter in a very long dream of automatic probity but these past few days I've been unable to see it that way. It's a bit of a stretch to see it otherwise, a bit of a reach, but that's my point. Did Dredj's hand deliberately, however automatically or ingenuously, stretch credibility to bestow an apt "ineptitude" upon the sketch, a fittingly suspect sketchicality limning a fittingly inflated claim? Bordering on tautology to avow an avoidance of tautology, it seems to say or to want to say that truth isn't identity or similitude so much as deepseated sleight of hand, as though a deepseated trickster twitch unsteadies all effort to gauge, grasp or take hold, a deepseated sketchical hedge allotting gestural suggestion, suspect largesse.

What if, soul to the inscribed balloons' body, spirit to the inscribed balloons' letter, the sketch were a pneumatic outline shadowing auto-inscriptive hush? Doesn't Dredj's drawing rightly shush its own claim, a claim it thereby leaves to the Kirlianish camera I've been wondering about?

Just a quick note. More later. I'm on my way out the door to rehearsal.

Yours,

N.

_____

Dear Angel of Dust,

It's been quiet the past few days, very quiet and very still, the proverbial dead of August: stark light, scorching heat, molten sun. The light, the heat and the sun seem to exact a stillness even amid movement, people and cars and trucks going about their business but subtly absent, a mirage of movement shadowed by bone-white light. Workaday bustle slows a bit of course, but it's not that I'm referring to. The sun's molten suffusion of every aspect of air, so that what wind or breeze there is has the feel of sunlight blowing, makes everything an antithetic silhouette, an inverse or antithetic extraction of animating shade. It's that I'm trying to suggest or give a sense of, a skeletal, x-ray stillness not so much at the core of anything as pervading everything, even as it shimmers, wavers and otherwise moves.

Spells of this sort bring the desert the L.A. Basin essentially is back to the surface. This is not without its quotient of ennui, attenuation, a condition I find instructively swung on the chaabi tape you sent me—swung on and swung by as well. I've been listening to it a good deal the past day or two and again those gritty vocalities get to me, repeatedly get to me, the "and" in the catch and continuity I mentioned a few letters ago an oddly enabling x-factor whose being swung dilates and dissolves. It seems the desert locale asserts itself, as though years of sand and unremitting sun had sown a tendency to swallow audibly, uneasily, husk of some sort caught in one's throat.

But it's not only that. The banjo's prominence conduces to a lead instrumental insistence upon something similar: tug, wrested utterance, pluck (both noun and verb, all its meaning as the former in effect). How the banjo came to be equated with easygoingness I've never quite seen and I'm even less able to see hearing its use in chaabi, Dahmane Elharrachi's music especially. The ictic, sweating pull and perspicacity of it, rattan and metallic by turns, bears on nothing if not effort, struggle, strain. The ka-noun's graduated provenance and chiming amenities on certain pieces only, by contrast, accentuate this. Ditto the spiked fluidity of answering violins.

No word from you for a while. What's new?

As ever,
N.

_____

Dear Angel of Dust,

Yes, the new mouthpiece is working out fine. Just as Fred said it would and just as Lambert found to be the case, it definitely opens you up. It demands more wind, which has taken some getting used to, but the old saw that the more wind you use the more wind you have turns out to be true. I like it that the reed vibrates against the lower lip with greater tactility and presence, that it seems more an extension of the lip than before, the lip more an extension of the diaphragm than before, diaphragmatic largesse extruding a shovel of sound. Shovel and shovelful as well I should say—a bigger, deeper, darker sound, a muddy sound, low but lifting end of a pout. One thinks of Turkish coffee or of someone dipping snuff, a sound suggesting sediment, even sludge, but not slush—not without edge, that is.

But I've actually been playing more trumpet since getting the new mouthpiece. A certain tendency toward bluster the new mouthpiece enables I feel a need to countervail or at least keep within certain bounds. Pursed, ironizing, acerbic, trumpet posits an alternate voice I want as counterpoint or antiphonal foil in actual interplay and alternation with the tenor and as instructive simple or salve or reminiscent pucker, an astringent or an aftertaste of sorts infusing my embouchure on tenor. As for the first, Don Cherry and Gato Barbieri on _Complete Communion_ are a good case in point, brass blare shadowing or shading saxophonic bluster and vice versa, though you'd have to imagine Don playing the date on pocket trumpet rather than cornet to get closer to what I have in mind. As for the second, think of the razorlike way recourse to a mute has of cutting both bluster and blare, cutting thru gruff coalescence; think too of what Frank Lowe says about using trumpet licks on tenor.

Complete Communion I mention for another reason as well. The four-in-one concept Don uses on the album, four pieces flowing together without breaks, worked very well, it turned out, with the four brass epiphany pieces I've been working on. I finally got the first three pieces written and I'm using, as Don does, the title of the first as a collective title: "Reverie's Reveille," "Hand Me Down My Silver Trumpet," "Accidental Divine" and "Sekhet Aaru Strut" all under the title "Reverie's Reveille." The same title identifying both whole and part resonates in interesting ways. The implicit equation of the two can be taken to say that a part is more than a part. That wholeness finds fault with itself, unity itself beset by strain or constraint, it can also be taken to say. The equation is a bumpy one. (It's even bumpier with *Complete Communion*, whose title identifies not only the album but the first of its two four-part compositions and the first part of that composition as well.)

The past week has proven to be a good time for getting things done. In addition to finally getting the first three brass epiphany pieces written I've written a new after-the-fact lecture/libretto. The seeds of it seem to have been planted by such reflections on whole and part as the above, the parsing or stricture wholeness exacts of itself in arrears and pursuit of an apparently parsimonious truth, an apparent pursuit bearing on relations between essence and accident as well, a bumpily sustained rapport having to do with accident-friendly heuristics, mistake-based or mistake-valorizing heuristics. The seeds began to sprout during our first rehearsal of the pieces, particularly during "Accidental Divine," in the course of each rendition of which, as I soloed, I couldn't shake the sense or, more exactly, sensation of a masonic expenditure we were privy to, a sonic structure of sand-castle provenance I instantly knew was Hotel Didjeridoo, the resurrection of which "further up the shore" ceaseless rumor and buzz instilled in the air itself it seemed. Lambert's contentious work on tenor, again picking the bone he's been picking with brass, probably had a hand in this. The walk I took with Djamilaa on the beach in Santa Monica the other day, passing, at one point, the big building that houses Synanon, the drug rehab group, might have as well. In any case, I'm enclosing a copy. A tape of the brass epiphany pieces I'm enclosing as well.

Yours,
N.

UNIT STRICTURE

or, The Creaking of the Word: After-the-Fact Lecture/Libretto
(Beach Variance)

"Mistakes have been made and more mistakes will be made." So declared the Hotel Didjeridoo Resurrection Project's Commission of Inquiry in the first and final sentence of its white paper. First and last, this was the sole assessment the Commission ventured, the only statement it deigned or dared to make. It comprised the entire paper, a fact by no means lost on the Commission's critics, who from day one had called the inquiry a sham, a palliative, a pretend investigation, shallow, nowhere near deep enough. The announcement of the Commission's membership had brought protests from all corners of the Kingdom, complaints that the members were no more than cronies, too close to the King. The white paper's terseness did nothing to rebut such complaints.

Bl'under, the Commission's chair, was indeed close to the King, considered by many the King's righthand man. A composite figure, Bl'under was a headless, two-torso'd houngan, a two-headed doctor despite having no head. His two torsos had once been separate but had merged in the interest of resurrecting Hotel Didjeridoo, a siamese measure having to do with beliefs that the hotel's fall had been a sundering, a lateral rather than vertical rift and collapse. While separate, they had been known as B'Loon and Djbouche.

Chief among the Commission's critics was an ex-con by the name of Djbot. The ghost of revolution according to some, he picked a bone not so much with what the Commission's report said as with its brevity, its parsimonious treatment of a theme very close to his heart. A wealthy tradition of such assertion existed but the Commission had failed to make use of or even acknowledge it. Djbot advocated a new mendicant order founded on Thelonious Monk's admonition: "You got to make mistakes to discover the new stuff." Something Miles Davis is reported to have said pertained as well: "When they make records with all the mistakes in, then they'll really make jazz records." Hotel Didjeridoo, Djbot was willing to admit, had been a mistake, its fall inevitable, dues eventually had to be paid.

Still, the possibility of a redeemed edifice persisted, Djbot believed, home and resurrected hotel rolled into one. The mendicant imminence he advocated he would house in home's roll away from home. The building permit, were it up to him, would begin with a quote, Monastic-Masonic Epigraph #1:

> There was the fleeting thought, at some point in the night, that, hidden in the intricate structures of boogie-woogie, Kansas City, New Orleans and, yes, the blues, was the image of an architecture. I recall fantasizing the picture of a man, both hands tied, trying to build a house with his voice while sitting on a cot in his jail cell.

A true house of allowances it would be were it his to rebuild. Hotel Didjeridoo, for all its reputed looseness, had proven too rigid when it came to the fault it rested on. An earthquake had taken it down. Were it his to rebuild, Djbot would make for more play between structure and seismic stress, build more give into its frame and foundation.

Djbot's head, as he pondered these matters, was a block of wood strung like a harp, an admission of otherwise unavailable sway. Breezes blew thru it. Birds flew in and out, black, red and blue, twigs and bits of straw in their beaks. His head was a piano, a grand piano. Birds nested under its lifted lid. He too was two-headed, one head harp-strung, the other a piano keyboard. What stayed with him, never left, was Alice Coltrane's *A Monastic Trio*, the record he'd been listening to when he got word of Hotel Didjeridoo's collapse. Her fingers' anansic tread, their traverse of keyboard and string, plied a monastic truth he'd emulate in the hotel's new design. Lateral versus vertical meant nothing as far as he was concerned—a moot distinction Bl'under tossed out like sand in everyone's face, obscuring the fact that both had taken part in Hotel Didjeridoo's fall.

"Brick by brick I'd build it were it mine to rebuild," he assured the crowd at the imaginary rally he repeatedly addressed. "Brick," of course, was only a manner of speaking, the threat of earthquakes being what it was. Still, his lips were all but glued to the bullhorn. He spoke forcefully, with almost no letup, exhorting the crowd to reject the Commission's white paper, the whitewash, he insisted, everyone knew it was. He sarcastically quoted the report now and again: " 'Mistakes have been made and more mistakes will be made.' " Each time he did so two notes from a tenor saxophone assailed his ears, Joe Henderson starting his solo too soon on Andrew Hill's "Refuge" (*Point of Departure* [Blue Note BST 84167, track 1]), cutting in on Richard Davis's bass solo. It was a low expectorant croak he'd heard a million times. Over the years he'd come to wonder was it really a miscue, Joe jumping the gun, albeit for years it'd seemed obviously so. Years of repeated listenings made it fit. It had come to be an essential part of the piece, a part he couldn't imagine the piece without. Thus he'd come to wonder had it been intentional, not a miscue at all, something Joe saw fit to throw in on the spur of the moment or even something they'd planned in advance. That it was a fortuitous miscue were it indeed a miscue was the least one could conclude he thought, though he couldn't help wondering was this merely the result of repeated listenings, familiarization or domestication, an acclimation of sorts ("The more you hear it the more harmony it has").

It was an abrupt, offhand aside even so, an ictic squib, all accent or emphasis, percussive, insinuative, bordering on snide. It seemed it said there're no accidents, that everything happens for a reason, that all's well that ends well, cliché atop cliché. The aggressive banality of it gave Djbot pause. He parted company with himself it seemed, a rift opening up inside which made light of the valorization of accident he was there to advance. He was no longer of one mind it seemed, the sarcasm he directed at Bl'under being met by sarcasm he directed at himself. Joe's two notes sounded more and more like a poorly suppressed belch, a half-baked or poorly digested supposition it would have been better not to bring up, better not to pursue. So it was that Djbot countered Bl'under's integration of B'Loon and Djbouche by taking issue with himself, tearing, in part at least, away from himself. The part that tore away went by the name Dredj.

For his part, Bl'under considered it a major breakthrough if not something of a coup (the word made him wince) that a government-appointed commission was admitting that the government had made mistakes and that it was prone to make even more. In a land in which might had always been taken to equal right the acknowledgement that might might on occasion equal wrong was an admission of no meager consequence as far as he was concerned. It was an act of unprecedented candor, hence the report's terseness. The Commission had thought to give its findings optimum weight by way of economy, saying without explicitly saying that nothing more needed to be said. Bl'under was genuinely startled by the charges of sellout which had greeted the report. What an op-ed piece in one of the papers termed its "blithe, blasé admission of fallibility" and what an editorial in one of the others called its "cozying up to incompetence" were anything but he would insist to the end.

Djbot was certain such candor amounted to a ploy. An authoritarian mea culpa was authoritarian nonetheless, nothing if not recuperative, a move to be held at arm's length. Admissions of error could become a new convention, he suspected, the government's adoption of a more human face all the more misleading if indeed it was even that. No, Joe's two notes now seemed to insist, the music was a model for nothing, the music was only itself; nothing could be based or built on it or fashioned after it, least of all executive conduct. Djbot shivered and shook his head and felt chided, caught out, guilty of not taking the music on its own terms. The guilty, chided part of himself took yet another name. What he and so many others did was the problem, digging for extrinsic meaning, hence the name this part was known by, Didj. The two expectorant notes attempted to clear themselves and the music of imposition, supposed import, the parallels, implications and analogies he, like so many others, insisted on eliciting from it. What he now heard was a cracked vocality, a music bearing too much baggage, cracking under the weight of it, crying out.

Joe's two notes went "What it is" one better, not only insisting "What it is is what it is" but verging on Trane's "It all has to do with it" as well. All-inclusive "it" was no less inclusive than circumlocutious, a circuitous "what," clairvoyance and occlusion rolled into one. It was all in his mind Djbot reminded himself, there and there alone, albeit Dredj pointed out at once it was a place even so. This observation caught Didj's ear in particular. It was a dry snap, a mere stick of a voice Dredj spoke with, a withered, broken twig a bird might have dropped.

"A twig snapping underfoot spoke for place," Didj prompted Djbot to announce to the crowd. Djbot pulled back from the bullhorn, surprised to hear the words leave his lips. He recovered quickly and pulled the bullhorn back to his mouth. "A twig. The beginnings of a nest," he added. "Only a bird's way of building will do." Djbot wasn't sure what he meant by this but Didj was. The twig spoke by inversion, not itself snapping but, read inversely, snapping the music's back, would-be baggage rendered otherwise moot. "Had the twig not broken it would've broken the bird's beak," Djbot heard himself explain to the crowd, Didj putting the words in his mouth.

Twig by twig Didj's bird built its humble nest, a far cry from Hotel Didjeridoo's former glory. Twig in its beak notwithstanding, it sang. More squeak than song but song even so, its music made no claim, no case for this, that or the other, a non-thetic nick of expelled air. "Free as a bird," Djbot could've sworn he heard someone say, but whatever emancipatory promise the bird carried it kept quiet about, as if to announce it was to annul it, which, as far as Didj could see, it was.

Djbot heard the music but he was haunted by the fear that he missed its meaning. He was nothing if not that fear, the very ghost he was reputed to be, prepossessed arrival's arrest. The squeak factor, however, he heard loud and clear. Had the bird been caught in Alice's harp strings it could not have concerned him more, though it fell to Didj to realize that the risk of being caught the bird ran was imposed by Djbot's conceptual schemes, the thetic motifs he insisted on hearing. Contemplating the matters Djbot seemed bent on contemplating called for tact and circumspection Didj pointed out. Resurrecting Hotel Didjeridoo would take a lot more than obvious analogies, he insisted, subtler shadings of export or exchange between musical and masonic motifs. One knew the blow by its repercussions, he never tired of cautioning, mystic imprint notwithstanding. This was Dredj's broken twig of a voice's impact or import as well, errant architecture's damped insinuation. Didj's diminution of Didjeridoo was lost on no one. No more stately mansions, it demurred.

Hotel Didjeridoo had been a refuge from the King's mistake-ridden regime most people felt. Illusory rather than real, it had been a refuge *within* the King's mistake-ridden regime its critics were fond of insisting. Joe's two notes, occurring as they did on a piece entitled "Refuge," appeared to be fraught with both prepositions, endorsing or enduring both views and thereby accenting, prematurely, the move into novelty whose need "New Monastery," the second track on the record, announced. Thus it was that the strings Didj's bird might have been caught in were bass strings rather than harp strings, squawk rather than squeak or squeak bound up in squawk, Richard Davis's intruded-on solo. Thus it was that the bird was not a bird but a frog or, if a bird, a bird coughed up by a frog. Djbot inwardly winced at the image, the conflictedness of it, the combativeness of it, adding a "D" and an apostrophe to Joe's name (D'joe), thinking of "dojo."

Intentional or inadvertent, D'joe's two notes threw down a gauntlet of sorts, demanding a new, non-stately refuge or resort, a new, non-churchical refuge or retreat, daring Djbot's crowd to work toward its construction. This was Djbot's reassurance or insistence to himself as he suppressed a belch, insurgent gas's loose way with public address for the moment thwarted, the bullhorn pressed more securely to his lips. It was the height of bodily projection and a salutary caution as well, constituent give's exponential receipt. What might have been sounded spoke for wax and retreat, ebb's logarithmic truth. Constitutive slippage upheld the technical-ecstatic edifice the music advanced. Translating this into wood, steel, concrete and such was the challenge the people would have to rise to, Djbot asserted, crooning into the bullhorn, exhorting the crowd. He was surprised to find he was actually singing, glossing over the would-be belch with a melismatic foray worthy of a Las Vegas nightclub act.

He was even more surprised to find himself playing guitar, accompanying himself on guitar, a far cry from Las Vegas it turned out, buoyed by a bossa nova swell in Rio de Janeiro, leading a bossa nova quartet. Listening closely, he detected Dredj's inimitable touch on piano, a watery-limbed way with time that had to be Didj on drums and a bounding forthrightness on bass he knew could be no one but D'joe (admittedly, by now, not so much Henderson as a faculty, a facet or, maintaining his architectural conceit, a facade of himself). He thought of something he'd read in the liner notes to a Luis Bonfá album, which he promptly christened Monastic-Masonic Epigraph #2:

> When the crudities of the Twist no longer lured writhing hordes to Peppermint palaces across the United States, the country was ripe for a change in its musical taste. The change that did take place—in the form of a refreshing tropical breeze from Brazil—turned out to be one of the most welcome trends in popular music in years. Assigned a flock of translations by attending doctors of lore, the Bossa Nova succeeded in eluding the semanticists and delighting the masses.

Still, he felt himself all but swept off the stage, buoyed but all but whisked off the platform he addressed the rally from. An elusive nonce beat or baton caught him and the others up in its inexorable advance, a solemn, salty-sweet furthering of itself that was celebratory and melancholy by turns if not both at once. An escort possessed of the evaporativeness of time (temporal escort, contemplative escort), it seemed to say, contra Bud, "Time waits for no one." This was a truth it purveyed as bearing good and bad news, each retaining a bit of the other, neither altogether unmixed.

Djbot's exhortative zeal wasn't dampened a bit by the recourse to song, nor by the nonce beat or baton's mixed-emotional remit. His voice found a certain chime at the upper edge of its middle range, endorsing the beat or baton's blue truth. Still, it wasn't what some have argued. Frustrated public speech was by no means the root of Djbot's contemplative croon. Nor was song public speech's frustration. It would have been easy to see it as compensatory, too easy. It would have been easy too, too easy, to view it as contestation. It was neither and both, neither albeit susceptible to aspects of both but accounted for not by one or the other wholly nor wholly by both. Other factors obtained, a splay, simultaneous relay of such factors, among them the furthering swell itself, exponential ebb notwithstanding. It was nothing if not momentariness, momentousness, momentum, the proverbial moment seized by opportune song. So in touch with apodictic swell or sway did Djbot feel as he sang he failed to notice that the bullhorn, now that his hands were occupied with the guitar, was attached to a harmonica holder which kept it within an inch of his mouth. He was by no means being swept off the stage. Adaptations had been instantaneously made, miraculously made, no matter how much he felt the stage might not hold him.

So it went on the fluid stage Djbot found himself on, the adaptable platform the quartet addressed the rally from. The poverty of antinomies and categories was nowhere more exposed. Ill-equipped to relay the music's nonce emolument, tenuous, moot, they fell by the wayside as the crowd found the recourse to song no problem at all. It was, on the contrary, a move to the crowd's liking, a move after their own collective heart. For his part, Bl'under got word of Djbot's rabble-rousing thanks to informants and secret police working throughout the Kingdom. He was nobody's fool and he wasn't a two-headed doctor for nothing. He was also able to read minds. The informants and the secret police were in that sense redundant, but there was no such thing as too much security he'd long since decided in his heart of hearts. He would brook no opposition. He was fully aware of Djbot's thoughts and doings and he was holding in reserve a statement by Charlie Rouse, Monk's tenor man, which would make mincemeat of Djbot's objections. He was prepared to issue it as an addendum to the Commission's white paper, though the idea of calling it an after-the-fact epigraph had occurred to him as well and had strong appeal. Indeed, it wasn't beyond him to call it an After-the-Fact Monastic-Masonic Epigraph and assign it a number like $2 + 3i$, a counter-quote and a complex jab at Djbot rolled into one. He was more than mildly tempted to go that way.

"There is no such thing," Rouse is reported to have said, "as a 'wrong note.' It's all in how you resolve it." As After-the-Fact Monastic-Masonic Epigraph #2 + 3*i* this would amount to putting quotes around the word "mistakes" in the Commission's white paper. It would give Djbot a taste of his own medicine, answering his Monk and Miles quotes with a contrary (or at least complicating) quote, wielding the musical analogy he was so fond of against him. Not only would it show Bl'under to be more conversant with the rich tradition of such assertion than Djbot gave him credit for, it would call into question the very term Djbot seemed intent on promoting. Were there no wrong notes there were no mistakes, much less a radically new epistemic order founded on mistakes as a revelatory device. If so-called wrong notes had a way of making good on themselves they were essentially empty of their ostensible meaning, gutted, one might say, by providential resolve. The same went for so-called mistakes.

After-the-Fact Monastic-Masonic Epigraph #2 + 3*i* would have the added advantage of complicating the white paper's relationship to itself, putting Bl'under at variance with himself. Its unsettling of the word "mistakes" would give the report a more equivocal spin than originally intended, making the report less the act of rare candor the Commission meant it to be. In so doing, it would answer Djbot's tactic of self-division in kind, fight fire with fire, putting the report at odds with itself, the Commission at odds with itself, Bl'under at odds with himself. Bl'under wasn't sure he wanted to go that far but in a sense he already had. The scheme itself was a form of self-division, his uncertainty a further such form. He was a two-headed doctor in more senses than one, by no means of one mind as to whether to resort to the Rouse quote. To undermine Djbot with it was also to undermine himself he couldn't help seeing. The mere thought of it had B'Loon and Djbouche beginning to pull apart again.

Djbot's quartet's bossa nova brought Djbouche's no-note samba to mind, arousing thoughts of a laboratory duet or pas de deux that had Djbouche pulling away from B'Loon only to be pulled back. It wasn't the case, Djbouche learned on listening more closely, that the nonce beat or baton bore the nonsonant brunt he sensed or surmised and sought to be the accomplice of. Bl'under was left, even so, with the sense that he himself was that duet or pas de deux, a dance of irreducible abstraction, prime auspice or indentation of thought. He saw himself in obscure cahoots with the quartet, base and exponent both, risen root. A last-ditch effort to regain control this might've been, for he saw the band as a precinct of soul set adrift for the occasion, a lifeboat of sorts—not surprisingly so, the piece they played being "O Barquinho."

But, no, it was next-to-last-ditch. Bl'under recovered and recalled the second quote he held in reserve, a passage in a book on black music that ran counter to Djbot's demotic aspiration, the populist claims he made for bossa nova. After-the-Fact Monastic-Masonic Epigraph #3 + 4i stood ready:

> Modern urban sambas cheerfully go on taking in influences from all over in true popular style, including jazz drumming licks, guitar phrases, and (when appropriate) piano stylings. The bossa nova seems to have remained a much less genuinely popular music. Sprung from an ultra-cool attitude to the samba and some rather tenuous connections with modern jazz, it has in fact developed into the "whitest" of styles, in which the rhythmic impetus and cross-rhythms of the samba have been schematized into a formula that (a giveaway, this) can pretty easily be handled by non-Brazilian musicians.

That the Commission's white paper would thus rebut Djbot and make the case for a blacker music as well was an irony Bl'under wasn't sure he'd be able to resist. Djbot's mistake was questioning Henderson's miscue, wondering had it been intentional, recuperating the intrusion it appeared to be on first hearing, refusing to simply take it at face value. In so doing, he allowed a foot in the door, left the door open to the ultra-smoothness and the breezy, light vocalities of bossa nova, its laid-back, unintruded-on providentiality, the recuperative croon (providential croon) he was surprised to find himself resorting to.

It would have been better to take up a saxophone and lead a sextet à la Archie Shepp's 1965 "cover" of "The Girl from Ipanema"—better and more consistent with Henderson's low expectorant croak, his two-note miscue. Archie's professed attraction to the tune and to the Brazilians' understanding of the minor seventh chord notwithstanding, it was hard not to hear the piece as a rejoinder to Stan Getz and the Gilbertos, a "reblackening" of bossa nova's "whitening" of samba. The horns' transit from their droll, bottom-heavy opening notes to a high-note spray that bordered on shrill appeared possessed of a snide, parodic aspect, an only-the-shadow-knows ominousness leavened by giddy marching-band twirl, section-happy chirp. Then, too, there was Archie's tone, its breathlessness that of an obscene phone call, the fractious growl he had recourse to a drunken slur. There was also the gruff stutter he resorted to at points, as though bossa nova's limpidity and mellifluousness were so much phlegm he eternally attempted to cough up.

Hearing it that way, Bl'under understood, ran the risk of conceiving it solely as reaction, solely in relation to something else that thus became or remained primary. To hear it that way was to hear it as negation and perhaps fail to appreciate the positive delight or elation it conveyed or advanced, the enjoyment of its qualities for and in and of themselves. To hear it that way was to lock it into a dichotomy, understand it only by way of antinomy and opposition, but it was Djbot, Bl'under insisted, who'd started this. He wasn't deaf to the whistle blown on dichotomous thought by the quartet's music, so to criticize or cast aspersions on bossa nova all the more amounted to an affront to unitary truth. That affront, though, had begun with the bone Djbot chose to pick with the Commission's report. That the quartet's critique of analytic division, its exposé of antinomic thought's poverty, came by way of Djbot's tactic of self-division bore a conjunctive truth Bl'under felt he had to be as ready if not more ready to partake of.

It remained to be seen how ready he was. The two After-the-Fact Monastic-Masonic Epigraphs lay in reserve should the need for them arise. Bl'under hoped to avoid pushing things to that point but in fact he already had, thought equaling commission in the thetic realm he and Djbot contended for. Djbot's four heads, that is, counted for something. A two-headed doctor at the very least, he too could read minds and he was already aware of Bl'under's contingency plan, the two complex-numbered quotes he stood ready to wield. Neither posed an insurmountable threat he assured himself. With regard to the first, Rouse's qualification of the term "wrong note" and, by extension, the term "mistake," he himself had allowed as much in his response to Henderson's miscue. As for the "whiteness" of bossa nova, he was, after all, a ghost or had seen a ghost, comprised or apprised of an airiness to which the music's breeziness was nothing if not appropriate, an airiness having nothing to do with skin; the nonce beat or baton accented floataway lack of attachment, the lightness of life itself. He stood ready to rejoin Bl'under's rejoinders and in fact, the realm they were in being what it was, he already had.

So went Bl'under and Djbot's thought war, raging as it apparently always had, raging as evidently it always would, the Kingdom's two most formidable houngans locked in head-to-head combat. Readiness wasn't all but it bore propensity, aspect, edge. Readiness and wont were a weather of sorts, coastal, mutable, on the move. It made thought more palpable, empirical. It left it inspired or inspirited nonetheless. All this took place close to a cliff overlooking the sea, on a pristine stretch of the Kingdom's rugged coast, the site, it had been decided, Hotel Didjeridoo would be rebuilt on. It took place during the groundbreaking ceremony Bl'under presided over, a ceremony at which the Commission's white paper, which had been released the previous week, was read in ringing, stentorian tones, followed by a proclamation declaring that a new Hotel Didjeridoo would be built. Djbot was among the dignitaries invited to sit on the canopied platform in front of the spot where the shovel would break the earth. He had in fact been accorded the honor of wielding the shovel, breaking the ground, turning over the ceremonial shovelful of dirt—a move obviously meant to placate if not co-opt the opposition.

It was a beautiful day, bright, hot, sunny, with a slight breeze coming in off the water—blue sky, white clouds, gulls gliding overhead. Waves audibly rolled ashore on the beach below the cliff, the beach to which access was planned but would have to be built, an eventually premier beach the hotel's patrons would flock to and fill. Hotel Didjeridoo would grace the cliff as if extending it skyward, samba's big-foot seismicity (Djbot thought, affected by Bl'under's dig at bossa nova) promoted upward. The air was glistening, vibrant, alive with Bl'under and Djbot's thought volleys, a veritable thought field, palpably fraught. The crowd which had gathered for the occasion felt it without knowing exactly what they felt. The dignitaries did as well. There was something in the air, they all knew, no doubt about it. Electricity most would have called it if asked to say what it was.

All this took place as Djbot sat among the dignitaries listening to speech after speech after speech. Once the white paper had been read and the proclamation had been read, speaker after speaker stepped up to the podium. Wittingly or not, they threw the terseness of the Commission's report into stark relief, each of them a bit longwinded. Djbot sat impatiently, fearing the speeches would never end. Speaker after speaker hyperbolically lauded the occasion, saluting and celebrating the Kingdom's resiliency and resolve, the "unbreakable spirit," as one of them put it, demonstrated by its commitment to rebuilding Hotel Didjeridoo. Speaker after speaker heaped unstinting praise on Bl'under and the Commission, applauding what one of them referred to as "the uncanny wisdom and the visionary drive nowhere more amply in evidence or more felicitously inscribed than in their painstakingly nuanced white paper." No rhetorical stone was left unturned. No fulsome paean was too fulsome, no panegyric too panegyric. Djbot could hardly stand it. He had a hard time sitting still.

Djbot sat anxiously waiting his turn, impatiently waiting to hear himself introduced and to stand up and take the shovel in hand. The brevity of the remarks he'd prepared for the occasion made the long speeches he had to sit thru that much harder to take. "Thank you for the honor of being chosen to break the ground for this grand and worthy project," he would say. "I hereby, with this plunge of the shovel, take the humble but indispensable first step toward the resurrection of Hotel Didjeridoo." That would do it. Unlike the speakers who preceded him, each of whom went to the podium carrying sheets of paper on which his or her speech had been typed, each inside a sheet protector, he would speak without text or notes, having committed his remarks to memory. As speech after speech rolled on he lost count of the speakers and his mind began to wander. Exactly where they were in the proceedings he no longer knew. How many speakers were yet to speak before it was time to break the ground he no longer knew. He grew more impatient, more and more set upon by an urge to go out of turn, bring the speeches to a halt.

Djbot saw himself hijacking the ceremony, rising from his chair holding a bullhorn he'd somehow gotten hold of, an iconic, insurrectionary bullhorn, addressing the crowd à la Linton Kwesi Johnson on the poster for the film *Dread, Beat and Blood*, à la countless radicals and agitators who had lifted bullhorns to their lips in hopes of stirring up the masses. He saw himself turn bossa nova singer but continue to address the gathering thru the bullhorn, the bullhorn losing none of its iconicity, continuing to signify. Bl'under got immediate, telepathic wind of this and he and Djbot volleyed thoughts, counter-thoughts, counter-counter-thoughts ad infinitum as Djbot sat ready to make a move but yet to decide to make a move. There wasn't a bullhorn within reach or, for that matter, within miles as far as Djbot could tell, so the bossa nova faded and his thoughts turned to simply rising and grabbing the shovel (rather than having it ceremonially handed to him), grabbing the shovel and, without so much as reciting the remarks he'd committed to memory, digging (sans oratory, contra oratory) into the ground.

Bl'under, of course, got immediate, telepathic wind of this as well and he immediately warned Djbot against it, telling him not to do it, that he would be digging his own grave. Though the bossa nova had faded the quartet had not disbanded and Didj, given new life and new meaning by Djbot's new thoughts and Bl'under's recourse to cliché, insisted he go ahead and do it, that he was already a ghost and that he hadn't simply seen a ghost, that it was better to be than see a ghost and that his grave, him being a ghost, had long since been dug. Dredj chimed in right away and agreed with Didj, resorting to the vernacular to announce, dryly, that he could dig it. D'joe, not to be left out and not to be outdone, announced even more dryly that, grave mistake or not, he too could dig it. Bl'under blushed and missed a beat coming back, that beat being all it took. Djbot made up his mind.

Bl'under's comeback, that it was graver than D'joe thought, no joking matter, no laughing matter, wasn't much of a comeback. Djbot had already decided to make his move. Perhaps decision was less what moved him than impulse, but when he heard the speaker who stood at the podium call the Commission's white paper "an ideal marriage of the pragmatic and the millenarian" he couldn't take any more. "When weari- / ness is let sit in the heart throne," he told himself, "as majestic as powerful as / mysterious as wrath," lines from a poem he'd read years ago and liked. "Is it weariness," he went on to ask himself, "or readiness? Could they be one and the same?" Not waiting long for an answer, he stood up, exclaiming, "I'm tired of this!" He stormed the podium and pulled the speaker, the Minister of the Interior, away from it. He took hold of the shovel, which stood leaning against the podium.

With everyone in attendance gasping and looking on in shock Djbot began to dig, plunging the shovel into the ground, pushing it deeper with his left foot, turning over a clump of earth. Having done so, he didn't stop, not letting matters rest with a simple ceremonial clump, not accepting the simple role he'd been invited to play. He continued digging, tossing dirt to the side as a hole began to be made in the ground. No one made a move, everyone in attendance immobilized by surprise and disbelief, but Bl'under pummeled him with thoughts insisting he stop. It was too late for that however.

The shovel was as iconic, it had already occurred to Djbot, as the bullhorn he'd seen himself addressing the gathering thru. He went on digging. The sharp edge of the shovel's blade was the lower lip of a saxophone's bell, the bell of Joe Henderson's jump-the-gun tenor. It was the lower lip of Hotel Didjeridoo's namesake ax (aboriginal brass, annunciative bell, apocalyptic blare). It was the lip of a conch-qua-cupping-horn, conch-qua-revolutionary-bugle. It was the harrowed, charismatic edge of Winston Rodney's voice, whose "People Get Ready" Djbot heard urging him on, the analytic scalpel of a speech by Walter Rodney: it wasn't groundbreaking alone he was doing, it was grounding.

The mound of dirt beside the hole grew taller and taller but Djbot would rebuild not by going up but by going down. He would dig and dig until he came out on the other side of the world, not the proverbial China but a truly new world or, if not new, at least distant, far away, far over.

NEW FROM NEW DIRECTIONS

Chuang Hua
CROSSINGS

"Chuang Hua's novel is a major landmark in Asian American literature.... And yet Chuang Hua's themes—crossing cultural barriers, crossing parental and conventional strictures, searching for a center within oneself from the past that is ever present—are not limited to Chinese Americans: rather, they are universal concerns."   —Amy Ling, from the Afterword

"Chuang Hua finished *Crossings* in 1968—a time of rampant social and artistic experimentation. She played with style and language to tell the modernistic story of Chinese becoming Western. A fascinating read."
                                        —Maxine Hong Kingston

Crossings, Chuang Hua's erotic semi-autobiographical novel, is widely recognized as the first modernist novel to address the Asian American experience. Its deeply imagistic prose, as haunting as the dreamlike visions of Jane Bowles, centers around the character of Fourth Jane, the fourth of seven children of a Chinese immigrant family, who becomes caught in an intense love affair with a married Parisian journalist. Jane's intimate encounters with her lover are collaged with recollections of her family, her homeland, and her constant migrations between four continents. What emerges is a deeply stirring story of one woman's chronological, geographical, and emotional crossings. Spare, lyrical, Taoist in form and elusiveness, visually cinematic, tender and sensual, Chuang Hua's powerful novel endures as a moving and original work of American literature.

NDP1076
ISBN 978-0-8112-1668-5

NEW FROM NEW DIRECTIONS

Alexander Kluge
CINEMA STORIES

Translated from the German by Martin Brady and
Helen Hughes

"Alexander Kluge, that most enlightened of writers."
—W.G. Sebald

"Alexander Kluge is a gigantic figure in the German cultural landscape. He exemplifies—along with Pasolini—what is most vigorous and original in the European idea of the artist as intellectual, the intellectual as artist.... Essential, brilliant."

—Susan Sontag

Each of the thirty-eight tales of Alexander Kluge's *Cinema Stories* combines fact and fiction, and they all revolve around movie-making. The book compresses a lifetime of feeling, thought, and practice: Kluge—considered the father of New German Cinema—is an inventive wellspring of narrative notions. "The power of his prose," as *Small Press* noted, "exudes the sort of pregnant richness one might find in the brief scenarios of unknown films." *Cinema Stories* is a treasure trove of strikingly original writing and cinematic lore.

NDP1098
ISBN 978-0-8112-1735-4

Also by Alexander Kluge available from New Directions: *The Devil's Blind Spot* (NDP1099), chosen as a Best Book of 2005 by *Artforum*.

New Directions Paperbooks—A Partial Listing

Walter Abish, *How German Is It.* NDP508.
Ilangô Adigal, *Shilappadikaram.* NDP162
César Aira, *An Episode in the Life of a Landscape Painter.* NDP1035.
How I Became A Nun. NDP1043.
Ahmed Ali, *Twilight in Delhi.* NDP782
John Allman, *Curve Away from Stillness.* NDP667.
Germano Almeida, *Last Will and Testament.* NDP978.
Alfred Andersch, *Efraim's Book.* NDP779.
Sherwood Anderson, *Poor White.* NDP763
Eugénio de Andrade, *Forbidden Words.*† NDP948.
Wayne Andrews, *The Surrealist Parade.* NDP689.
Guillaume Apollinaire, *Selected Writings.*† NDP310.
Homero Aridjis, *Eyes to See Otherwise.*† NDP942.
Paul Auster, *The Red Notebook.* NDP924.
Gennady Aygi, *Child-of-Rose.* NDP954.
Field-Russia. NDP1085.
Jimmy Santiago Baca, *Martín and Meditations.* NDP648.
Honoré de Balzac, *Colonel Chabert.* NDP847.
Carol Jane Bangs, *The Bones of the Earth.* NDP563.
Djuna Barnes, *Nightwood.* NDP1049.
Willis Barnstone, *To Touch the Sky.* NDP900.
H.E. Bates, *A Party for the Girls,* NDP653.
Charles Baudelaire, *Flowers of Evil.*† NDP684.
Paris Spleen. NDP294.
Bei Dao, *At the Sky's Edge.*† NDP934.
Midnight's Gate. NDP1008.
Unlock.† NDP901.
Gottfried Benn, *Primal Vision.*† NDP322.
Nina Berberova, *The Accompanist.* NDP953
The Book of Happiness. NDP935.
Adolfo Bioy Casares, *A Russian Doll.* NDP745.
Carmel Bird, *The Bluebird Café.* NDP707.
R.P. Blackmur, *Studies in Henry James.* NDP552.
Johannes Bobrowski, *Levin's Mill.* NDP817.
Shadow Lands: Selected Poems. NDP788.
Roberto Bolaño, *By Night in Chile.* NDP975.
Distant Star. NDP993.
Last Evenings on Earth. NDP1062.
Wolfgang Borchert, *The Man Outside.* NDP319.
Jorge Luis Borges, *Everything and Nothing.* NDP872.
Labyrinths. NDP1066.
Seven Nights. NDP576.
Kay Boyle, *The Crazy Hunter,* NDP769.
Death of a Man. NDP670.
Kamau Brathwaite, *Ancestors.* NDP902.
Black + Blues. NDP815.
DS(2). NDP1061.
MiddlePassages. NDP776.
Edwin Brock, *The River and the Train.* NDP478.
William Bronk, *Selected Poems.* NDP816.

Christine Brooke-Rose, *Textermination.* NDP756.
Buddha, *The Dhammapada.* NDP188.
Mikhail Bulgakov, *The Life of Monsieur de Molière.* NDP601.
Basil Bunting, *Complete Poems.* NDP976.
Frederick Busch, *War Babies.* NDP917.
Can Xue, *Blue Light in the Sky.* NDP1039.
Veza Canetti, *The Tortoises.* NDP1074.
Yellow Street. NDP709.
Hayden Carruth, *Tell Me Again How ...* NDP677.
Anne Carson, *Glass, Irony and God.* NDP808.
Mircea Cartarescu, *Nostalgia.* NDP1018.
Joyce Cary, *A House of Children.* NDP631.
Mister Johnson. NDP657.
Camilo José Cela, *Mazurka for Two Dead Men.* NDP789.
Louis-Ferdinand Céline, *Journey to the End of Night.* NDP1036.
Death on the Installment Plan. NDP330.
René Char, *Selected Poems.*† NDP734.
Inger Christensen, *alphabet.* NDP920.
Butterfly Valley. NDP990.
it. NDP1052.
Chuang Hua, *Crossings.* NDP1076.
Jean Cocteau, *The Holy Terrors.* NDP212.
The Infernal Machine. NDP235.
Maurice Collis, *Cortes and Montezuma.* NDP884.
Cid Corman, *Nothing/Doing: Selected Poems.* NDP886.
Gregory Corso, *An Accidental Autobiography.* NDP974.
The Happy Birthday of Death. NDP86.
Julio Cortázar, *Cronopios and Famas.* NDP873.
62: A Model Kit. NDP894.
Robert Creeley, *Life & Death.* NDP903.
Just in Time: Poems 1984-1994. NDP927.
Edward Dahlberg, *Because I Was Flesh.* NDP227.
Alain Daniélou, *The Way to the Labyrinth.* NDP634.
Guy Davenport, *DaVinci's Bicycle.* NDP842.
7 Greeks. NDP799.
Margaret Dawe, *Nissequott.* NDP775.
Osamu Dazai, *No Longer Human.* NDP357.
The Setting Sun. NDP258.
Madame De Lafayette, *The Princess of Cleves.* NDP660.
Tibor Déry, *Love & Other Stories.* NDP1013.
H.D., *Collected Poems.* NDP611.
Hippolytus Temporizes & Ion. NDP967.
Trilogy. NDP866.
Coleman Dowell, *Mrs. October Was Here.* NDP368.
Edouard Dujardin. *We'll to the Woods No More.* NDP682.
Robert Duncan, *Bending the Bow.* NDP255.
Ground Work. NDP1030.
The Opening of the Field. NDP356.
Selected Poems. NDP838.

For a complete listing request a free catalog from New Directions, 80 Eighth Avenue, New York, NY 10011; or visit our website, www.ndpublishing.com

†Bilingual

For a complete listing request a free catalog from New Directions, 80 Eighth Avenue
New York, NY 10011; or visit our website, www.ndpublishing.com

†Bilingual

For a complete listing request a free catalog from New Directions, 80 Eighth Avenue New York, NY 10011; or visit our website, www.ndpublishing.com

†Billingual

For a complete listing request a free catalog from New Directions, 80 Eighth Avenue
New York, NY 10011; or visit our website, www.ndpublishing.com

†Billingual